Desert Flower

A FIVE DIRECTIONS PRESS BOOK

Desert Flower

A NOVEL

C. P. LESLEY

TARKEI CHRONICLES 1

ISBN-13 978-0692264485
ISBN-10 0692264485

Published in the United States of America.

A Five Directions Press book

Cover images: fantasy desert landscape © diversepixel/ Shutterstock; ballerina in silhouette © OSTILL/istock.

Book and cover design by Five Directions Press
Five Directions Press logo designed by Colleen Kelley

FIVE DIRECTIONS PRESS

Contents

MORE BY C. P. LESLEY
Legends of the Five Directions
The Golden Lynx (1: West)
The Winged Horse (2: East)

The Not Exactly Scarlet Pimpernel

Tarkei Chronicles
Kingdom of the Shades

All my books are available in print, and most of them can also be found in Kindle and ePub formats. To stay up-to-date on my publishing plans for this and other novels, check my blog at blog.cplesley.com or my publisher's site (www.fivedirectionspress.com). I love to hear from readers, so if you have any questions about my books, please e-mail me. You can find current contact information on my blog.

Choli

FABRIC GLEAMED IN THE flickering candle flame. Shadows danced on the cave walls. Blush pink ribbons slid through her fingers—soft and smooth. Once, before her mother died, she had stroked a *m'retta* with fur like this.

"What are these?" Entranced, Choli held out her find to the man who sat cross-legged in the corner, who had watched without speaking while she rummaged through his few possessions. Tall and slender, dark-haired, dark-eyed, olive-skinned, austere in his charcoal robe, he looked like the men of her world. But no man of her world would have tolerated her presence, never mind giving her free run of his home. This one sat, still as the rocks at his back, hands folded like a scholar or a priest. Or so they said, the people of the caves.

Choli wondered how they knew. Scholars were rare among the Kazrati. In her thirteen years, she had not met a single one. Priests were not so rare, but they were intimidating. Danion, of course, was not Kazrati, although he appeared to be.

His deep, cool voice answered the question she had almost forgotten asking. "They are shoes."

A lock of straight dark hair fell into Choli's eyes as she squinted at the shoes. Restless hands pressed them, prodded them. The uppers were soft, the soles like blocks of wood in her palms. "They're so hard. Who wears shoes like that? Are they yours?"

"Not mine." The man before her did not smile; he seldom smiled. Still, a note of something that might have been amusement tinged his voice. "Ballerinas wear them, so they can stand on their toes, like this." He took one shoe from her and stood it on its toe, balancing it with a long slim finger, then handed it back. "As you see, that one is not new."

Examining it more closely, Choli saw he was right. Someone had scraped satin off the toe, scored the sole with a knife, sprayed the front with varnish. The ballerina, she assumed. Whatever that might be. She asked.

"A human dancer," Danion said. "Usually, anyway. Not necessarily human." He flicked the shoe. "It is difficult to dance on your toes. The shoes must be just right—not too hard, not too soft. They prepare a dozen pairs at once, wear each one for a single performance, then throw them out."

"I have never seen a ballerina." Under the pressure of her hands, the shoes became more malleable: warm, flexible, alive. What would it be like—to dance on her toes? "These were not thrown out."

"No," Danion said. "Because she cannot wear them again, the ballerina sometimes gives them away, to mark a special performance. That is how they came to me."

As though they had a will of their own, the shoes turned in her grasp, ribbons spilling toward the floor. Anxious, she leaped to catch them, but Danion stopped her with a touch. "It's all right, Choli."

Someone had written on the pink satin, flowing passages of Tarkei script. Choli put her head on one side and pondered. Would Danion be angry if she asked what they meant? But he was teaching her to read, so perhaps he would not mind.

She held out the shoe with the writing on it. "What does it say?"

In the candle flame, garnet flashed in one diamond-shaped ear. Danion reached for the shoe. He did not look at it, but his long fingers encircled the satin, caressing it. With his thumb, he pressed the heel inward, winding the ribbons into a neat circle around the arch. "Come here," he said. When she stood beside him, he pointed the letters out to her, one by one.

"'For thee, *kaleita*,'" she read, "'may the stars always smile.' I can't read the rest. It's not Tarkei."

Choli looked at her mentor, eyes wide. "Who wrote it?" Then, considering what he had taught her, "Stars don't smile."

For an instant, she was sure, his lips curved. "Not literally," he said. "But life is not always literal, my child, even on Tarkei. The shoes were given to me, long ago, by a great ballerina. Some say the greatest ballerina of the century."

"Really? But who was she?"

"Her name was Alessandra Sinclair. That is her signature, the part you can't read."

Alessandra Sinclair. A name like music. A human name. And Danion sounded sad, more sad than she had ever imagined he might feel.

The child stared at this teacher who never failed to surprise her. "And you knew her? But how?"

"Sit down," he said, "and I will tell you."

1. Suns' Rise

LIFE SEEMED SO SIMPLE then, years ago when his story began. Every day the same routine: up before dawn, he washed quickly in the stone basin in his cell, chose the cleaner of two identical white linen robes, ate whatever the temple servants had prepared, and left to meditate in the desert. He returned to hours of study and contemplation, rarely encountering another being. Days blended into weeks, then months and years, a progression as eternal as the three suns of Tarkei, to whose service Danion had devoted his life.

This day began like every other, with Danion perched on a great block of granite arching over the desert. Orbfire glowed crimson against its maroon sky. Soon it would slip beneath the horizon, giving way before the rising suns. Already, luminous fingers stretched around the side of the world. The nighttime chill had begun to lift. The rock beneath him gave off a warm glow even after hours of darkness.

He could smell the morning dew on the rocky soil around him, the only water much of this land ever knew. It trickled into small pools under the ground, giving rise to the occasional vine he could see tumbling from cracks in the stone.

The suns crept closer to the horizon, chasing Orbfire before them. The sky paled from maroon to scarlet and would soon match the ground, ocher soil extending dust-dry to the horizon. Granite, sandstone, obsidian, quartz lay everywhere. Danion, a scientist once, recognized them without difficulty. He knew more of them than of himself, his mentor said. Danion was not sure what that meant.

The three suns rose—glittering Father Danar, who had given Danion his name, a yellow-white ball too brilliant for comfort; Selassa, mother star, a softly glowing red dwarf; and Kana, white dwarf, child star of this holy trinity. They rounded the horizon in tight formation; pursued their separate paths throughout the day, rays interlacing across the sky; then set, one by one, in a prolonged and multicolored twilight.

As the flush of dawn turned the sands to pink and Orbfire slid from his sight, Danion began the ritual that led to contemplation. He touched the garnet in his left ear. Just a stone with backing, it marked him as a junior priest of Selassa—second rank, second tier.

The suns' rays strengthened, heating the sands. Insects skittered against a distant rock. Danion stopped his silent chant and looked up. On the solar-induced winds silver birds glided. They soared above the barren landscape, glistening, translucent wings etched against the reddening sky. Quantum particles of light shimmered around their delicate heads. The damp, earthy smell of morning turned to steaming dust with a hint of sulfur. Against a rock far below, ivory flowers bloomed.

Danion closed his eyes, breathing deeply. A quiet sense of certainty filled him. Today he would succeed.

The skittering became clearer, more pronounced. His concentration shattered. Danion came to himself, fighting irritation. The noise increased, deflecting his annoyance. Not insects, nor the lizard-like creatures that scurried among the rocks. Something larger.

He froze, listening. Predators existed even here, close to the sanctuary and far from the inhabited areas, in the most inhospitable section of the arid lands. The sound originated below him, perhaps a third of the way down the hill. He would have to pass it to get home, and he needed to leave soon. What should he do?

The noise sounded like a small carnivore. With skillful tracking, he might catch it before it caught him. And so, abandoning his attempt at meditation, Danion slipped silently down the path.

He was close. The noise had stopped. Danion squatted behind the largest boulder he could see and waited.

It took some time, and he became concerned about the rising suns. Then he heard it, no more than a whisper on the breeze but enough for his quick ears to identify. On the other side of the boulder, a narrow crack cleft the hill. Whatever it was waited there.

The whisper came again. Danion pounced, grabbed, and almost fell off the hillside. His prey wriggled loose, and he snatched at her. She fought him with a strength he had not anticipated, squirming with the lithe agility of a desert cat. When at last he pinned her against the rock and held her, she glared at him, gray eyes wild in her heart-shaped face.

Danion sat back on his heels to examine what he had caught and nearly lost his grip on her again. A human woman, as slender, light-boned, and elegant as the silver birds that flew overhead. It seemed impossible that she could have fought so hard.

Dark hair tumbled over her shoulders and down her back. Her heart-shaped face was the palest rose, cheeks flushed now with anger but bearing no evidence of the sunburn that hours in the desert would have brought. Dust smudged her face and covered her clothing, a result of their struggle. Even so, she was beautiful—the big gray eyes that glared at him ringed with dark lashes, her nose short and straight, her mouth well-shaped. What had brought her to the barren lands he could not imagine. More improbable still was her attire: the omnipresent red dust stained a navy-blue leotard and black wool tights—and stranger yet, pink satin pointe shoes.

Briefly he wondered if she were a mirage, the result of too much time in the desert heat. But the skin under his hands was soft, the muscles beneath taut as tempered steel, and if he loosened his grip she would be halfway down the hillside before he could catch her.

"Who are you?" she said sharply in English. "What planet is this?" Her voice, beneath the edge caused by fear, had a rich, mellow ring. A contralto voice.

Danion felt his mouth drop open. He understood her words—before joining the priesthood he had worked at the Tarkei Academy of Sciences, where he had often encountered humans—but he was out of practice, and the response he needed eluded him at first. After a while, he said, "What planet is this? You don't know?"

Already taut muscles tensed under his hands. The woman pulled her feet closer, pressing her back into the rock. Danion tightened his hold before she could break free, earning himself another scowl. "No," she said. "How would I?"

Her reaction surprised him. True, he had attacked her, in a sense, but he had no intention of hurting her. He would release her if he could convince himself that she would not run away. Danion forced himself to relax, to look nonthreatening. A hint of amusement entered his voice. "You are in the most inhospitable section of one of the least hospitable planets in the galaxy. Is it unreasonable to expect you to have planned your trip?"

The humor did not have its intended effect. The woman pulled as far from him as she could. "Are you going to tell me where I am, or do I have to guess?"

"Tarkei," Danion said, puzzled.

All the hostility went out of her, like the air from a toy popular at one of his friend's children's birthday parties. "Tarkei," she said. "Truly?"

Danion sat back on his heels, loosening but not removing his grasp on her wrists. He could not rid himself of the conviction that she might bolt at any moment. "Truly. Why do you doubt me?"

She did not pull free, although she could have. Instead, she dropped her head on her raised knees. It made her look as though she had no bones at all. Was she, perhaps, mentally disturbed?

After a while, she straightened. Amid the grime, twin tracks marked pink passageways down her cheeks. One wrist tugged at his hand, and he released it. It brushed through her hair, pushing the heavy dark mass from her face. "I won't run away." Her rich, musical voice shivered, like the strings of a Tarkei lyre. "I'm sorry. I was mistaken."

"About what?"

Instead of an answer, she produced more questions. "Where did you come from? You don't live here, do you?"

At first, he misunderstood. "I do. I am Tarkei."

The woman brushed her hair back again. In the strengthening light, she looked tired, her face drawn and pinched. "I can see that." The hand he had released brushed against his arm. "I meant here in the desert, not here on the planet."

Danion pointed to the mountain sanctuary where the sun priests made their home. "There. I live there."

The woman's other wrist rested in his hand. He let go of it, then stared at her in shock. Between them, clear and unmistakable, a gold thread stretched. A mind link. Something that could not happen between strangers but had.

Memory flicked at his brain, an old story, not heard since childhood. Danion's insides gelled. No, it was impossible. Legend, not reality.

The woman, mulling over his last remark, had not noticed the thread. Her forehead furrowed as she examined the mountain, then the desert. "There? It doesn't look any more inhabited than this. Do you live alone?"

Danion pushed at the thread, willing it to disappear. It did not. *Break,* he thought, but it did not break.

Head tipped to one side, the woman awaited his answer. He cleared his throat, found his tongue, and said,

"I am Danion, one of the sun priests. That mountain is our sanctuary. It is larger than it looks. The priests built into the rock to protect themselves from the heat."

Kana's strengthening light forced Danion to squint against the glare. He had to move fast—and bring his peculiar companion with him, whether she liked it or not. The desert in full daylight was a death sentence.

The thread remained. He tried once more to break it, then bowed to the logic of approaching day.

"We must go," he said. "The suns rise. Come with me, and I will take you to the sanctuary. You can tell me on the way who you are."

He held out a hand to help her down the mountainside. She caught it, then let go, leaping from one rock to the next with the grace of the desert cats she so resembled. Halfway down, she turned, her tired face little more than a blur against the dark gray stone behind her.

"But I don't know who I am," she said.

2. Sanctuary

DANION FOLLOWED THE WOMAN down the mountain as swiftly as his dignity allowed, not sure where, or if, he would catch up with her. When he reached the bottom of the hill, he found her sitting on a rock, waiting for him. Her shoulders were hunched, and she regarded him warily, more like a wild animal than a person, but when he approached, she rose, as if ready to accompany him. He noticed that she had stripped off the wool tights and wrapped them around her waist, revealing a fine pair of long legs covered in pink.

True to his oath, he ignored them. Almost. Even priests have eyes.

The woman held up her palms. "Where do we go next?"

"Here," Danion said, leading the way. She kept up with him without difficulty, dancing across the rocky plain. Only when confronted by a rock that reached her chest did she falter. Danion came up behind her and put both hands around her waist. As his grip tightened, she bent her knees and jumped, clearing the rock with ease. He let go and hoisted himself up, then stopped, staring at her. The thread was stronger than before.

The woman frowned. Danion, filled with a warmth that had nothing to do with the desert, touched her arm. Her thoughts brushed against his: What's happening? Why is he looking at me so strangely? What is this?

Danion pulled back. The thread remained, clear as the one spun by Rumplestiltskin. He dropped onto the rock, too heavily for comfort.

Rumplestiltskin. It was worse than he thought. There was no Rumplestiltskin in Tarkei folklore.

The woman, whose name he still did not know, sat beside him, her eyes fixed on his face.

"It's nothing," he told her. "An odd coincidence. We must get to the sanctuary, and soon."

Danion stood, pulled her up with one hand, then started up the path. "Come. It is not much farther now."

Her footsteps padded on the trail behind him as he climbed the last hill.

Leaving the woman in the hosteller's care, Danion took refuge in the temple. His mentor found him there, one standard unit of time later. Sendar knelt on the cool, stone-flagged floor and lifted the meditation medallion at which Danion had been staring with little effect.

"I hear you acquired a companion in the desert this morning," Sendar said.

For a moment, Danion considered pretending he was so deep in trance that the words had not reached him, but he doubted Sendar would believe him. Instead, he chose the most noncommittal response he could find. "In a manner of speaking."

His mentor glanced at him. "In what manner are you speaking?"

Danion gave up. Sendar placed the meditation medallion in his student's hands and said, "That's better."

"Is it?" Danion said dryly. "You weren't there."

Sendar tapped the center of the medallion. "I wasn't, was I? Perhaps you could tell me what happened."

Danion fixed his gaze on the intricate web of silver wire, studded with glass of many colors—ruby and emerald, sapphire and amethyst, rich golden topaz, amber and quartz. Where to start?

"It didn't sound like much." Sendar's voice acquired a hint of concern. "What troubles you?"

Danion dropped the medallion. He was being foolish. What had happened, after all? "Nothing, Sendar. You were right. I encountered a woman while I was meditating. A human woman. I brought her back to the sanctuary and left her with the hosteller."

Sendar raised his right hand, as if signaling a stop. "A human woman in the desert? Who is she? What was she doing there?"

Danion felt his cheeks warm. Against his will, he remembered the woman vividly: her lithe form, her lilting voice, the way her gray eyes sparkled in the rising suns.

"She didn't tell me," he muttered. It sounded pitifully inadequate.

"She didn't tell you? Did you ask?"

Danion quelled his instinctive defensiveness. "Of course. But she told me nothing, not even her name. The suns were rising. I was concerned for our safety, so I rushed her back here."

Sendar's face set, every muscle in place. "I see."

Danion pulled himself together. "Sendar." His mentor lifted an interrogative eyebrow. "She was afraid."

"Ah," Sendar said. "You have decided to be sensible. Explain."

"She didn't know where she was." Danion concentrated on the medallion. Suns' rays and desert, reflected in its multifaceted spectrum, evoked memories of early morning. He spoke slowly, pulling forth perceptions registered but not processed while he focused his attention on capturing what he thought was a predator before it caught him. "She was hiding, and when I found her, she fought me."

"You?" Sendar's amusement was audible. "She fought *you*? A human woman? She must be half your size."

"More than that," Danion said, although it hardly mattered. The woman's head had reached his chin, and lifting her over the rock had not strained him one bit. "It startled me, though. Especially when she came close to escaping me. Twice."

"Twice." Sendar looked deep in thought. "Why?"

Danion shook his head. "I cannot guess. In the desert at daybreak? She must have recognized the danger, but she acted as though I were her enemy."

Sendar's eyes met his. "Really?"

"Really." Her enemy. Against the screen in Danion's head, pictures flashed, one after another, pieces falling into place like the facets of a kaleidoscope. "At first, I thought she was angry," he told Sendar. "She did her best to escape from me, although she had nowhere to go. But she wasn't angry. She was afraid. She asked me where she was. No, what planet this was."

"What planet?" Sendar sounded as surprised as Danion himself had felt. "That *is* odd."

"I thought so, too."

Sendar picked up the meditation medallion Danion had dropped, twirling it in his long fingers. "And you told her?"

"Yes."

"And then?"

Above Danion's head, a mobile delicate as the wind dancers, as the woman he had found, spun in a passing breeze. "She collapsed. Not into unconsciousness, but as though relief overwhelmed her."

The kaleidoscope twisted, and the crystals fell into a new pattern, one that he could identify. Glancing at Sendar, he realized that his mentor, too, had seen it. "She didn't know I was Tarkei."

Sendar again placed the medallion in his hand. "Yes, I think that also."

He stood, and so did Danion. Relief filled him as his calm returned. Now the bond would break. It was good that he had not revealed its presence to Sendar.

One more thought required expression. "I can think of only one reason that would frighten her."

Sendar, halfway to the first set of pillars, turned. "So can I, Danion. And that disturbs me greatly."

❀

The thread did not dissolve as Danion expected. The next morning, he returned from the desert to visions of sunlight glinting off stone walls and realized he was observing the mountain through the woman's eyes. The room he saw was serviceable, by sanctuary standards comfortable, with fine linen sheets and a stuffed mattress. It seemed to be rising and falling, as though the eyes he had borrowed were moving up and down. He sensed pleasure, although fear lingered in the corners of her mind.

The incident unsettled him. Legend said that the bond developed in this way—first the thread, then moments of shared experience, then mental conversations. Emotional connection and physical attraction, all the elements of life he had set aside to join the priesthood. A face from his past—tight with unexpressed anger, green eyes cold—rose to taunt him.

Danion shuddered and pushed the face away. The thread was a legend. Not something for which he wished to sacrifice his future. It could disappear at any moment, and then where would he be?

The woman awoke in a tangle of bedclothes. Choking hands dissolved into a sheet wrapped around her throat. The shackles that in the dream had prevented her from running turned out to be a voluminous white linen robe, which had somehow entwined itself about her hapless feet.

Shaking, she buried her face in her hands. Wisps of fog swirled in her brain, clawed hands reaching for her across the swamp of nightmare.

Silence surrounded her—soft, peaceful, reassuring, broken only by the hoot of a distant bird. A breeze blew past her cheek, bringing the aroma of vegetables cooking, the scents of an unseen garden. She straightened, looking about her. The room itself was dark, but outside a large moon glowed crimson. Stone walls and long narrow windows, open to the cool night air, signaled solidity and serenity.

Silhouetted against the moon, a man sat, not moving. In one diamond-shaped ear sparks flashed from a garnet earring. His robe glowed red in the crimson light, but the angles of his face lay in shadow. The woman gasped and tried to burrow under the tangled sheets. It was impossible.

"I will not hurt you," the man said. His voice, deep and cool, broke through her panic. She stopped trying to hide and stared at him.

He walked toward her. Panic rushed in again; she gripped her hands together, pulling her knees up to her chin. The robe covered her from throat to ankles, but this provided small comfort. She scrambled as far away from him as possible, wedging herself between the headboard and the wall.

He sat at the end of her bed. Once he no longer had his back to the moon, the dim light revealed enough of his features that she could recognize him as the man she had met in the desert.

Her brain bounced back and forth like a ping-pong ball. She closed her eyes, trying to breathe slowly and remember his name. Dan something. Danny. Daniel. Danyon. No, that wasn't how he had said it. Dan-EYE-on. Accent on the second syllable. That was it.

As she reached this point, he said it. "I am Danion. We met in the desert."

The woman opened her eyes. "I remember." Something else seemed called for. Her thoughts felt fuzzy, even her name uncertain. That scared her, too.

She went for the most important point, although she thought he had confirmed it during their earlier encounter. Yesterday? Her memory presented her with overlapping images, like a malfunctioning computer program. "This is Tarkei?"

"I told you before. Yes." He did not sound impatient, as a human might under the circumstances. Puzzled, perhaps. But then he said, "You are quite safe."

So he did understand. "I know," she said. "That is, I know it here." She touched her head, then her heart. "But for some reason I don't know it here." He nodded. "And you frightened me. What do you want? It's an odd time to visit, the middle of the night."

"Sendar asked me to talk to you." The deep voice was reassuring, level and measured as though nothing disturbed him.

An illusion: she sensed that she herself troubled him, despite his surface calm.

"Sendar?"

"My mentor. My sponsor, here on the mountain. After five days, we have learned no information about you. As for the hour, I apologize. This is my normal time of rising."

Five days? When had five days tumbled into one? The woman watched Danion tuck his hands into the long sleeves of his robe. "In the middle of the night?"

"It is later than it seems. Orbfire will set at any moment." One arm emerged from its sleeve to point at the window. "When I saw you were asleep, I turned to leave. But you thrashed about as if you were in trouble. So I changed my mind."

Orbfire. The moon, probably; it hung low on the horizon. The woman pulled her wispy thoughts together. If only everything would stop pressing in on her at once.

"You were dreaming," he said. It was not a question.

She pulled her knees closer to her chin. "I was." The pile of tangled covers caught her eye. "Did I cry out?"

Danion shook his head. "But you seemed distressed. Do you remember anything?"

"No." She shuddered. "Except that it was bad." Her head ached, and she pressed a hand to it. "I don't remember much, to tell you the truth. My thoughts are muddled, as if half a dozen versions of reality are piled on top of one another. I'm not sure where I came from, let alone what I'm doing here. My name is Sasha, I think."

"You don't know?"

"I can't be certain. Other names keep pushing it aside."

"Interesting. What sort of names?" Danion leaned back against the footboard of the bed. It made him look less priestly and more approachable.

Sasha scowled at her feet, crossed at the ankles. "Dove. *Petite. Belle.* A few things I'd rather not share."

"That's quite a collection. But no surname?"

"No."

"Then I will call you Sasha, if you do not object."

Sasha nodded. The names she half-recalled kicked against the side of her head, creating waves of agony and a queasy feeling in her stomach. She had no energy to protest, whatever name he chose to use, and Sasha suited her better than the alternatives.

"Your dream had something to do with us," Danion said. "People who look like us."

That startled her. "Yes, it did." Fragments of the dream returned, dancing in her thoughts. And something else, the thread she had noticed before but lost track of in the ensuing chaos. "You didn't get that from watching me."

He blushed, she was certain. His olive skin made it hard to tell, and the dim light didn't help, but she would have sworn she saw him blush. It was the most endearing thing he had done yet.

"No," he said. "I did not."

She waited for him to continue, but instead he stared at his hands.

"Well?" she said at last. "Are you going to explain? I can feel it, you know. We're connected somehow."

The thread quivered like a plucked harpstring. What was happening? Were her muddled memories affecting her imagination? But if so, how could Danion describe her dream? "What is it?"

"I can't say for certain." His face looked strained.

"I don't believe you."

In response to her flat statement, Danion squirmed against the footboard. So there was something. This time she waited longer, watching him try to wriggle out of the question, until he gave up and answered her.

"There is a Tarkei legend," he said, "that two people who are very compatible can create such a bond the first time they touch. We call it the joining. But it's only a legend. It can't affect us."

A bond? Compatible? He had to be kidding! "Why can't it? What would it mean if the legend were true?"

"Excuse me?"

"I'm not an idiot," she said. "If you really thought it couldn't affect us, you wouldn't have mentioned it. So what you mean is that you believe it is the joining, and you don't like the idea. Why?"

He looked, if possible, even more uncomfortable. "Forgive me. Many years have passed since I worked with humans. I had forgotten how sophisticated your emotional reasoning is compared with ours."

Sasha's head spun: too many rapid shifts of feeling, too many blank spots mixed with new information, too much confusion. "Just tell me the truth. Life can't get much crazier."

Danion bowed his head. He seemed unaware of her volatility, or perhaps he was being polite. The link did not reveal which.

"You are correct," he said. "I suspect it may be the joining, because I have heard my whole life that it occurs in this way. Yet my friends, my family—people talk about it as one speaks of legends from the remote past, not as part of everyday life. As for what it means, it means marriage."

That was too much. Sasha pressed herself against the headboard; the stone wall bit into her spine. "Marriage. You're joking."

"Please. I am Tarkei."

"Sorry." The dizziness returned with a vengeance, and she dropped her head onto her knees. She would *not* faint.

A hand touched her hair, or was that her faulty memory at work?

"It is too much, too soon," Danion said. "But do not fear. I cannot permit the joining to take hold. I am a sun priest, sworn to celibacy. I will break it."

It helped, if not much. Sasha straightened her neck. Danion sat at the end of the bed, watching her. She saw no evidence that he had touched her.

Overwhelmed by this latest bombshell, she fought an urge to drop her head on his shoulder and cry. How he would love that, this priest of the Tarkei.

Although he seemed quite sympathetic, in fact. The thread that linked them had cotton-wool edges, as though he understood how she felt. It was not what she would have expected. Danion himself was not quite what she expected.

The swamp mists were rising again, but Danion's last words seeped through the fog that surrounded her. "*You* can't permit it," she said. "How do I know I'm not married already?"

"It would not matter. The joining, if it exists, supercedes all other unions. It is a mental link that cannot be broken. No ordinary marriage stands a chance against it."

Sasha gripped her thumb with her teeth. Didn't he hear what he'd said?

Her mind whirled, but she pushed the overlapping possibilities into a corner, clinging to the reality represented by the taste of her own skin. Drawing on some hidden reservoir, she managed to keep her voice steady as she asked the question that he should have asked himself. "If it cannot be broken, Danion, then how will you break it?"

As they talked, the moon had set. The suns were rising, and in the strengthening light she could not mistake the return of Danion's blush. This time she did not find it endearing. On the contrary, she felt distinctly uncharitable.

"I don't know," he admitted, cutting the rope of her irritation in one swipe. "I will ask Sendar, and if it is not the joining, I will break it. Perhaps I should have said that I would not impose it on you. I do intend to keep my oath."

So she had misjudged him. Inevitable, perhaps: they seemed quite different in personality.

Although the bond existed. Two people who are compatible, he'd said. She wouldn't have guessed that anyone would describe them that way.

He had been waiting—for an answer, she assumed—but now he stood. "I have overstayed my welcome. I came to ask about those you feared. Sendar and I had an idea, but we need confirmation, the more spontaneous the better."

The realization that he was leaving sparked an odd combination of regret and relief. Since her arrival, she had seen no one except the hosteller, who had fewer words than a Trappist monk. Only Danion had taken time to talk to her, disturbing as his revelations had been. Sleep brought nightmares; and solitude, pleasant in small doses, had become oppressive.

Although it might help her now: she wanted nothing more than to pull the pillow over her face and hide.

Still, she didn't want to end on an ungracious note. "Thank you, Danion," she said. "I'm sorry I misjudged you. If I do remember anything, should I let you know?"

At her doorway he turned, mouth quirked in a half-smile. In the dawn light, she saw him clearly. An attractive man, with his sharp-angled face and his pulled-back hair, especially when he smiled. "I would appreciate it," he said. "If you follow the link, you will have no trouble finding me."

3. Altanai

FIVE WEEKS PASSED. DANION shared Sasha's nightmares, spoke to her in passing, tried to ignore the strengthening bond. Until one morning a scuffling sound distracted him as he settled into yet another attempt at meditation.

He gazed down from his height and saw a woman kicking the sand. He had arrived as dawn broke; the backdrop created by Danar's fiery entrance revealed only her outline, but the link conveyed her identity. He would have guessed even without the bond; Tarkei seldom danced, and never in anger.

Multicolored sunlight split the sky in prismatic hues as Selassa and Kana joined Danar in their daily climb. The morning dew evaporated, soft clouds of mist dissipating in tendrils that drifted around Sasha's dancing body, then vanished. The power of the rising suns exposed every detail to Danion's watching eyes.

The silver birds soared, but Danion did not notice them. He gave his full attention to the woman who stalked with controlled menace, grace and fury blended in steps at once slow and fierce. She could be a Tarkei warrior in training, a fighter as savage as the spectral enemies she fought. She kicked and turned, her hands slicing the air. In the light of the rising suns, triple shadows surrounded her, phantom opponents matching her every move. Through the link, glittering scarlet, Danion sensed rage, pain, a grief too deep for words, and fear—powerful emotions cut off from their source. A mirrored room with wooden floors, dimly perceived in Sasha's mind, offered no hint of trouble, yet sparks of horror flashed like lightning in a summer sky, revealing glimpses of faces without names. They blended and morphed like words in an ancient script, distorted beyond recognition.

The experience made him uncomfortable, like mental eavesdropping—and not only because he was, willingly or not, invading her boundaries. How often in the last six years had he encountered a person expressing her feelings in vivid color? Not once.

Nor before, in truth. His father, by greeting such displays with rigid distaste, had taught Danion early to conceal his emotions.

The image of green eyes, cold with fury, displaced Sasha's dancing form. The eyes belonged to Reilu, the woman forced on Danion by custom. How she had glared at him the day he told her he planned to enter the priesthood. To leave her, in short. The stream of complaints she had produced about his abandonment, his irresponsibility, still stung.

Her voice had not risen; the rigid expression on her face had not changed. But looking back, he recognized that Reilu had felt every bit as angry as Sasha. More, perhaps. With someone as controlled as his ex-wife, it was difficult to tell.

Reilu had a right to her anger. He had defied her expectations, unilaterally changed the conditions of her life. And he had not wanted to explain that he acted less out of irresponsibility than from a profound antipathy for Reilu and what she represented. He accepted her criticism and did not try to justify himself, but his acquiescence had not lessened her rage.

Enough. Reilu was, thank the three suns, part of his past. Meanwhile, Sasha danced at the edge of danger. Danion, yielding to the needs of another, stopped pretending to meditate and walked down the path.

Sasha did not notice him at first. The silver birds, oblivious to the small drama being played out beneath them, swooped and dipped as the desert thermals rose and fell. A vithra slithered by; Danion stopped with one foot in midair, unwilling even to breathe. He had come far too close to stepping on it.

Judging by the bulge in its mid-section, the reptile had fed a short time ago. Danion returned his foot to the path and watched it slide into a crevice. He—and Sasha—had been lucky. Hungry vithra were attracted to movement, and even a medium-sized one like this could disable an adult Tarkei or human with its poisonous bite, waiting for its venom to dissolve flesh and bone before consuming its victim.

Vithra usually hunted alone, but others might live in the hollow. Danion scanned the area where Sasha was dancing and found it devoid of obvious reptilian life.

But the desert contained other hazards, including a variety of carnivorous plants, some with tendrils thick enough to capture a man, long enough to snap around a leg before its owner had warning of the plant's existence. Scattered about the sands, he saw several of the depressions in which such vines lurked. So far Sasha had kept her distance from them, but her drumming feet would send vibrations through the ground.

He had made the right decision. On his hill, he could not have reached her in time to assist if danger threatened.

The suns cleared the highest peak, and Sasha stopped to watch them. Her right hand pulled the heavy black hair away from her face and twisted it in the nape of her neck. He called her name, and she whirled in place, hands clasped into fists, hair tumbling around her.

"I startled you. I'm sorry." His voice sounded loud in the silent desert. He conducted another quick search of the area, in case the vithra reacted to the noise. When it did not leave its crevice, he returned his attention to Sasha, who leaped up to join him.

"I'd forgotten you were there," she said. "I noticed you when I arrived."

She sat on a nearby rock, her feet dangling, her face aglow with perspiration. Head on one side, she examined him. The scarlet glow of the bond faded to a warm, peachy pink—the color of the shoes she often wore, although she was not wearing them today.

"Are you watching over the insane?" she asked. "To make sure I don't hurt myself? Or is it merely my lot in life to interfere with your studies?"

"I was watching. The desert can be quite hazardous."

"Tactful." Sasha surveyed the orange sands, the graceful birds, the brilliant rainbow sky. "It's lovely here. So peaceful. I can see why you like it."

Uncertain of how best to proceed, Danion said, "You were angry, but I could not tell why."

Sasha watched the gliding birds. He had stopped expecting an answer by the time she said, "I wish I knew." She turned to face him, twisting her hair back into its knot. "My memories are mixed up. I feel the anger. I feel sad and scared, but when I probe for what lies beneath, I see only disconnected images—like pictures on a screen, like a nightmare. I recognize the places and faces as familiar, but they have no names, no context—other than an overwhelming sense of dread. Or many names and many contexts, which bothers me just as much. If I push, my head aches and I feel sick. Then I get more frustrated than ever. That's why I came here: so I wouldn't take it out on the people in the sanctuary."

Danar lit her cheek with his golden glow. Danion resisted the urge to trace the line with his finger. "The suns are rising. We should return. Have you danced enough for the present?"

"I suppose." Sasha rose in one fluid movement and leaped from the rock. Her arms stretched in a vee before her, her legs formed a straight line. Like the wind dancers, she could have been flying. For an instant, she hovered in midair, like a Terran humming bird. Then her left leg hit the sand, knee bent, toes pointing sideways.

From the nearest depression in the ground, waving green tendrils erupted and shot toward her. Danion jumped from the ledge, grabbed her around the waist, tossed her onto a free-standing rock, and scrambled up beside her. One stretching vine touched his boot, and he pulled the knife kept in his belt for emergencies and slashed at it until it pulled back.

"What was *that* about?" Sasha demanded.

Gasping, he pointed to the plant, which, having reached its fullest extent without capturing them, had initiated a retreat. "You can't do that in the desert," he said when he could speak. "Those plants will eat you, if a vithra or kantela doesn't get you first. I kept expecting the vines to react to your dancing."

"Oh." Sasha sounded chastened. "Thank you. Is that why you came down from your height? What you meant by hazardous?"

He nodded. "Next time, stay in the sanctuary." Her expression became mutinous, but she didn't protest. He sensed that she accepted the necessity, whether she liked it or not. But it didn't matter whether she liked it, so long as it kept her safe.

He slid from the rock, taking care not to disturb the sands, and held up his arms. "Let's go back."

❀

Another interval followed in which Danion's and Sasha's paths did not cross—ten days, perhaps longer. Yet despite his best efforts, the golden thread did not break.

When she reappeared, Danion, preoccupied with the philosophical treatise Sendar had assigned him, heard nothing until her voice sounded from the doorway to his cell.

"I have information for you," she said. His handheld reader clattered against the stone windowsill.

"I'm sorry. I didn't mean to startle you." The anger was gone, and the distress; Sasha seemed relaxed, almost happy. "Did the bond not warn you to expect me?"

The simple statement added to his confusion. How easily she accepted this reality that was not part of her culture and that he, who should know better, refused to face!

"It would have," he said, "if I hadn't been concentrating on something else. Come in." He gestured to the window seat. The two chairs next to his stone table were piled high with computer equipment and the week's unfinished assignments, and the wooden storage trunk was studded with nails, whereas the stone of the window seat boasted a brightly covered pallet. It doubled as his sleeping space, but he saw no need to mention that to Sasha.

She stayed in the doorway. "You're busy. Would you rather I came back at another time?"

"No." Danion stood, retrieved the ill-used device— which appeared unharmed—and again pointed to the window seat. "I can finish this later. Would you like some tea?"

"Thank you," Sasha said. He watched her cross the floor and settle herself on the window seat. Today she wore the usual sanctuary garb—loose blue cotton pants, tied at the waist, and a matching jacket, round-necked and short-sleeved. The color suited her. Danion permitted himself a moment of aesthetic appreciation.

Sasha kicked off the standard-issue thong sandals and crossed her legs like a novice. He went to the flat panel inserted in one wall and ordered the tea. When it arrived, he carried the tall glasses steaming in their brass holders to the window seat and handed one to Sasha, who sniffed it with every appearance of enjoyment.

"It smells like orange blossoms," she said, "and vanilla. Like drinking candy."

"The herbs grow here, in the sanctuary garden," Danion told her. "I don't think they are a form of citrus, but if it pleases you, I am content."

"Thank you." Her eyes sparkled in the afternoon suns. The solemnity of his answer seemed to amuse her; she was teasing him, but so gently that he decided he did not mind.

"Am I mistaken," he asked, "or are you in better spirits today?"

It seemed like a simple question, but Sasha took a long time to answer. Danion, watching her sip tea, tried to disentangle the unstable compound of emotions that bubbled at the other end of the bond.

"Today," she said at last.

If she did not want to share her feelings, he would not pry. "You had information for me, you said."

"Yes." Sasha drained her tea, balanced glass and holder on the windowsill, and straightened her legs.

"It was another dream," she said, "but clearer this time. You weren't aware of it?"

"No," Danion said. "I was studying. It happened just now?"

She nodded. "I saw a man. He looked Tarkei, but he wasn't." She assessed him with the impersonal glance one might give clothes in a shop window. "Close to you in height, I think. Not unlike you, in fact, but crueler. And he had blue eyes."

"Crueler." Danion repressed a shudder. A more brutal version of himself, with blue eyes. It was not a pleasant thought. "Did this person have a name, in your dream?"

"No name," she said. One avenue closed, then. "He wanted to shoot me. With a laser gun. I tried to run away, but I couldn't. My feet wouldn't move."

"That happened before, too."

"A few weeks ago. Yes, I remember. And many times since. It's quite common, though, in dreams—the feeling that you can't escape from the whatever-it-is."

Dreams. What good were dreams when he and Sendar needed facts?

But Sasha could not give them facts. That became ever clearer as the days turned into weeks and months. For whatever reason, her experience had stripped her—not of emotions, not of memories, but of the links between them.

As a result, even facts distorted by dreams would give them more to go on than they had at the moment. Danion bit his tongue, then released it to ask, "Was anyone else in the dream? Where were you? Who were you?"

Sasha pointed and flexed her feet, paying close attention as they moved. She had beautiful feet, with high arches and well-defined muscles, although the toes were callused and bruised. One touched Danion, and she pulled it away.

"I'm sorry," she said. "I was stretching. I haven't used them enough the last couple of days, and they hurt."

The brief physical contact strengthened the link enough for Danion to see in her thoughts the man she had described. "Kazrati."

"Kazrati?" Sasha's pupils dilated until they almost obscured the gray irises. He was right, then, and at some level she knew it. He walled off the terror that tugged at the corners of his mind. She did not need a partner in panic.

Her stance, back pressed against the wall, reminded him of their earlier encounters. Would she always fear him?

Danion pushed the thought aside. "The Kazrati are ancient enemies of ours. Long ago, they rejected worship of the three suns for a cult of violence. Once Orbfire was habitable, and they lived there, but they destroyed their environment through constant wars—some of them with us. Whenever we dare to hope that they will leave us alone, they resurface with some new plot aimed at our destruction. It appears that this time they have involved you."

An old memory, not permitted to surface in more than a decade, floated at the edges of his vision. A little girl with short blond hair and honey-brown eyes filled with the same primeval fear that he sensed in Sasha. A secure haven ripped apart—no one to help her, no one to mourn. Except Danion. Remembered sadness ringed his thoughts.

"Who is she?" Sasha asked.

"It doesn't matter," he said. "That was a long time ago."

The bond, rainbow spikes of curiosity, probed his thoughts, but instead of an answer, he sent reassurance.

After a while, he sensed the spikes dissolve in a soft golden glow. Sasha relaxed, closing her eyes and sliding down the stone to curl up against the cushions. He sensed gratitude, and relief that he had not judged her.

"You did not answer my question," he said.

"Question?" She sounded drowsy.

It did not surprise him. From what he'd observed, the deluge of nightmares cut short her every attempt to sleep. "Whether anyone else was there," he said. "Where it was."

"Or who I was. I remember. I could see green sky. What else?" Her voice sharpened again. He should not have asked. "Crushed flowers." She shivered. "Pink ones. Dead bodies. People I loved."

The bond had developed angles, like broken glass. "This man was responsible? The Kazrati? He threatened you?"

"He did." She sounded scared. The angles glittered, glacier blue.

"You are safe now." Without thinking, he rubbed her feet. The angles melted, the harsh blue softening to a rosy glow.

"Yes," she said. After a while, she fell asleep. Danion leaned back and considered what he had learned.

After a while, Danion stood, covered Sasha lightly with a blanket, then picked up the e-device he had been reading when she appeared and went to sit at the stone table. One pile of equipment and assignments went to the left of the wooden chest, the other to the right.

He could not concentrate. A jumble of thoughts and feelings—some his, some hers—mingled with data points that demanded elucidation. After fifteen minutes of staring at the same page, he gave up and went in search of Sendar.

He found his mentor in the sanctuary garden, clearing weeds from a plant wedged into the shadow of a granite block, a small version of the hill on which he liked to meditate. The whole garden was a miniature desert, austere and beautiful: rust-colored sand, broken in places with dark spires and crystalline formations that sparkled in the suns' light. Few of the plants were green. Some matched the sands, but in a profusion of shades from pale orange to dusky brown. On others, big yellow blossoms hid dull gray leaves. One group had nothing but spikes. Paths of basalt pebbles wound among the rocks and plants. Danion stood on one, regarding his mentor.

The plant Sendar was tending was different. Dark gray-green leaves, spiky like those of the aloe vera an Academy colleague had kept, gave rise to multicolored blossoms— pink, white, and blue.

A plant Danion had, until now, seen only on computer screens. Even a 3-D image did not do justice to the original— the austere beauty of the foliage, the lush profusion of contrasting flowers. Where had Sendar found it?

"An altanai," he said, "and in bloom. Your gift?"

Sendar put down his hand fork. "Danion. I planted it, yes. It grows well. Come and admire it."

Danion joined the older man, dropping to one knee beside the plant. "It is lovely."

"Thank you," Sendar said. "Then I am well served. And what can I do for you? Have you finished Chelaya-*chan* already?"

A thousand pages of metaphysical theory in less than a week? His mentor must be joking, but Danion refrained from insulting Sendar by suggesting such a thing.

Besides, he had more important information to convey. "The woman I met in the desert came to visit me."

Sendar sat back on his heels, his face intent. "While you were studying. How did she find you?"

So direct a question demanded an answer. Danion controlled his embarrassment with three deep breaths. "We are bonded. I fear it is the joining."

Sendar's face did not change. "I see. Well, you are a fount of revelation today." He picked up the hand fork and removed another weed. "What do you intend to do about it?"

"I don't know. Can I break it?" Danion crumbled sand between his fingers, releasing a root ball. He handed the weed to his mentor.

The question earned him an arched eyebrow. "The joining? What do *you* think, Danion?"

Danion had no answer.

"You mean you wish to break it, I suppose," Sendar said. "An admirable devotion to duty, but misplaced. I think you had best introduce me to the lady, and we will see."

"I left her sleeping in my room." Danion could not meet his mentor's eyes. "She has been plagued by nightmares, so I doubt she will awaken soon. I came to find you because she brought me new information. There is no doubt that the man who attacked her is Kazrati."

"Ah." Sendar stood, tucking the hand fork into the belt of his robe. "The altanai will survive another day. Let us return to the sanctuary. We have much to discuss."

❈

When Sasha woke, she found Danion talking to a person she had not met before. The two men sat around the stone table in the center of the room, drinking tea, heads together over the computer terminal. The stuff that had lain on the chairs and table was piled in three towers on the floor. At the top of one pile rested a hand fork tipped with dirt.

She sat up. Her hair uncurled from its coil at the back of her neck, and she shook her head to free it, then braided it. Without a tie, it wouldn't hold, but it would have to do.

The stranger spoke first. "I am Sendar, Danion's mentor. How do you do?" His English seemed adequate, although he had a much stronger accent than Danion.

"Well, thank you. And you?" She articulated each word with extreme clarity, but despite that, she saw he needed time to decipher the simple phrases. While waiting, she examined him. Easily twice Danion's age, he was smaller, agile and lean, with bright brown eyes and graying hair. He, too, wore a coarse white linen robe, although his ear stud was ruby, not garnet. He had a desiccated air, like a lively mummy.

An absurd image, Danion said in her thoughts, but accurate.

An oxymoron, she agreed, wondering if he knew what that was.

Only after answering did she notice that they had communicated without words.

How could that happen? What did it mean?

"You still don't have a name?" Sendar asked.

Caught up in the strangeness of the joining, Sasha struggled to untangle the question from his accent. Danion unraveled the sentence for her, adding to her sense of disorientation. She thrust the idea aside for the moment. This conversation threatened to prove challenging enough.

"Danion calls me Sasha," she said. "It feels right."

"Sasha," Sendar repeated. "Danion, you are more familiar with human customs than I. Does it sound like a complete name to you?"

"At a minimum, I would expect a family name as well." Danion typed something into the computer terminal and stared at the results. "I see lots of Sashas. Millions. We need more than that."

"I don't have more." Sasha pressed her palms against her aching forehead. Could Danion sense the confusion in her mind, as if multiple films ran simultaneously on a single screen?

These men were Tarkei; it should be safe to confide in them. Yet it did not feel safe.

Danion had turned his head and watched her with narrowed eyes, but Sendar, intent on his impromptu interrogation, appeared impervious to her distress. "Sasha will do," he said. "Until you can give us more. We need the full name to identify you, not to place you. Since you and Danion have joined, you belong to his house."

Danion had discussed the bond? *Danion,* who kept insisting he meant to break it, that the strange gold thread existed only in their imaginations?

Danion, who minutes ago had spoken to her without words? His assertions that he could break the link seemed less plausible than ever.

Which might be what this Sendar wanted them to hear.

Danion emitted a small sound of protest. Sendar lifted the hand fork from the pile of equipment and waved it inches from his student's face. Danion shied away, and Sendar dropped the fork with a muttered apology. "But really, Danion," he added, "stop behaving like a child. I expected better of you."

Danion glowered at his terminal, not answering, and Sendar turned to face Sasha. "You cannot escape it," he said, gesturing at Danion before extending his hand to her. "Whatever he told you. Nor should you wish for escape. The joining is like the altanai, rare and beautiful, a gift of the desert—desired by many, bestowed on the few."

"Altanai." Sasha, brain spinning, found herself focusing on the foreign word, as if the whole concept were not impossible to grasp.

"A plant." Danion sounded grudging—suitable for someone who had had his deepest hopes crushed, she supposed. "He was weeding one earlier today."

The bond, which moments ago had permitted a short unspoken conversation, had narrowed to a single thread, no wider than a hair. As if Danion were blocking it.

Sasha, pushed even more off-balance by the vagaries of her shifting connection to him, felt the band of pain tighten around her head.

"Come and join us, Sasha-*chan*." Sendar remained oblivious to her discomfort, so far as she could tell. "We are trying to identify a green-skied planet that might fall within Kazrati space, at least as defined by the Kazrati."

Danion rose to his feet. "You need not, if it will cause you further pain." His voice exuded concern, and the link thickened again. His flash of resentment had vanished as if it never existed.

"Pain?" Sendar asked.

"Her head aches." Danion's cheeks flushed, as they had the day he woke her at dawn.

Sasha closed her eyes, shutting Sendar out. Danion remained at the edge of her consciousness—drawn, it seemed, by his awareness of her discomfort.

A reaction he could not block? What *was* this thing that bound them?

"I see no reason to torment her," Danion said. "We have already established that we have too many possibilities. Until we can narrow the search, we are wasting our time— and hers."

Sasha opened her eyes. Sendar stooped and picked up the garden fork, holding it in a loose clasp. He glanced at her, then at Danion. "Very well. I have a meeting with the council soon. See what you can learn, and we will discuss your situation tomorrow."

Danion thrust his hands into the long sleeves of his robe. "You and I? Or you and the advisers?"

"I meant the three of us, Danion. I see no need to trouble the advisers at this point, do you?"

"No," Danion said. "I intend to keep my oath."

Sendar waved the hand fork at him. "That remains to be seen."

He left, without a farewell, without even an acknowledgment that Sasha remained in the room.

She watched him go. After weeks among the Tarkei, she had learned not to take their abrupt arrivals and departures personally, but the lack of small talk unnerved her. Every encounter felt incomplete.

When Sendar had vanished into the corridor, Danion turned to face her. "Can you find your way back?"

"No," Sasha said. "The place is a maze. If it weren't for the link, I'd still be out there wandering."

His face relaxed. "It is overwhelming. You cannot imagine how often I get lost, even now."

Sasha forgot her troubles long enough to produce a small smile. "Could you show me the way? And the altanai? If I must endure someone spouting metaphors for an experience that seems like magic to me, at least give me an original to envision."

"That I can do. But don't misunderstand. It seems like magic to me, too. The joining is a tale from the remote past. Ordinary marriages are planned by one's parents."

"Seriously?" The alternative to a bond thrust on a couple out of thin air was an arranged marriage? What was *wrong* with this planet, that it lacked a concept of personal choice?

They had reached the doorway. Danion extended a hand, inviting her to precede him. "I did not take that path. My parents' selection had no use for me, nor I for her. I left to become a priest, and here I am."

Sasha stopped in the corridor, at a loss for words. The unspoken phrase—And here I will stay, despite you and the joining—hung in the air, as if written in lightning.

He had every right to reject her. It didn't even qualify as rejection by normal standards. Despite the demands of his culture, Danion *had* found a way to follow his own path. Who could blame him for preferring the life he had chosen to a wife forced on him by circumstances?

And what was she thinking? She didn't want a near-stranger as a husband, let alone one assigned to her by fate. So why let his flat statement unsettle her?

Danion had again withdrawn into himself, his thoughts hidden. Then, for no reason she could discern, a glint lit his dark eyes. "Perhaps you would like to have dinner with me."

If she had the sense God gave a baby bunny, she would refuse. The joining bewildered her, Danion perplexed her, the whole planet of Tarkei threatened to send her into a mental cyclone from which she might not emerge unscathed. Let him lead her back to the guest quarters and spend his evening huddled over the reader he'd dropped in the early afternoon in preparation for convincing his mentor and the advisers that the joining would not deflect him from his purpose. She had better things to do with her time, if she could only remember what they were and where they lived.

"Please." Danion's fingers brushed hers. "I did not intend to be rude."

He was reaching out. It wouldn't kill her to respond in kind. And the guest quarters, although comfortable enough, had one huge disadvantage. She had no one to talk to.

Besides, if Sendar was right about the joining and Danion wrong—an outcome that appeared more likely with each day that passed—she and Danion could be spending a lot of time together. She might as well put in the effort to learn more about him.

"Thank you," she said. "I don't think I've ever spent so much time alone in my life."

❋

The garden in red–white twilight was lovelier than Sasha had expected: arranged and manicured with such pristine clarity that it made her think of a collector's piece or a glass ornament, precious but not real. For a moment, memory stirred, and she saw a large crate filled with sand arranged in intricate patterns; three rocks provided contrast. Behind the sand garden stood a narrow vase containing one spray of flowers.

"Japanese," Danion said. "I've seen one. They are similar."

That caught her attention. "You've seen one? Where?"

"I did not always live here," he said in what might have been a quiet rebuke. She felt rebuked, in any case. "I used to work at the Academy of Sciences, where there were many human visitors. One of my colleagues was Japanese."

"I'm sorry," she told him. "Of course, you must have had a life before this, but you seem so at home here. It's hard to imagine you anywhere else."

The bond gleamed silver; she had pleased him. Yet he looked more rueful than delighted. "My friends thought otherwise," he said. "They could not understand why I left."

The garden was settling into night. Selassa set in a blaze of glory, and only Kana lit the maroon sky, its brilliant white too small to keep the shadows at bay for long. Birds sought their nests, their songs silenced until morning. The heavy scents of evening filled the air.

Sasha and Danion stood alone, facing each other. Obeying an instinct she did not understand, she put her hands on his chest and looked up at him. "They had never seen it, then?"

He did not touch her, but she heard him wondering if he should, how it would feel to kiss her; wondering why he wanted to, when it was not Tarkei custom; rejecting the idea as unworthy of a sun priest but drawn to it at the same time. She felt the moment when he pushed the thought away.

Danion, hands clasped behind his back, turned toward the sanctuary. "No. The sun priests do not admit casual visitors. Come and have dinner with me."

Without speaking, Sasha walked beside him down the path.

Dinner was steamed vegetables and unleavened bread. These priests did not live on their stomachs, as the phrase went. Sasha, belatedly remembering the bond, hoped she had not offended her rather touchy companion. The glint was back in Danion's dark eyes, so she decided that she had not.

Surely she could get through one meal without creating a social disaster. In pursuit of an impeccable topic that would lead her toward that goal, she settled at last on the philosophy of the mountain.

It worked. Danion explained, at length and with minimal prompting, how the priests, through their extensive study of philosophy, freed themselves to enter the place of light.

It was more interesting than she had expected. Sasha walked the salt shaker in circles round her plate, trying to capture memories of a human discipline with a similar goal. Something to do with movement, disciplined movement not unlike her dancing, but directed inward.

Unlike the philosophy of the sun priests, which focused on the intellectual as its pathway to the divine, the discipline she half-remembered began with the physical, then moved to the emotional, and finally to mental and spiritual harmony. She tried to explain it to Danion, but she saw that the connection escaped him.

"It cannot be," he said. "How can one achieve transcendence through movement?"

"Well, I do." Drat. Now he would ask her what she meant, and she would not be able to tell him. Where did these thoughts pop up from, anyway?

"You do?" His eyebrows had disappeared into his hair. "Through this discipline of yours?"

"Yoga," Sasha said, capturing the name at last. "Not exactly. I have, I think, achieved it through yoga, but the reason I was taking yoga was to improve my alignment."

That confused him, she saw. "My physical alignment," she explained. "The placement of my body. Shoulders over hips over feet." He still looked blank. "It's essential for dance," she said. "Essential for balance. It was through dance that I achieved transcendence."

Danion swallowed a mouthful of vegetables the wrong way and choked. She tried to help him. It would not have been kind to laugh.

4. Transit

THE NEXT DAY SASHA was standing on pointe, watching through the window as Danion began his daily trek down the mountain. He must have started later than usual, for the suns were rising. She could track his progress quite clearly.

Someone behind her said "Good morning" in a deep male voice. Deeper even than Danion's, bass to his baritone, but with a subtle warmth not unlike the man they insisted was her husband in those moments when he forgot his obsession with self-control.

"Good morning, Sendar," she said. With her feet crossed in fifth position, turning was easy—so instinctive, in fact, that until Sendar remarked on it, she did not realize she was balanced on pointe.

"That does not hurt?" he asked.

Sasha looked in astonishment at her feet, as though they had no connection to the rest of her, then rolled smoothly through her arches to stand flat. Her toes pointed sideways in a sloppy fifth. "Not really. I'm used to it."

"Incredible," Sendar said. "May I interrupt you, then?"

She gestured at the window seat. Like Danion's room, this one had few alternatives in terms of furniture, although the upholstery was more comfortable. "Please, come in. You're not interrupting. I hadn't started yet."

"You were watching Danion, I think." Sendar took the seat she had pointed out, crossing his legs under him. It made him look like a spare but spry Buddha.

Sasha smiled, sheepish at being caught. "I was. It's difficult to dance here—there's not enough space, although at least the room isn't crowded with furniture." That was an understatement, all right. "And the floor's too hard."

Sendar's eyes twinkled. The spry Buddha became a mischievous elf. "And that is why you were watching Danion, because you could not dance? Do I look that old?"

One on one, it was easier to get past his accent. "Ouch, rude as well as dishonest," Sasha said. "No, you don't."

"Good," he said. "Let us talk."

She sat beside him, at the other end of the window seat. One leg curled under her, the other dangled toward the floor, pink satin toe skimming the stone flags. Out the window she saw Danion striding toward the granite rock where he had caught her. Mingled scents drifted up from the garden far below. Much closer, a bird trilled.

"I will show you a place where you can dance," Sendar said, "but first I want to talk about the bond. Your bond with Danion. Has he explained it to you?"

"He said it was a legend, something called the joining— that it links people spontaneously and cannot be broken. He keeps insisting he will find a way to break it even so, but I don't think he can. If anything, it's becoming stronger."

Danion had reached the rock and started to climb it. She knew it was he only because she had watched him;

from this distance, he had shrunk to no more than an inch in height.

"Would you break it, if you could?"

Sasha turned to find Sendar with his chin on his hand, his elbow resting on the windowsill.

"Of course," she said. His brow furrowed. Her certainty puzzled him, she guessed, and she hastened to explain. "How can I commit to anything when I have such a fuzzy sense of my past?"

Sendar tapped the fingers of his free hand against the stone. "It is a difficulty. But perhaps not an insurmountable one." He pointed at her feet. "You recall some parts of your past. Otherwise, you could not stand on your toes."

Sasha considered his statement. On the distant mountain, the minuscule Danion sat, hands palm upward on his crossed knees. It must be part of the priestly training, that way of sitting. Sendar, too, seemed perfectly comfortable; he had not so much as shifted a toe since he sat down. His self-possession impressed her.

"Yes," she said. "I remember lots of things. I can use equipment, respond to music, dance whatever I want. I sense what I like—and what I don't. And it's not true amnesia. I see faces and places, but the names have become so garbled I can't attach them to their objects. Most of the time, my head aches to the point where I don't dare make the effort. I knew enough to be afraid of Danion when I first saw him, and enough not to be afraid when I learned he was Tarkei. I recognized your moon and the style of your planet, although I don't think I've visited it before. Danion says the joining supercedes all similar relationships, but I asked more as a 'what if'—I don't believe I'm married or involved with anyone else."

He folded his hands in his lap, increasing his resemblance to a statue. "What, then, is the problem?"

It wasn't easy to explain. "It's so sudden," she said. "More like a novel than real life."

Sendar frowned, and his resemblance to a statue vanished. "True. The situation cannot continue as it is, however. Danion wants to remain a priest, but the time has come for him to face reality. The bond would not have formed were he not open to it, and you. We will discuss it, we three, but I think you must go forward. The path back is already closed."

Path closed. Time to face reality. Never mind Danion. Could *she* face the reality of a marriage she had not chosen? And Sendar must be mistaken. How could she and Danion have welcomed a bond that formed within seconds of their meeting?

But welcome or not, the bond had persisted for weeks. Soon it would be months. Moreover, the contact between her and Danion had strengthened during that period despite his rejection of the joining.

Time to face reality, indeed. She didn't have to like the truth, but she did have to cope with it. Life might surprise her. Her jumbled memories suggested it had done so before.

She shrugged, bowing to the inevitable, hoping for a best she could not yet perceive. "*Que sera, sera.*"

Sendar quirked an eyebrow at her.

"What will be, will be."

"An admirable philosophy," he said. "I see I have underestimated human potential. Let us go and convince Danion."

Danion returned to his cell as Kana cleared the distant hills. Once again, the light had escaped him. The sight of Sendar and Sasha sitting cross-legged like bookends in his window seat did not alleviate his glum mood. The promised talk had arrived, and Danion did not know what to say.

"Well?" Sendar began, as usual, without preamble. "What next?"

Danion took his place between them, wishing that his own people shared his human friends' regard for preliminary courtesies. "I told you. I will remain a sun priest. It does not violate my oath to help Sasha find her family. Then she can return to her own world, while I resume my studies. She wants that, too."

When he glanced at her, verifying that he spoke the truth, she lowered her gaze to her satin-clad feet. He touched the bond. Dove gray as a Terran morning, it exuded, from beneath a blanket of fog, trails of insecurity ringed with sadness.

A hand tapped his elbow. "Pay attention," Sendar said. "And stop feeding me nonsense. The joining does not work that way."

"How can you know?" Even to himself, Danion sounded churlish. "No one marries that way now. If they ever did."

"I did," Sendar said.

Danion straightened, startled out of his resentment. "You did? What happened? Did you break it?" A flash of hope surfaced. If Sendar had joined, yet remained a priest, Danion could do the same.

Sasha inhaled—a sharp intake of breath. Only when he twisted sideways to look at her did he realize she was responding to his unspoken thought. She uncrossed her legs and hugged her knees to her chest. The soft gray of the bond thinned almost to nothingness, but one stubborn golden thread remained.

What had he missed? She had told him she had no desire for a closer relationship, so why did she react as if he had stabbed her each time he expressed, even in his own mind, his devotion to his chosen path?

Sendar interrupted this train of thoughts. "My wife died, Danion. That is something I hope you never have to endure."

The pain, however far in the past, was tangible. Danion apologized.

"It does not matter. You meant no harm. My point is, the joining happens. It has happened to you. Accept it. The question is how to proceed, since you cannot remain on your present path."

"What bothers you, Danion? We are strangers, but we need not remain so. Given a choice, I would have preferred to marry another way, but we can define the relationship to suit ourselves, can we not, even if you must leave the mountain for a while?" Sasha's voice, warm and liquid, touched him in ways he did not want to acknowledge. Somewhere, deep inside, he knew Sendar was right. Such feelings did not bode well for his oath of celibacy.

He could not tell her that he feared she would vanish, leaving him with neither the priesthood nor the world. Nor how much he desired her, although he suspected she knew. Her uncertainty, refracted in the shimmering thread that bound them, drew him even as it widened the current that he at times welcomed, at others sought to resist. He reached as if blind for an answer, but his tongue could not form the words.

Sendar again broke the silence. "The advisers have authorized me to decide, and I have. I am releasing you from your oath of celibacy and sending you into the world. Find out what the Kazrati are doing. Stop it if you can. This is not a trivial assignment. The future of Tarkei and its allies depends on what you discover."

"And the marriage?" Danion's throat closed, choking the question off at the source.

"As Sasha said, that depends on you. By the time you complete your task, you will have discovered what you want." He bent forward, seeking Sasha with his eyes. "And you," he told her, "I charge with helping Danion find his path. Will you do that?"

"If he will let me," she said.

Danion bowed in her direction, his palms pressed together. He had hurt her enough for one day, even if he had yet to figure out what he had done. "It seems I have no choice."

"There are always choices, Danion," Sendar said. "Surely you have learned that by now."

❀

Sendar sent Sasha away, saying he needed to talk to Danion. The younger man watched her leave, graceful and balanced, comfortable in her own skin despite the demons that plagued her. When the door closed behind her, he turned his attention to Sendar, fighting waves of emotion that roiled in a dozen different directions. After six years, he was leaving, and not by his own choice.

"It is time to part, then," Danion said. "I did not think this day would come."

Sendar, too, seemed subdued. "Let us say that it is time to move on, Danion. You are always welcome here."

"It will not be the same." Danion felt Sasha brush his thoughts. Her sympathy touched him and withdrew, leaving the sadness less overwhelming than before.

"Things change, Danion. It is their nature. I will miss you, too, but the joining is a remarkable experience. You cannot imagine what you would give up if you rejected it. If you find happiness, my faith in you will be rewarded."

"Happiness." A goal as rare as the altanai, as the joining. Tarkei did not seek happiness but order. How different might his life have been, had his father viewed the world as Sendar did?

"Happiness," Sendar said firmly. He paused, as though searching for words, then added, "Danion."

Danion gazed at him.

"I have not asked you this," his mentor said, "because I wanted you to discover the answer for yourself. But before you go, I would like you to consider it. How much of your desire to join the priesthood, especially your determination to take and keep the oath of celibacy, grew out of the situation you were in before you came here?"

A difficult question. Danion rested his head against the granite wall and cast his mind back six years, remembering how he had felt then, comparing it with the present. Words came slowly. "I no longer know. More than I understood at the time, I think."

Sendar nodded. "I had the same impression. Not then, although sometimes I wondered. Now, definitely."

The past, clear as yesterday, rose up: angry faces, and one in particular, cold in its fury as the desert was hot. Sasha touched him again, questioning. Like balm, the link thawed the ice and cooled the excessive heat.

Should he give in to the attraction he felt for her? If he did, would he lose the self he had created here? Would the gains be worth the loss, as Sendar promised?

His mentor sat silent, watching him. "You may be right," Danion said. "Is that why I was open to the bond?"

"I believe so." Sendar extended a hand, flicking the tip of Danion's ear. The gesture of farewell, used within families.

Touched, both literally and figuratively, Danion stood and bowed, then held out both hands to Sendar, palms up signaling respect and thanks.

Sendar placed his own hands, palms down, on Danion's. "Care for her well," he said, "lest you lose her. The day my wife died haunts me still."

"I will," Danion said. Somewhere deep within, the promise awakened a dream, forgotten so long ago that even its existence had vanished from memory. Perhaps, after all, life had more to offer than patterns.

✳

Danion arrived before long, a single bag over his shoulder. He had cut his hair and exchanged his robe for civilian clothes. Dark trousers and boots set off his lean frame, and the contrast between the white shirt and his olive skin was striking. The short straight hair emphasized the planes of his face and those elegant ears, as well as the garnet earring he still wore. Sasha, deciding she liked the effect, wondered if it indicated his determination to remain a sun priest or was merely a personal choice. The bond did not enlighten her.

He took the bundle of dance clothes that comprised her possessions and added it to his own, then led the way down a narrow stone staircase that wound through the mountain. Some time later, they emerged onto a wide flat plain, open to the hot desert winds. The smell of sulfur was overpowering. Sasha wrinkled her nose, and Danion's thin face looked pinched. They walked briskly toward one of about six small craft that sat side by side by the sanctuary wall.

The shuttle he picked had white paint and red trim. The door opened upward, allowing a small flight of steps to descend. Sasha entered and found the cabin small but comfortable: red fabric-covered seats and a polished wood console. The lettering on the console was in English.

She took the passenger seat and strapped the belt around her waist. Danion threw the bag into a locker behind the seating area and climbed in. When she questioned him, he said, "It's not mine. Someone I knew at the Academy stopped by last month. He's on retreat. When we reach Tarkakhan, I will return it."

"Tarkakhan." She frowned, but then the name stopped playing games and revealed its identity. "The capital. Is that where you're from?"

"I have family there," Danion said. "And property. It has been held in trust for six years. I must speak to the estate agent about occupying the house, but it gives us a place to begin."

Why not say yes? If he had family and property there, wasn't that where he belonged? Sensing resistance, Sasha did not argue, and after a moment's consideration decided that maybe she understood after all. "You see the mountain as your home."

He glanced at her then—surprised, she thought. "Sendar is my family. My mother died when I was sixteen, and my father cast me off when I rejected the wife he had chosen for me and joined the priesthood."

He had said something similar before he showed her the altanai: "My parents' selection had no use for me, nor I for her," or words to that effect. And about the joining superceding other relationships. She had thought he was making a general point, but perhaps not.

"Are you still married, in your father's eyes?" she asked.

The shuttle jerked sideways as his hands lost their sure grip on the controls. Danion hurriedly righted the small craft. "I suppose." He glanced at her. "In everyone's eyes, now."

"Will he accept me?" Surely she had enough on her plate without having to handle a hostile family as well.

"It doesn't matter." Danion appeared transfixed by the unrelenting sameness of the desert. "I don't intend to ask him."

"I see." She should be grateful that she was not being submitted for examination, but Danion's family situation did sound rather bleak. Her memories of her own family remained jumbled, warmth intermingled with images of sadness and pain. But she could not reconcile her image of a loving father with someone who would cast off his son over an issue of preference, especially so personal a preference as marriage.

"He is a Tarkei father," Danion said. "He expects compliance."

"Oh." What else could she say? "Is that why you joined the priesthood?"

"Yes." Danion tapped the console with one long brown finger. "My life seemed to be slipping out of my control. I wanted to do something that had meaning. Escape from the patterns. I was tired of having to conform to my father's expectations, even if it meant being married to someone for whom I felt no connection. Tired of experiments that confirmed laws already proven and a life lived like everyone else's. I didn't think of it that way at the time, but looking back, I can see it."

"Did you find it? The meaning?" Outside the window, the desert stretched in all directions. Uncovering meaning in such sameness seemed unlikely, but what did she know?

"To a degree," Danion said. "I have not progressed in my studies as fast as some of the other initiates. Were it not for Sendar, the advisers would have sent me away. They say I lack focus. But I love the sanctuary and the serenity of life there."

"I'm sorry," Sasha said. He questioned her with a raised eyebrow. "For coming along and taking it away from you."

"It's nothing," he said.

"Danion, please. Don't lie to me. You've told me a dozen times you want to stay."

He flinched, then stared straight ahead, not answering, refusing to meet her gaze. She waited, and at last he seemed to reach a decision. "I did," he said. "I still do, but Sendar was right in this. I need to understand why I joined the priesthood in the first place. That's what he wanted to tell me. You did not hear?"

He thought she would pry into his life? Bond or no bond, she had standards. "I did not listen. You felt sad, and I tried to help, but I don't eavesdrop on private conversations."

He looked at her then. "Sendar asked whether I took the oath of celibacy because I believed in it or because I wanted to escape. An oath of celibacy is not easily contradicted. Even my father could not overrule it; he could only do his best to threaten me into obedience." His half-smile slipped out. "He is good at asking awkward questions, Sendar."

Her irritation vanished. "To escape your marriage, you mean?"

As he talked, she watched the long brown fingers play over the controls, admiring his skill. Piloting seemed an unlikely accomplishment for a priest.

"Everything," Danion said. "When I took the oath, I left the Academy. I closed up my house and came to the mountain. The priests, too, have patterns, but at least I chose them for myself."

"Doesn't everyone? Have patterns, that is?" Thinking of his marriage, she didn't bother to elaborate. "There's no divorce on Tarkei?"

"No." Danion stared straight ahead again. "Our parents signed the contract, and like the joining, it cannot be broken. Except *by* the joining—which is ironic, I suppose."

Sasha pressed both palms against her aching temples. Memories of beloved faces pressed in on her; incoherent voices surrounded her. Cruelty, longing, grief, fear: tangled emotions and images provoked by ... what? Danion's experience?

"Your head hurts," he said, concern in his voice.

"Family," she said, dragging the images out by their heels. They kicked and screamed like toddlers after too much birthday cake. "Something to do with family. Families that act like that, families that don't act like that, something that happened to family that didn't act like that—I'm not sure which. Something hideous, whatever it is. How could your father disregard your interests in that way, then cast you off for defending them?"

"It is our way," Danion said. "In any case, the oath served my immediate purpose but not, perhaps, my ultimate one. I have paid the price for escaping: meditation does not bring me what you find in dance. Sendar says we would give up the opportunity of a lifetime if we refuse the joining. Let's see if he's right." He brushed his fingers against the back of her hand. "You seldom sleep. We will not reach Tarkakhan for hours, and the desert, while lovely, becomes monotonous after a while. Maybe you can conquer the nightmares."

"I wish," Sasha said, but he had a point. Her eyelids were drooping. She hadn't realized the sanctuary lay so far from any inhabited area. Only luck, or a guardian angel, had brought her and Danion together; she could have wandered in the desert until she collapsed from thirst. She was imagining Danion with big fluffy wings when she fell asleep.

❋

Danion flew the shuttle arrow-straight across a roadless expanse that stretched to the horizon. It was a lovely craft, light and responsive; as always, when he returned to flying, it surprised him how much he enjoyed it. Not that he had much opportunity to fly these days—the four or five times a year that allowed him to keep his pilot's license pushed the sun priests' tolerance to its limits. They permitted it because they needed to leave the mountain sometimes, and pilots did not often present themselves for ordination. Tarkakhan lay several hours in the distance; he could afford to indulge himself for once.

After a long period of silence, he glanced at Sasha. She had pushed her seat back as far as it would go and lay curled up, one hand pillowing her cheek. In sleep, she looked utterly at peace, in a way Danion could not imagine feeling.

Great winged creatures filled her dreams. Creatures of human folklore. At least they neither crushed bodies nor threatened mayhem, like the ogres of her nightmares. He turned back to his piloting, considering what awaited him in Tarkakhan.

Escape had served its purpose. It had extricated him from an impossible relationship with a woman he did not want, who wanted him only because her parents had commanded it. It had taken him out of an unsatisfactory environment with limited possibilities and sent him to the mountain, where infinity waited behind each desert rock. It had shown him that life went on outside the confines of his family and its punishing expectations. It had, he hoped, given him the resources he would need to tackle a situation he had not known how to confront six years ago.

He would need those resources. For the truth that neither Sasha nor Sendar had been unkind enough to mention was clear: all that he had run from still existed, and he was heading right for it. With another wife who did not want him, and a legacy of failure in his pocket.

Danion glanced at his companion, curled up in the seat, in temporary reprieve from the torments that plagued her. In his mind, he returned to the sanctuary garden. Sasha's gray eyes sparkled in Selassa's sunset; her gentle hands touched his chest. If he had kissed her, would she have objected?

Danion thought not. He sensed her attraction to him. Sasha's problem with the arrangement lay elsewhere: she wanted to make no promises she could not keep. She was not like Reilu, who had wanted a façade of commitment without the substance.

As for failure, he could imagine what Sendar would say to that. Failure is part of life, Danion; without mistakes, how would we learn? The future begins now.

Danion shrugged. He could not undo his years on the mountain, and would not if he could. At the time, he had seen no other exit.

The shuttle responded to his touch, clearing a small mountain not unlike the one on which he used to meditate. Before him, faint in the distance, an adobe circle, edged in green, marked the outskirts of Tarkakhan. What should he do when they arrived? How many of his Academy friends remained, and who could best help him?

A name came to him. He nodded and reached for the handset.

The adobe circle grew larger as he flew on. The winged creatures in Sasha's dreams mutated into wind dancers, then human women dressed in white tulle and feathers, odd parasol skirts. Tutus: the word sprang from her mind to his. They're called tutus. Which sounded stranger still. But they all danced on their toes, and they all danced beautifully.

5. Tarkakhan

THE TREMOR IN THE dream resolved itself into a hand shaking her shoulder. Danion's hand, Sasha realized as she forced her eyes open.

"We are here," he said cryptically as soon as she could see him. She sat up, rubbing her eyes, and looked around. Danion pulled the bag from the back of the shuttle and disappeared through an open gate in a wall of solid clay—no windows, no tiles, not so much as a peephole. Only a tub of big yellow flowers distinguished this house from its neighbors. Even the gate would be invisible when closed.

Sasha pushed herself away from the seat, fighting pins and needles in feet that, like their owner, had gone to sleep during the long journey. She had reached the bottom of the steps when Danion returned. He stretched past her and punched a series of codes into the console. The shuttle door closed, narrowly missing her head, and the small craft turned and zoomed away. Back to the mountain, she assumed.

Danion seemed even quieter than usual. Stress at returning home, she decided, and left it alone. Curious, she followed him through the gate.

The sight on the other side stunned her. In contrast to the drab outside, the garden was a riot of colors and scents. Flora of a dozen planets mingled in beds separated by paths of crushed black pebbles like the ones in the sanctuary garden. Here no attempt had been made to reproduce the desert. Except for the absence of grass, she might have been back on the green-skied planet she had seen so briefly.

In the middle of the garden stood a triangular house: adobe like the red-brown walls, but with clean lines and wood trim that made it appear delicate against its solid background. One side, in permanent shadow, had long glass windows; the other, narrow slits to protect against the suns' onslaught. A covered porch of dark red wood surrounded the house. White cane furniture with pastel upholstery welcomed visitors to admire the garden.

On the far side of the house, a bank of pink azaleas covered half the walls. Sasha took one look at them and dissolved in tears.

Danion was pleased to see that the estate agent had taken her duties seriously. The house looked to be in good repair, and the plants showed signs of careful tending. It was remarkable, in fact, how well the bushes had grown during his six years away. If the house's internal condition matched its outside, he must certainly call the estate agent and compliment her. Even Tarkei like to know that their efforts are appreciated.

A wave of grief washed over him. Startled, he dropped the bag on the porch and turned. Sasha stood at the end of the path, tears flowing down her cheeks. Preoccupied with the house and grounds, he had missed the cues that would have warned him.

He walked toward her. The overwhelming sense of a home destroyed poured across the bond, threatening to engulf him. When he reached her, she threw her arms around him. Intense loneliness washed over him, a sense of being torn from everyone he knew. It awoke an old, almost forgotten wound, the horror and grief of his mother's death—never healed, seldom acknowledged. The little blond girl again slipped into his thoughts, weeping tears no one else would comfort.

Danion pushed the image and the pain away. Sasha pressed her face into his shoulder, and, feeling somewhat awkward, he wrapped his arms around her. Slowly, the tears ebbed. Her dark hair, tightly bound when they left the mountain, had worked its way loose while she slept; he rubbed it between his fingers, sending thoughts of safety.

"Well, well, Danion," a cheerful male voice said in English, "there's hope for you yet."

Sasha twisted in Danion's arms. He promptly released her, although she could feel him, a bulwark against her back. The world was pressing in on her again, making demands faster than she could meet them.

In the open gate a man was lounging, arms crossed over a well-muscled chest. He had curly black hair and dark brown eyes, chocolate skin, and what looked like an ever-present grin. If she had to guess, she'd place his age, like Danion's, between thirty and forty.

"Shouldn't leave the gate open when you're kissing beautiful ladies," the man said. He separated himself from the gatepost and sauntered down the path. "You never know who'll drop in."

"I wasn't kissing her." Danion sounded amused, light-hearted almost, as though the teasing was an old, familiar game.

"Your loss," the newcomer said. In three steps he had joined them. "I would." He dropped a kiss on Sasha's cheek and held out a hand to Danion. "Welcome home, brother. Dare we hope you've come to stay? And who is the lovely lady?"

Brother. Not literally, obviously: the man was human. A close friend, then. Interesting. On brief acquaintance, he seemed wholly unlike Danion in personality.

Danion shook the hand. "Thank you, my friend. I am pleased to see you also. But so many questions at once. Which would you like me to answer first?"

Dark eyes rolled heavenward. "Well, you haven't changed, I see. Why not start at the beginning and answer the lot?"

"I have left the mountain," Danion said, the unexpected warmth in his voice undiminished. "Whether I stay depends on what happens next. The lady you were kissing is Sasha, my wife. Sasha-*chan*, this is Geoffrey Anderson, a friend of mine from the Academy."

"Pleased to meet you." Sasha hoped she spoke the truth. Geoffrey's effusive compliments had raised her hackles.

Ignore him, Danion said in her thoughts. Geoffrey means no harm. When he realizes he's upsetting you, he will stop.

Perhaps Danion was right, for this time, Anderson did not even look at her.

"Same," he said absently, frowning at his friend. "I thought you..."

He stopped in mid-sentence.

"You thought I what?" Danion asked.

Really, Danion, Sasha said, don't be dense. He thought you were married already, or that you took an oath of celibacy. He's trying not to embarrass you by spilling secrets you haven't shared with me.

Oh, Danion said. Should I tell him?

Later, she said. I'm sure he'll mention it again when you're alone. At the moment, it would just get in the way.

"Never mind," Anderson said. "So what brings you back, Danion? I couldn't believe it when I got your call."

You called him then? Sasha asked. Why?

He can help us, Danion said. I know he has not made a good first impression, but you will see. Beneath his frivolous manner, he is a loyal friend and good at his job. "Come in, Geoffrey, and I will explain. We require your assistance, but as you see, we have just arrived. I did not expect you so soon." He gestured at the door.

"Sure thing," Anderson said. "I think I'll shut your gate for you, though. You never know what riff-raff may show up." He grinned again. "You can't have everyone kissing your wife."

Sasha shook her head at him. "Silly." She let Danion lead her into the house.

❅

The front door revealed a dark hallway, sepulchral rooms opening at angles from the main entrance. Off to the left, just beyond a curve in the passage, she saw a staircase, granite risers contrasting with a banister like a polished tree limb. Closed shades and covered furniture explained the darkness, but the non-human design was reflected in oddly shaped corners and slightly out-of-proportion fixtures: doorknobs too high or too low, handles that did not turn in the direction one expected, and so on. It should have been familiar after her weeks on the mountain, but subconsciously she had assumed a private home would be different.

Sasha moved among the rooms, opening shades and removing covers, fluffing pillows and nudging ornaments out of their oppressive symmetry. Behind her, Anderson and her husband were talking, the human's voluble diatribes contrasting with Danion's occasional calm remark.

Anderson was discussing the details of a project he was running, with occasional asides into Academy politics. Listening in as she passed them on her self-appointed rounds, she realized Danion was right. Anderson had a gift for observation, as well as an enviable ability to identify and analyze political factions. He would make an effective ally.

Danion had dropped the bag in the front hall. Sasha left it there and continued her explorations. Upstairs she found three more rooms—two obviously bedrooms, sheets piled at the ends of bare mattresses, and the third a bathroom, impeccably clean but otherwise unremarkable. Discovering the Tarkei version of a linen closet, a large wooden chest perfumed with a local variant of cedar, she selected a towel and went to wash the desert grime from her hands and face.

A second staircase descended beyond one of the bedrooms. Sasha followed it down and found the kitchen. It, too, was spotless and well-appointed, although the service panel contained a limited amount of food. On one counter she spotted a box of Tarkei tea. Hoping it had not sat there for the last six years, she hunted down a teapot, boiled water, and brewed tea. Tray in hand, she walked back to the front of the house, where Danion was enlisting Anderson's help in identifying green-skied planets that might be missing a dancer.

She handed Anderson a cup, relieved to notice that his flirtatious air had vanished. Danion sat on the edge of a couch cushion, elbows balanced on his knees. He thanked her as he took the cup. Cradling her own mug in her hands, she sat next to him.

"Green sky." Anderson raised the teacup to his nose and sniffed. "Nice. Lemon something. Or is it peppermint?"

"Both, according to the package," Sasha said. "Not too ancient, I hope."

"It belongs to the estate agent," Danion said. "What do you think, Geoff? I found too many possibilities and no way to distinguish one from another."

"We need the Academy computers," Anderson said. "Offhand, I can't tell you. Green skies aren't that uncommon: anything yellowish in the atmosphere and there you are. But green skies and a human dancer should turn up something. What kind of dance?"

"What kinds are there?" Danion asked.

Anderson leaned back in his chair and stretched out his legs, heels on the carpet. "One or two, old buddy. Flamenco, square dancing, English country, Indian, African, about a million other folk traditions, jazz, modern, postmodern, post-postmodern, expressionist, impressionist, Highland, Graham-Tharp, Sokolnikov ... Shall I go on?"

Danion rubbed his forehead, as if overwhelmed by the number of options. Sasha sympathized.

"She dances on her toes," Danion said.

Anderson straightened, his face intent. "A ballerina, by God. Why didn't you say so in the first place?"

Danion shrugged. "I didn't think it significant."

Anderson groaned. "I shouldn't have asked." He stared at Sasha as though she were jewelry in a store window. "Well, that ought to narrow things down."

"Why?" Danion asked.

Anderson didn't answer. Instead he continued to stare at Sasha. "Come to think of it, you do look familiar. Are you famous?"

She spread her hands. "I don't know. It's like my memory stopped working. It's not that I've forgotten, but I have two or three different versions of everything in my past. They fight with one another, and most of them are too scary to contemplate."

"Must be rough," he said, but his intense focus didn't shift. "Are you good, then?"

The tea had a delicate tang that echoed its subtle aroma. The cup warmed hands that had inexplicably gone cold—not an easy trick, on Tarkei. "How can I tell? I have no basis for comparison."

Her voice sounded shaky. Danion shifted his cup to his left hand and leaned back. She kicked off the thong sandals she had worn from the mountain and curled her feet under her. Her collar bone touched his shoulder.

Anderson, lost in thought, paid no attention. "Oh, come on. Has anyone seen you?"

She tried to clear the fog that swirled in her head, to concentrate, to respond. "Dance, you mean?"

"Yes," Anderson said.

Sasha sensed his irritation. At her literal-mindedness, probably, but trying again to explain how muddled she felt would be a waste of time. Better to answer the question, on the assumption he had something specific in mind.

"No," she said. "Except Danion."

"Why will it narrow things down?" Danion asked.

Anderson waved the question aside, intent as a terrier on a mouse. "Parts? Styles? Reactions? Anything?"

A stageful of characters ran through her head, each name as clear as if they held placards in front of their faces. She read them off. "Giselle. Aurora. Juliet. Odette/Odile. Hester—"

He held up his hands. "Enough! I don't need the whole pantheon. Do something. You're wearing pants, right? Never mind the pointe shoes. Strike a pose."

"A pose," she said. Beyond the couch, near the window, she saw an area with minimal furniture. She walked toward it. How good was she, anyway? Curious that this Geoff believed he could tell. He didn't seem the type, somehow.

Her chosen section of floor was carpeted. That meant she couldn't turn in bare feet unless she wanted to risk an

ankle. No fouettés, then. Too bad. That would show him. What else could she do?

Her face lit up with mischief. She thought of long red skirts: Kitri. Two running steps and she jumped. Her back leg flicked into the air, almost touching her head. She landed on the front foot, not making a sound, and brought the back foot down and through to the front, knee bent, right arm over her head. She was standing on the spread toes of her right foot.

"Not bad," Anderson said. "Not bad at all." He started to clap and laugh at the same time. Danion reached to catch him before he fell off the couch, but at the last minute Anderson recovered.

Sasha returned to her seat, comfortable for the first time since she'd met him. "You did ask," she said. "I didn't expect to send you into hysterics."

His face creased in a charming smile. For some reason, he reminded her of a children's story, something about a cat who vanished, leaving only his grin. "Doesn't matter, beautiful," he said. "It was just what I needed."

He turned to Danion. "She's a classical ballerina, brother, and one good enough to dance leading roles in nineteenth-century productions. There aren't half-a-dozen companies in the galaxy who do that, and if one of them's missing a prima, you can bet they have put out the word. Give me a couple of hours, and I'll tell you which one."

Danion raised an eyebrow. "Excellent, my friend. And how is it that you know so much about dance?"

Already on his feet, Anderson produced a rueful smile, not the Cheshire-cat grin but a twist of the lips that suggested real feeling. "You didn't know? My sister Sara began studying ballet when she was eight. She joined the corps at Xantera Ballet six months ago..."

Sasha missed the rest. The word "Xantera" flooded her with memories more excruciating than any she had experienced so far. Desperate to escape the pain, she buried her head in her hands and screamed.

Danion jerked as though bitten by a vithra. Geoff said something unprintable and grabbed Sasha's hands. Danion snatched them away from him. The shrieks continued, the sound of a hunting cat. Or its prey.

"Well, don't just sit there!" Geoff said. "Help her!"

Danion thought, not quickly enough for his friend. Geoff made a sound between a snarl and a hiss, pushed Danion aside, and put both hands on Sasha's shoulders.

"Stop," he said. Then, more gently, "Stop. You're safe. No one's here but Danion and me. We won't hurt you."

After a while, the screams stopped. Sasha pressed her fingers into her cheeks until the tips turned white. She made no sound, and she did not weep. Instead, she rocked back and forth, as human mothers rock their babies.

Danion touched the edge of her collar bone, where Geoff's hands did not reach. His friend stepped back, and Sasha turned her face into his shoulder. He wrapped his arms around her for the second time that day.

"Damn, I knew I should have called Sara," Geoff said, his voice flat—a tone Danion had heard him use only once before, the day a close friend died.

He started for the door. He'd almost reached it when Danion called to him. "Geoffrey, where are you going?"

His friend turned. His face, rigidly composed, shocked Danion more than Sasha's screams. "To the Academy. I have to find out what's happened on Xantera." He made a helpless gesture. "It's probably too late for Sara, but it will help the two of you. I've seen your wife. I just don't remember her name."

With that, he left. Danion looked down as Sasha lifted her head from his shoulder. "You should go with him," she said, her voice trembling. "I'll be fine."

A questionable assertion, but the bond confirmed her determination, at least. "If you are certain," Danion said, "I will. The sooner we find out who you are and what happened, the sooner we will know how to proceed." Geoffrey would undoubtedly castigate him for leaving her, but she was his wife, not Geoff's.

"Go." Sasha moved to the far side of the couch, freeing him to stand. "Then come back and tell me what you find out. I'll be safe here."

Danion studied her. She sat, straight as the path to the mountain, hands wound in her lap, staring at him. There was so much he could not say—how he grieved for her pain, how he wanted to help her untangle her past, how he regretted the pressure placed on her by the joining, how he would remove that burden, too, from her if he could.

But to start such a discussion would delay what aid he could provide, and she might not understand, as she had not before. In that case, he would only add to her troubles. He rose to his feet, pressed his hands together, and bowed.

"May you bask in Danar's rays." The farewell to those one held dear.

Sasha did not react. She did not recognize it, then. "I'll be here," she said.

He didn't have time to explain. "I will return soon," Danion promised as he hurried out the door to catch Geoff.

The front door clicked. Sasha leaned back against the pale blue cushions of the couch. Pictures elbowed their way into her thoughts, cutting one another off at the corners and falling over one another, heightening the chaos that had afflicted her since her arrival on Tarkei eight weeks ago. Crushed flowers and dull silver laser guns, scowling faces and ripped leather armor, bodies of people she had loved crumpled lifeless on a bare wooden floor. They swirled and leaped like flames in a pit, then rolled up and away before she could capture them.

Danion reached for her along the bond, and she clung to the sense of him until his thoughts displaced the tortured images. He strode down the street, moving fast enough that Anderson had stopped to wait for him.

"What did you do, just leave her there?" Anderson asked as Danion approached.

Danion flinched. Don't take it personally, Sasha told him. Chances are he's angry with himself for not protecting his sister.

Thank you. Danion's confusion ebbed.

Good. Her own was more than she could bear.

"I wish to help her," Danion told his friend. "She needs support, as you say, but she needs information more, and the sooner we have it, the better."

Anderson sighed. "Come along then, brother. I'll reintroduce you to the Academy computers."

6. Academy

THE ACADEMY HAD NOT changed. The pyramid of glass and steel evoked the past as even his house had not done. If Danion closed his eyes, six years would vanish into dust.

The building exuded an air of functional splendor. Opaque glass, fortified against the suns' glare, shone black as the obsidian that littered the desert. Shot through with the rays of three suns, set against the brilliant rust sky of late afternoon, the glass gleamed. Danar rode low on the horizon; his bright yellow glowed around the second floor. Selassa hovered over him. Kana topped the pinnacle, a star impaled, alien rendering of a Terran Christmas tree.

Sentient beings of many species traversed the concrete steps leading to the main door. Danion, fighting a wave of nostalgia, distracted himself by quizzing his friend.

"Hardly anyone," Geoff said in response to a query as to who remained from six years ago. "All the humans have left, except me. Most of them were interns, you know."

Danion nodded. He had expected nothing else.

"Thuja's here, with a new crop of Pannthu in training. That may prove useful, if you're planning to go after these guys. Are you?"

"Good question." Pannthu were warriors almost from birth; science came distinctly second. If he and Sendar had drawn the right conclusions, a group of Pannthu would indeed prove useful. "It depends who they are. But the preliminary evidence suggests that they're Kazrati. If so, we must go after them. Otherwise, they will come after us."

"Kazrati," Geoff said, repeating the expletive he'd used when Sasha screamed. "I don't like the sound of that. Especially if they've got Sara."

"Nor do I, Geoffrey." Danion placed a hand on his friend's shoulder. "I have not said so, but I deeply regret that Sara is involved."

"Thank you, brother." Geoffrey held the door for him. "By the way, Reilu is here."

Danion froze with his foot on the top step. "She is not."

"She is. Gunning for you, too, I'd say." Geoff walked through the door and held it open from the other side.

"After six years?"

Geoffrey waited, one hand on the door. Danion forced his feet into motion and followed his friend through. The corridor beyond was dark and pleasantly cool, but he lacked the serenity to appreciate it.

"Some people have long memories," Geoff said. "Women scorned in particular. And the new wife isn't going to help. Does she know?"

"Sasha knows." Danion touched his earlobe, where the garnet stud anchored him to the mountain. "What do you take me for, Geoffrey?"

"I meant Reilu."

"I arrived this afternoon," Danion said. "I haven't told anyone except you. And she wasn't scorned. She did not want me either; she made that clear."

"That's not her story, according to Thuj. Not that I care; I'm on your side either way. But you did surprise me. Frankly I didn't know you'd divorced."

"I didn't."

Anderson groaned.

"Forgive me, Geoffrey." Danion ran a hand through his hair, aware that he was acting more like a human and less like a sun priest every minute. It had been a long day. "Do you mind if I explain later? It is complicated, and I have no wish to shout it to the Academy." He cast an apprehensive glance over his shoulder. "Dodging Reilu is enough stress for one visit, don't you think?"

Geoff's hearty laugh burst out. Anyone within six parsecs could have recognized it and come running, but fortunately no one did. He smacked Danion's back and pointed to a door just ahead. "In here, my friend. Hide away. I won't spill the beans, but don't think you can dodge the explanation."

"Fair enough." No point in arguing, when Geoff and Thuja would have it out of him anyway.

The door opened onto an office so crowded it was difficult to imagine anyone using it. Printouts, disks, computer equipment, handwritten notes, even old-fashioned paper books were piled high on every available surface. Chairs, desk, floor were barely visible under the heaps, while the bookcases that lined the five walls bulged at the seams. On the far side, a pair of purple antennae peeked above a computer monitor, their owner a mere reflection against the glass.

"Good afternoon, Thuja," Danion said. "I trust that life has treated you well."

"Danion!" A navy-blue head, attached to the purple antennae, popped up from behind the computer terminal like a lizard from behind a rock. Thuja hurtled over desk and piles in a single leap and threw both long skinny arms around Danion's neck. From there she dangled until he gently disengaged her.

She produced a series of exclamation points. "Danion! You are back! But I have missed you! How pleased am I!"

It was exhausting but pleasantly familiar. Danion said, "I too am pleased, Thuja. I see you have not changed."

"That is a compliment, I hope." She cleared two chairs by the simple expedient of knocking their piles to the floor. Danion raised an eyebrow at Geoffrey, who shook his head.

Thuja leaped back over the desk. "But sit," she said, "and tell me what I can do for you. Would you like some tea?"

"No, thank you," Danion said quickly. Six years were not long enough for him to forget Thuja's tea.

"We had some at Danion's house," Geoff added. "He's back from the desert—and remarried, to boot."

Danion scowled at his friend. Geoff grinned. "Don't act like an idiot, Danion. Sasha's the reason we're here. You can hide from Reilu, but you can't hide that. Not from Thuja, if you want her help."

"And why would you wish to hide from Thuja, no matter what?" the Pannthu asked. "Are we not friends?"

"Because you gossip, Thuj," Geoffrey said. Danion forgave him. "This is confidential, at least till Danion breaks the news to his family."

"But he is not divorced. How can he have remarried? Tarkei is not Panntha." Thuja's antennae waved as if blown by a breeze emanating from the window behind her.

Danion sighed. "I see I must explain after all."

"It's about time," Geoff said. To Thuja he added, "She's a real stunner, the new wife. I must admit, I'd trade Reilu for her in a second, myself."

"Oh, do tell." The purple antennae stood straight up. Thuja's arms followed, throwing piles of material off the desk—so she could get the full benefit of his explanation, Danion assumed. The Pannthu looked 100 percent engaged.

He leaned back in his chair, hoping it would not collapse under him (as Thuja's overstrained furniture had a tendency to do), and explained the joining as succinctly as possible. His friends oohed and aahed in a very non-Tarkei manner, but when he reached the end they seemed satisfied. They stopped interrogating him about his marriage and turned to the question of Xantera.

Thuja's computer resisted her attempts to gather information, and in the end she gave in to Danion's urging and ceded her seat to him. Geoff hung over his shoulder making suggestions while he poked and prodded and bypassed security protocols, looking for the data he sought. The longer it took, the more convinced he became that Xantera was their goal, for why would an ordinary planet be blanketed in such secrecy?

At last, he hit on the right combination. The screen cleared its lines of irritating mumbo-jumbo about missing passwords and produced a picture of a green-skied planet. In the middle of grasslands as lush as the Tarkei desert was dry, a glass-walled dance studio gleamed in the sun. Outside the windows, a bank of pink azaleas climbed halfway to the sky.

"Bingo," Geoff said. Danion, his stomach tight with a tension that did not originate with him, could not find words to reply.

But the best, or worst, was yet to come. "Show us the principals," Geoffrey told the computer.

"Principles?" the computer said.

"Principal dancers," Geoff specified through gritted teeth, "of the Xantera Ballet Company. Start with the prima."

"Ballerina," he added hastily.

The computer choked off its reprimand concerning the use of "prima" and flashed another, smaller picture onto one corner of the screen. A lovely dark-haired woman with gray eyes stared at the camera.

"Alessandra Sinclair," the mechanical voice said. "Age twenty-eight. Prima ballerina five years, principal dancer before that, daughter of the company founder and of its first prima ballerina, Lucia Sinclair. Sister of the present company director. Born on Xantera."

"Current status?" Geoff asked. Danion could not speak.

"Unknown," the computer said.

Two hands touched Danion's shoulders. One belonged to Geoffrey; the other, thin and bony, to Thuja.

"That is his wife?" the Pannthu asked across the top of his unresponsive head.

The question, like Geoffrey's answer, came from far away. "That's his wife," he said. "I knew I'd seen her before."

"He is in shock." Thuja sounded strangely dispassionate for so volatile a creature.

Geoff's hand tightened on his shoulder. "Hang on, buddy," the human said. "Now we're going to find out what happened."

While she waited, Sasha, plagued by disconnected visions, alternated between burying her head in the cushions and wandering around the house, looking for something to do. She made beds and dug out enough of the estate agent's supplies to produce a tolerable dinner. Eating it almost choked her, but somehow she managed. She put the rest away for Danion, recycled the dishes, then gave up and went to bed.

Silver laser guns, bodies sprawled on a wood floor, ripped leather armor, and glowering Tarkei-like faces mingled in her thoughts. A person who looked like her mother dissolved in an angry blue blaze; it turned to engulf her father as he ran to save his wife. In the dream, she whimpered and tried to run, but her feet, chained to the grass, would not move.

A whisper of sound woke her, and she sat up in a single movement, terror spilling over from the nightmare that clung to her like a straitjacket. Danion sat at the edge of the bed.

"Do not fear," he murmured. "It is I. I did not intend to wake you. You were dreaming again."

Shaking, she clung to the closest object. It happened to be his shirt. She pressed her face into it, fighting for control.

"Hush." He pressed her fingers apart, and she realized she had wound them in his collar, tightly enough to prevent him from breathing. He did not protest, just loosened them and held them close to his chest. "Lie down," he said. "I will stay with you, and you will be safe."

Sasha took several deep breaths. Her heart stopped trying to break through her ribs, and her stomach left her throat and returned to its usual place. "You don't have to. I'll be fine."

His eyes lightened with the glint that so appealed to her. "Actually, I do have to. Geoffrey has the other bedroom, and I do not wish to sleep with him, whereas I think you would benefit from my presence. Or have you not noticed that your dreams cease to plague you when I am nearby?"

It was true. She did feel safer when he was there. "Geoffrey is staying here?" she asked. "I thought he had his own home."

"He does, but he lives on the other side of the planet. He came to Tarkakhan because I requested his help. Does it trouble you, that he should stay here?"

"No. If he has no home in Tarkakhan, he must stay. I misunderstood." She moved closer to the wall to make room for Danion.

"I can sleep on the floor," he said.

Sasha examined the floor. True, the priests' cells were far from comfortable. True, the floor had a carpet. It still seemed extreme, even for someone sworn to celibacy. What did he think she would do to him?

"You look exhausted," she said, and he did. The angles in his face were sharply drawn, and deep lines cut from nose to mouth. "You can sleep here. I'm sure nothing will happen. Besides, if your friend finds out you slept on the floor, you might as well have stayed with him."

"He will not find out from me," Danion said, but he made no attempt to move. He looked as though he might not have the strength to do more than fall down if he tried.

"Did you learn anything?" she asked, then regretted the question as soon as it was out of her mouth. She stroked a finger down his cheek, and he caught her hand and held it. The garnet earring pressed against her fingers.

"I will tell you the rest in the morning, but we did discover who you are. Alessandra Sinclair, the prima ballerina of the Xantera Ballet Company."

All the blood left her head at once. Had Danion not caught her, she would have tumbled off the bed. As it was, he pulled her against his chest and lay down beside her, cradling her against his shoulder. Her body trembled as if she lay in a blanket of snow, and tears pooled against Danion's shirt. He fumbled in a drawer with his free hand, retrieving a box of tissues, which he handed to her. Minutes passed before she could calm herself enough to use them.

"I'm sorry," he said when the tears gave way to sobbing breaths, then silence. "I thought it would help."

She didn't know what to say. "It's not your fault," she whispered at last. "Someone else did this, whatever it was, and I have to find a way to make sense of it, whether I want to or not. It does help, truly."

Danion stroked her hair, and she relaxed against his shoulder, grateful for his support.

Danion awoke to an urgent hand on his shoulder. The mattress under him felt soft, too soft, and the weight on his chest should not be there. About to shift it off, he stopped. It seemed to be calling his name.

Whispering his name, in fact. "Danion, Danion, are you awake? It's morning."

He opened one eye. Sasha's face—no, Alessandra's— filled his vision, her eyes huge in the dim light. Outside the window, Orbfire hung low on the horizon. She was right; it was his usual time of rising.

Yet he felt grumpy. Yesterday had dragged on forever. "Did you not tell me this was the middle of the night?"

Sasha pushed a fist against his chest. "Don't joke. This is serious."

Danion caught her hands. His irritation dissipated as he became more alert. Across the bond, a maelstrom of emotion boiled, held in check by the most fragile of barriers. At any moment, the storm could sweep the levee away. "What is, Sasha-*chan*?"

Now that she had his attention, the urgency seemed to leave her. She released the elbows that had been propping her up and fell forward onto his chest, eyes closed against the storm's onslaught. "I remembered," she said, muffled, into his shirt.

Tempted to jump off the bed, Danion restrained himself. "Indeed," he said, a little breathless. "And what did you remember?"

The answer came through the bond. The storm was gathering; he could sense it. I can't say it, she said, but I'll think it and you'll see.

Very well, he said, bracing himself. Just in time, for the images poured over the bond like rain through the desert, sweeping all in their path. Nightmare images of gratuitous cruelty and vicious hate—shrieking demons, human and Kazrati—swirled and mingled, the man Sasha had seen earlier at their head. His name was Tendak. Friends murdered, family tortured, leather restraints against her hands, cold electrodes at her temples, secrets shed, screams of anguish, tears and heartache. Here, in the actions of the sect his own people had rejected, Danion saw what they might have been, what he might have been, had his own long-ago forebears chosen that other path. A world farther from the mountain, it was difficult to imagine.

Alessandra, not even crying, lay with her head pillowed on his arm, curled against his side, trusting him. Danion sifted the pictures she had shown him, comparing them with what he and Geoff and Thuja had discovered, and mastering the fury that made him see the world through a haze of Orbfire's crimson.

After a while, he flicked the tip of his wife's ear. "Time to get up, Alessandra. We must talk to Geoffrey. Can you do that?"

Alessandra sat up, one hand pulling the dark hair into the nape of her neck. She looked drained past the point of exhaustion yet somehow relieved, as though a huge burden had been lifted from her. "I can do it."

Danion started to rise, but her hand on his shoulder stopped him before he made it more than halfway. Behind her, the suns were rising. Danar's first beams cut through the glass behind her head. Danion watched and waited, probing the bond for clues to her intent.

She kissed him. A real kiss, with her arms around his neck and her lips, slightly parted, moving against his. It was much more pleasant than he had anticipated. Danion pulled her closer. She touched one hand to the tip of his ear, Tarkei-style, then wriggled free. He stared at her, his emotions in turmoil.

From the doorway, she smiled at him, a half-smile worthy of the Tarkei. "Thank you, Danion," she said. "And *not* Alessandra. It's my name, of course, but my friends call me Sasha."

She whisked through the door before he could produce a suitable response.

7. The Lion's Den

NO INCURSION ON THE estate agent's supplies could produce a morning meal for four people. Leaving a note with the promise of reimbursements, Danion and Sasha, with Geoffrey in tow, joined Thuja for breakfast. Geoff suggested the Academy cafeteria, a suggestion Danion rejected with the closest approximation of loathing Sasha had seen in him, so they wound up at a small café about two blocks from Danion's house.

"No sign of Reilu here," Geoff announced, after a certain amount of theatrical peering behind every pillar and potted plant, of which the café boasted a good number.

Danion glared at his friend. Thuja—a skinny lavender being almost as tall as Danion himself (and he topped six feet), with navy-blue hair, no eyebrows, and a magnificent pair of purple antennae—laughed. An odd sight in someone who had no lips.

"His first wife," Thuja told Sasha. "He fears she is chasing him."

Sasha sent her husband an amused but sympathetic glance. "A bit late, isn't it?" she said to Thuja, who laughed harder, displaying half-a-dozen rows of pointed lilac teeth.

"Not to mention somewhat obsessive. How does she know he's not still on the mountain?"

The bond glowed gratitude.

"Ah, but that's the best part," Thuja said. "She doesn't. He merely fears that he will run into her. She frequents the Academy, you know."

"Then we shall have to hope that either he will not, or she will see reason, won't we? There's not much she can do, is there?" Sasha directed this last at Danion, who shook his head. The gold thread flowed between them like a glittering stream.

He touched the tip of his ear where she had stroked it earlier. "Thuja, your love of gossip is insatiable, even if you must fabricate it. Please, turn your appetite to more prosaic forms of nourishment."

Thuja, as immune to rebuke as a rubber ball, responded by burying her nose in the menu. The waiter appeared. Geoff ordered coffee and a donut, earning a protest from Danion that he staunchly ignored. Thuja selected tea, together with something unpronounceable and, from the image in Danion's head, likely to be squirming when it arrived from the kitchen. Danion chose vegetables and fruit juice. Sasha, thinking of the squirming dish, decided on cheese and fruit, although the coffee was too good to pass up; she hadn't had so much as a sip since she reached Tarkei, or for some time before.

That thought made her shiver. The waiter asked if she were cold as he collected the electronic touch pads that served as menus.

"No," she said, and he went away. Danion was gazing at her, concern in his eyes.

"It's nothing," she said. It wouldn't convince him, but it might distract the others.

Until the food arrived, they stayed on neutral topics, mostly current events at the Academy with occasional jabs on the subject of Danion's first wife. Since none of it had anything to do with her, Sasha let her thoughts drift. The café in early morning was pretty, an adobe grotto decorated with the pillars and plants Geoff had made such a show of searching. Some of the plants had bright-colored desert flowers, in yellows and reds. Their rich scents reminded Sasha of the sanctuary garden, but she saw no altanai; Danion had said they were rare.

So soon after the suns' rising, the restaurant had few customers; no one but themselves sat at the white bent-cane furniture at this end of the room. Outside, wispy rust-colored clouds sprayed across the lightening sky, but by midday they would dissipate. The rainy season was not due for months.

A milky tang wafted past her nose, accompanied by the smell of cut tropical fruit and the delicious, unmistakable aroma of fresh-brewed coffee. Sasha, looking apprehensively at Thuja's plate, was relieved to see that the whatever-it-was did not move, although that shade of puce was quite revolting.

Grateful, she switched her gaze to Danion's vegetables, sitting on their plate and exuding a delicate garlicky scent. Her husband's thoughts touched hers, and she raised her eyes.

Just don't drink her tea, he said, referring to Thuja, whose antennae wove side-to-side in his mind.

Thanks for the warning, Sasha said. The waiter delivered Geoff's donut, which did indeed look like a donut, although it was more the size of a dinner plate.

"Geoffrey," Danion said, his tone one of a disappointed parent, "you are not going to *eat* that, are you?"

Geoffrey took a hearty bite, and a good sixth of the donut vanished. "Sure am, brother," he said through the mouthful of pastry. "Besides, why get on me? Look at that mess Thuja ordered. Although at least it isn't trying to escape this time."

"You are right, Geoffrey, it is not fresh," Thuja said. "I must remember that if I come here again."

The waiter left. "Enough teasing," Danion said. "We must plan."

Thuja's flightiness vanished. Even the purple antennae became intent. "You have news, Danion? Last night we did not know enough to plan."

"I have news," Danion said. "More accurately, Sasha has news, which, with what we learned last night, tells us much of what we need to know." Again, his thoughts flicked at the edges of her mind. Do you wish to tell them, *kaleita*?

Kaleita? What's that?

Bond mate, he said. Soul mate, if you prefer. The other half of a joining, whether male or female.

Thank you! It was such a beautiful word, and it surprised her that he would use it. Was he growing accustomed to the idea of the joining, then? Did she want him to?

But he had asked whether she wished to tell the others her story, now that her mind had made sense of it at last.

No, I can't, she said. I'd be in hysterics.

Very well. Danion twirled an eating utensil in his fingers, one of the china spoons Tarkei used. I will do it. I just hope I don't break anything—or anyone.

It is dreadful, isn't it?

Danion's fingers gripped the spoon. Unconscionable, he said.

Geoffrey was staring at them. "What are you doing when you look at each other like that? Are you just making sheep's eyes, or is something else going on?"

Danion jerked his head as if startled, then relaxed. "Of course, you would not know. We are mentally linked, Geoffrey. We talk to each other."

"Honest?" Geoff looked from one to the other. "That's part of this joining thing?"

Danion nodded.

"Useful," his friend said, "but I didn't mean to get sidetracked. What did you find out?"

Danion clasped his hands together, wrists resting on the table. Thuja and Geoff gave him their full attention, and Sasha listened for the information he had promised to share last night.

"Here's what I put together from the Academy computers and what Sasha told me," he began. "Some time ago—it's not clear how long, but some weeks after your sister's arrival, Geoff—the Kazrati invaded Xantera, where Sasha lives."

Geoff groaned. "I am sorry," Danion said.

His friend nodded, and Danion went on. "Why they chose Xantera remains unclear, although it is a habitable planet with a low population density located not far from Kazrati space. They may not have launched a full-scale operation. Sasha can identify only one leader, a man named Tendak."

"Could be a scout," Geoff noted.

"True," Danion said. "In any case, it doesn't matter. Even if Tendak is a renegade, allowing him to succeed encourages others to try."

"And if he isn't, the government will disavow him if he's caught." Thuja's antennae curved forward, almost touching her nonexistent eyebrows. It made her look like a cat with its ears perked.

"Precisely." Danion took the interruptions in stride. With such voluble friends, he must be used to them. "In any event, the invasion caused considerable loss of life, especially among the rural population, which, lacking sophisticated weaponry, attacked the invaders with rocks."

Anderson made a small sound, and Danion held up his hand. "Not including Sara. She was alive and in no worse condition than anyone else when Sasha left." Geoff subsided into silence again.

"Sasha's parents were killed," Danion said.

"Ouch," Geoff said. "I'm sorry."

"I also," Thuja added. Her perked antennae drooped toward her tea.

Danion ignored them and continued his story. "Another outbreak occurred when the dancers mounted a rebellion, about three months into the invasion. Sasha's brother organized it, and in the aftermath she fears that she betrayed him. She was tortured with a device that manipulated her memories, and she believes that Tendak, who was operating the device, may have forced a 'confession' from her that he used as an excuse to kill her brother. Because the false memories overlap the true ones, she finds it difficult to separate them, especially since much of the truth is unbearable."

Presented as this dry recitation of facts, it sounded worse, even, than when the memories had overwhelmed her in a cascade of grief. Sasha closed her eyes, breathing in the flowers' perfume and feeling the chair solid against her back.

At the end of the link, she sensed Danion, but he had his work cut out for him to keep his own fury in check. She would not ask him for help.

Gradually, the mist cleared and she could again focus on his words. "It seems that the Tarkei government and its allies must be aware of the situation," he was saying. "Otherwise, they would not have shrouded the planet in such secrecy. Had I not had the proper connections, we would still know next to nothing."

This caught Sasha's wandering attention. "What connections?"

"His father's prime minister," Geoff said. "I guess he didn't tell you."

Too overwrought to respond to this except in the most literal way, Sasha exchanged glances with her husband. "It hadn't come up."

Danion leaned back, balancing his chair on one of its three legs. The pose made him look younger, almost boyish, although that wasn't an adjective that she would normally apply to him. "I'll have to talk to him."

On the whole, he sounded as though he'd prefer major surgery. Geoffrey said, "Must you? I don't think he's going to kill any fatted calves."

He understood, then, that Danion and his father did not get along. She recalled the gruff tone in which Danion had announced his refusal to seek his father's approval of their marriage, his statement that his father had thrown him out for having the nerve to disagree. It would not be an easy meeting, she guessed, but he was willing to take on an unpleasant task to help her. His *kaleita*.

Or to fulfill his mission from Sendar. She should not read too much into his decision. Yet the warmth provoked by the thought remained.

"Calves?" Thuja asked. "But what is this? They are vegetarians."

"It's a human story." The weight of the world, briefly lifted from Sasha's shoulders, landed back down with a thump. Given a choice, she'd go back to bed and pull the covers over her head. "The prodigal son returns, having done everything his father warned him not to do, and begs forgiveness, so the father throws him a feast. Killing the fatted calf was the ultimate in those days."

"Well, I don't intend to beg forgiveness," Danion said, "so my father can refrain from slaughtering any unfortunate bovines on my behalf. Talk to him, however, I must, for no doubt he knows far more than we do about what is happening on Xantera."

"Not to mention how the allied governments plan to respond," Geoffrey added. "Alas, brother, you're right." He toyed with the last of the enormous donut. "I wouldn't be in your shoes, though. He's gonna have a conniption when you walk in that door."

"No, he won't." Danion sounded resigned, if not depressed. "He will freeze me with one glance and make me wish I were part of the furniture, which is how he will treat me."

Sasha brushed his left ear with one finger. "Would you like me to come with you?"

Danion clasped her hand and held it under the table. "Not today. If he doesn't throw me out, I suppose I'll introduce you sometime, but you have enough to deal with for the moment, I think." His half-smile peeked through. "I have had years of practice, after all. And before I go, I will call Sendar."

It was pleasant to see Sendar's familiar face. "I did not expect to hear from you so soon, my son," Sendar said. "Are you well? And Sasha-*chan*?"

"We have made progress," Danion said. "Sasha is the name her friends and family use—more comfortable, safer to recall. Her full name is Alessandra Sinclair, and she comes from the planet Xantera. Have you heard of it?"

"I have not." Sendar extended his fingers, forming a steeple with his hands. "Impressive progress, for such a short time. How did you accomplish it?"

"I contacted my friends from the Academy, and we discovered a little. Who she was, among other things. One of my friends had seen her; his sister dances with the same company. When I told her, it seeems to have triggered the rest." Thinking of that "rest," Danion shuddered.

"It was that bad? And how is she?"

Danion spread his hands. "She will recover, but it will not be easy. They manipulated her memories until she could not distinguish illusions from reality. That's why she could produce no coherent explanation of who she was or how she reached Tarkei. She remains confused, although I suspect the most painful memories of being the true ones. That story hangs together, as the other does not."

"We also have some acquaintance with the Kazrati and their rule," Sendar said. "They punish innocents; they do not protect them."

"And whether the horrors are true or false, the Kazrati have inflicted a vicious form of torture on this particular innocent."

It was good that he had called Sendar. Sasha had enough to handle without Danion imposing his fury on her. Even Geoffrey, under normal circumstances a willing and responsive listener, struggled with anxiety for his sister.

"And I cannot spare her, Sendar. I find that more distressing than her experiences. I wasn't there. But yes, from the images I saw, it was horrific."

"And you and she?" Sendar's steepled fingers touched his chin. "Do I sense progress there, too? She communicated through the bond, I assume."

"She did. The joining exists. It grows. I can't tell you more than that, Sendar, except that I am resisting it less than before."

Less? As Geoffrey would say, who was he kidding? The warmth of Sasha's lips, the pressure of her mouth, the way she nestled into his hold—he had not resisted those developments in the least. Had welcomed them, in fact. The joining beckoned, holding out a potential for joy Danion had not imagined, if only he could trust it not to evaporate when he needed it most.

He did not share those thoughts with Sendar, although he suspected his mentor understood all too well.

The steepled fingers pointed toward the screen. "I am pleased. What will you do next?"

The one thing he least wanted to do, now inescapable. Unless Sendar could suggest an alternative.

Possible, but not likely. Danion knew where his duty lay. "That's why I called. I must speak with my father."

"Indeed?"

"Yes." Danion forced his hands out of the fists they formed whenever he faced that unwanted reality and placed them, palms down, on the desk that supported the communications console. "You can't imagine what I had to go through to break the security protocol, and I was using an Academy terminal with the highest clearance. Sasha can't tell me what the Kazrati wanted, let alone what anyone might be doing about it, and if I try to bypass my father it will be worse than if I approach him directly. You know how he is."

"Of course," Sendar said. "Courage, Danion. I did not mean to give you quite so difficult a task." But his mentor's eyes twinkled, and Danion did not believe him.

"Give my regards to Sasha-*chan*," Sendar said, the hint of levity gone. "She has suffered much, and no doubt will suffer more before we bring the Kazrati to justice."

Danion agreed, then switched off the console and went to find something in his tiny wardrobe that would not cause his father to throw him out on his ear.

❀

Prime Minister Jenat of Tarkei had not mellowed with the years, his son decided within the first ten seconds of their encounter. Jenat, an imposing man of middle age, heavier-set than Danion but the same height, looked down his Roman nose, brushed back his silver hair, and conspicuously refrained from offering his son and heir a seat. Frosty glares were far from absent, although the voice was closer to a bark than to its usual iceberg variant.

"Well?" Jenat said by way of greeting. "I have a meeting in twelve minutes. Have you come back to fulfill your responsibilities to the clan, or is this more of your priestly nonsense? I see you're still sporting that earring."

And good morning to you. So delightful to see you again, father, after six years. Danion bit his tongue and prayed for patience. Aloud he said, "I have left the priesthood for now, but I could not live with Reilu if I wished to. I have a wife by joining."

The bark rose to a roar. Danion, reading the signs, gripped his hands behind his back. "She is human," he said before his father could order him out, "and a survivor of the Xantera invasion. That's why I'm here. I would like to trade information, mine for yours."

"Trade. With a child like you." The roar gave way to the more familiar freezing tones.

"I am thirty-two." Danion's fingers were losing sensation, his clasp was so tight, but the strength of his grip enabled him to unclench his teeth and pretend to match his father in indifference. "If you're not interested, I can introduce Alessandra to the leader of the opposition party."

"Don't blackmail me, Danion," Jenat said. "Sit down."

Danion collapsed onto the nearest chair, trying to ensure that it didn't look like a collapse. His father pushed a glass in his direction, and he sipped it, grateful for the cool liquid.

"A wife by joining, eh? The suns must love you, Danion. Are you sure?"

Danion shrugged one shoulder. "As certain as I can be. I did not seek it. We bonded spontaneously, and I have tried for weeks to break it, but instead it strengthens. What else could it be?"

"Sendar said that, I expect." Jenat snapped a pen against the desktop. "He's probably right, though. Well, so be it. I'll inform Reilu's parents. Your cousin will have to take her."

So simple. Your cousin will have to take her. As though he couldn't have taken her six years ago and spared Danion the trouble.

Although the cousin might not have wanted her either. Without knowing which cousin his father had in mind, Danion sent his absent relative a silent apology and returned his attention to the present.

Jenat twirled the pen between his palms and did not meet his son's eyes. "Your wife, then, who is she?"

Danion sipped the juice, then placed the glass on the table, careful not to mar the wood. "Alessandra Sinclair, nicknamed Sasha. The lead dancer at the Xantera Ballet Company. Her brother heads the company, unless the Kazrati have killed him. He plotted an uprising against them. Or so we think. The Kazrati leader, Tendak, subjected Sasha to a memory manipulator, so the sequence of events remains hazy."

"Brave man, the brother," Jenat said. "If so. Foolish, but brave. How did she get here, this Alessandra Sinclair?"

"She stowed aboard a cargo ship, in one of the containers, and escaped when it stopped to deliver goods to the sanctuary. She ran into the desert, where I was meditating. But she thought I was Kazrati, that she had landed on Kazratan, so she hid from me. I thought her a predator on my trail until I captured her."

Jenat dropped the pen and leaned forward, elbows on his desk. "Quite a story. Quite a woman, from the sound of it. Most resourceful. Why didn't you come to me at once?"

Because you swore that you didn't want to see my face again unless I was ready to bow to your every command?

Although accurate, that statement would not secure the answers Danion needed. "Because we lacked hard information," he said instead. "Sasha couldn't face her story, never mind tell it to us. Sendar and I suspected Kazrati involvement from the beginning, but without proof of what had happened, it seemed premature to bring our suspicions to you."

"Yet you are here. What changed?" A buzzer sounded, reminding Jenat of his meeting. The prime minister punched the button, saying to the person at the other end, "Don't interrupt me. I am speaking with my son."

"Yes, prime minister," an abject voice replied.

"Idiots," Jenat muttered. "Well, don't just sit there, boy! I have a meeting to attend."

"Yes, father." Danion picked up the glass and studied it. The suns' rays cast patterns on the green glass until it seemed to glow from within. The worst was over. His apprehension melted, and his father's abrasiveness acquired the comfort of familiarity. "I searched the Academy computer and discovered an inordinate amount of security."

Jenat picked up the pen and shook it at him. "Which you cracked, of course. I suppose I needn't ask who your partners in crime were."

Danion, assuming this comment was rhetorical, ignored it. "When I told Sasha her name, it helped her disentangle the multiple versions of her past. She shared her story with me, and I brought it to you. Because there is much we do not know, and I suspect that you do."

His father punched the button again. "Reschedule the meeting for half-an-hour from now," he told the abject voice.

"Yes, prime minister," it said.

The prime minister poured more juice into Danion's glass, then leaned back, hands clasped behind his head. "All right, boy, tell me the whole."

Altogether, the meeting between Danion and his father lasted more than an hour. The voice became more abject as it received repeated orders to postpone the assembled council of ministers, but Jenat was, as ever, unrelenting. In the end, he dismissed his son with a stern injunction to present himself and his wife at the family home for dinner at the earliest opportunity.

"Very well, father," Danion said, "but I make no promises as to when that will happen. Sasha has endured a great deal, and we must first complete the task you have set us."

Jenat rose, accompanying his son to the door. He slapped a firm hand on Danion's shoulder. Danion managed not to flinch. "I know, boy, but when you return, I expect to see you. Is that clear?"

"Yes, father," Danion said, tongue well in cheek.

"Impudent pup." Jenat's hand bore down on one shoulder, making Danion feel like a hunchback. But as he was about to leave, his father dropped his hand and flicked his son's ear. "Welcome home, Danion. I'm glad to see you. You stayed away too long."

When Danion entered his home, he found Sasha stretched out on the chaise longue that overlooked the garden. Geoff sat next to her, spread across two chairs, his mouth open.

Sasha padded over to him as he released the gate, one finger in front of her mouth. He stopped. She stood on tiptoe to brush her lips across his cheek. Danion caught her around the waist, steadying her.

Don't say anything, she told him through the bond. I'm convinced Geoff is going to drop right through those chairs at any moment. I tried to give him the chaise, but he wouldn't take it, and I was too tired to insist.

He will be fine. He makes me nervous, too, but I have not seen him fall.

There's always a first time, Sasha said. How was the lion?

Bearded, Danion said, in his den.

How quick you are! Did Geoff teach you these colloquialisms?

Most of them, Danion admitted. As I'm sure you've noticed, he has an abundance of them. In the beginning he teased me mercilessly, so I had an incentive to learn fast.

Ah, yes, she said. Throw them in the deep end and see if they can swim. A venerable human philosophy. Tell me, what did you learn from your father?

He has assigned us to reconnoiter the situation on Xantera. To end it if we can. Thuja will help; the Pannthu are natural warriors. We will try to rescue your brother and those you care about, as well as Geoff's sister and as many others as we can transport. You are sure she was alive when you left?

Almost certain. Sooner or later, I talk to everyone in the company, but a new corps member I might not meet at once. I think I noticed her, though, because she showed real talent. I hope the Kazrati didn't hurt her.

I, too. Danion cast another glance at his sleeping friend. Geoffrey appears volatile, but his feelings run deep, and his family means a great deal to him.

Sasha turned halfway toward the porch, following his gaze, then looked up at him. When she stood on the tips of her toes, her eyes were at the same level as his. And *your* family? she asked. Your father treated you well?

As well as he treats anyone, Danion said. He sent his laughter along the link, pleased to have someone with whom to share it. Better than his miserable assistant, I assure you. He has promised to release me from the contract with Reilu, and he wants to meet you.

Alarm flickered at the end of the bond, although it was more a spark than a flame. Not today, he told her. When we return from Xantera. Sasha's anxiety gave way to relief.

Let us wake Geoff, he said. We have much to do, and only a few days to prepare.

8. Iqara

PROMPTED BY A CALL from Danion, the estate agent had stocked the house with several days' worth of supplies. These did not include dinner for a citizen of Panntha, so Thuja went off to forage on her own. She returned less than fifteen minutes later carrying a plate of what looked like live spaghetti. Sasha showed her the kitchen and left, hoping the spaghetti would give up the ghost before she saw it again.

Geoff and Danion sat in the garden, heads together over plates of sandwiches. Sasha joined them. Maybe if she ate quickly, she could finish before Thuja came out. Not high on the politeness-to-guests scale, but higher than the reaction she would have if she had to eat while the spaghetti was fighting its destiny.

Halfway through twilight, the garden gave off an air of quiet opulence. Sasha relaxed into her chair. The array of sautéed vegetables, wrapped in a flat Tarkei bread not unlike whole-wheat tortillas, had a spicy aroma and enough bite to pique the taste buds without overwhelming them. Behind her, the voices of the two men, discussing strategy and tactics and where they could find a ship, blended into a reassuring purr. The pink azaleas evoked sadness, but the peaceful atmosphere muted her sorrow.

What a day. Eyes on the flowers, she allowed herself to think of Xantera, of what had happened there, of those she had lost and those who might be alive.

Thuja joined the discussion, but Sasha did not hear her. The sounds of the garden died away, the shadows lengthened, the three friends withdrew—she did not notice. In the quiet of late evening, Sasha wept.

Danion stayed with Sasha again that night, and he did not offer to sleep on the floor. Thuja, despite assurances that crime did not disrupt life on Tarkei, had refused to walk in the city at night—some Pannthu superstition, he said. He did not explain further, and Sasha supposed it didn't matter, if even the possibility of an escort (Danion and Geoff had both volunteered) could not counteract whatever previously unsuspected evil lurked in Tarkakhan's streets. As a result, Thuja was ensconced on the couch in the living room, as well as Geoff in the spare bedroom. If the household continued to grow at this rate, they would need tents in the garden by the end of the week.

Sasha stretched out on the mattress and admired her husband's lean frame, clad only in a pair of beige cotton trousers. He was sitting at the end of the bed, staring out the window in a preoccupied way, and the bond gave her no clue to what he was thinking.

Why did it do that, open and close in such unpredictable ways? At first, she had expected to lose her privacy, that Danion would hear every passing thought.

It didn't work that way, though: rather it resembled nothing so much as a private conversation—more intimate, more inclusive of emotions sensed but not shared, but still under the participants' control.

"Quite a day," she said, hoping this extreme understatement would jar him loose from whatever gremlin had seized him. "You aren't still making plans, are you? Anxious as I am to get started, I'm sure they can wait till tomorrow."

He lay down beside her. "I was thinking about my father. How much easier it was to talk to him this time. How difficult I found it before. Wondering why we don't get along better, and how much of it is my fault."

"The mountain changed you, then." Sasha tapped the end of his nose. He caught her hand in his and rolled over. His body pressed her into the mattress. His eyes had lost their solemnity, acquiring a gleam that did not reflect the crimson glow outside.

"So it would appear," Danion said. He tapped her nose in turn with the clasped hand he held. "This morning, when you kissed me, were you having fun with me?"

His tone suggested idle curiosity. He was not human, and Tarkei did not kiss, so it might be only curiosity, although Sasha sensed a current he had not acknowledged.

"No," she said. "You stayed with me and helped me through a horribly difficult time. I remembered, from the day you showed me the altanai, that you wondered how it would feel. I wanted to say thank you." She rubbed the clasped hands against his ear. "And I wanted to find out for myself. Kissing one person is different from kissing another. Did you like it?"

"It was not unpleasant," he said with a casualness that dismayed Sasha, who considered pleasant much too mild a word to capture her experience. Then his lips curved, and she heard the laughter through the link.

She pinched his earlobe, catching the rough edges of the garnet between her fingers. "You're teasing me. Wretch. I thought Tarkei didn't make jokes."

Danion shook his head. "My association with you and Geoffrey, I fear, has undermined my principles."

"So sad," Sasha said. "Should I return you to Reilu for your own good?"

His eyes widened in pretended alarm. "A dreadful idea. Have I been so unkind?" His voice dropped half an octave, becoming husky, soft. "That must be corrected."

Even in play she didn't want him to think she could not appreciate what he had done for her. She stroked his ear.

"Are you all right?" Danion asked. "You were crying earlier. I didn't know if you wanted comfort, so I decided to take Geoff and Thuja away instead, so they would not trouble you."

"I noticed." Sasha tangled her fingers in his hair. "Thank you. The crying helped. I expect it will happen again before I'm through." A smile peeked through her lingering sense of grief, and Danion responded. "Comfort's good, too," she said, "if you feel so inclined."

"I will remember that," Danion said. His hand slid beneath her waist, narrowing the small distance between them. "As for the kissing…"

"Yes?"

"I require more data," Danion said, pursuing his research with considerable fervor. The link, Sasha discovered, more than compensated for any inexperience on his part.

In the morning they separated. Thuja went to the Academy to interview her trainees, Geoffrey to begin negotiations with a friend who might provide transport, and Danion, with permission from his father, to discuss the Xantera situation in greater depth with the diplomat in charge. Sasha volunteered to remain at the house to inventory the items they had on hand, a suggestion Danion accepted so readily that she suspected he guessed how far she had to go to overcome the shock caused by yesterday's revelations.

Her husband, bless his considerate heart, had bought her some coffee. Sasha wandered from room to room, mug in hand, sniffing the steam that rose from the dark liquid and considering their most urgent needs.

Both lists had clothing at the top. After six years on the mountain, Danion's wardrobe fit in a single carry-on, while her own was scantier still. Her dance wear had frayed from overuse; she owned no pointe shoes worth the name; and the rest of her clothes consisted of one set of pants and tunic, one nightgown, and some underwear in need of a wash.

She had turned on the computer, hoping that her bond with Danion would supply enough of his language for her to discover where in Tarkakhan one went to buy clothes and wondering how, under the circumstances, to pay for them when a voice she did not know said, "Good morning, Alessandra-*chan*."

Sasha sprang to her feet. The cup slid across the desk, but she snatched at its handle and caught it before it reached the edge. In the doorway stood a young Tarkei woman, very attractive, with short blond hair and honey-brown eyes. She had an ivory complexion, deepening into pale brown on lips and cheeks, and ears that could have passed for a porcelain casting of Danion's. Pearls on gold wires dangled from each delicate lobe, and she wore a peach dress that, unlike the clothes Sasha had seen on everyone else, stopped four inches above her knees. She had the slinky figure of a fashion model, but the brown eyes showed a mischievous delight in having startled someone that Sasha might have expected from a five-year-old child.

A teenager, she decided, perhaps eighteen or twenty—maybe a bit older, since Tarkei matured more slowly than humans. Unmistakably, a grown-up version of the little girl Sasha had seen in Danion's thoughts.

"How you startled me!" Sasha said, further delighting the newcomer. "How did you get in?"

"Through the gate," the young woman said. Her English, like Danion's, was fluent and so lightly accented that it had a certain sophisticated charm.

The answer, however, left much to be desired. Tarkei, while free of crime, had not abandoned locks. Sasha waited.

The tactic proved its worth. After less than a minute, the girl threw up her hands and said, "I am Iqara."

She seemed to think that explained everything. "And?" Sasha said, when no further revelations presented themselves.

"Your sister," the young woman said. "Your sister Iqara."

"My sister." Light dawned. "Danion's sister? My sister-in-law?" Another "detail" her husband had failed to mention. Really, Danion, she said through the bond, what else have you left out?

There was no answer; he must be too focused on his task to listen.

"Your sister." Iqara waved both hands, her face alight with joy. It made her look less like a stereotypical Tarkei than anyone Sasha had met since her arrival. "I wanted so much to meet you!"

"I'm glad to meet you, too," Sasha said. Which was true, more or less. Danion had not identified Iqara as his sister, but Sasha had recognized that the blond child held a particular significance for him.

Her new sister made a graceful descent onto the couch. "Is that coffee? May I have some?"

Sasha pushed her mug to the center of the desk. "Sure. How do you like it?"

"I don't know," Iqara said. "I've never tried it. It smells good, though. How do most people drink it?"

"With milk and sugar, or one of those, or none. It depends how good the coffee is and how much they like the taste. Wait here," Sasha said, "and I'll bring some the way first-timers like it. I warn you, though: good as this is, if you've never drunk it before, you may find it bitter."

She returned with the coffee, doctored until it resembled coffee ice cream, to find that Iqara had left the couch and was examining the ornaments, one by one.

"You shifted them," Danion's sister said as she took the coffee. She sipped it, made a face, and sipped it again.

Sasha tried not to laugh; Iqara looked like a cat not too confident of the tuna.

"I did. I like symmetry, but in moderation." Sasha picked up her coffee. It had begun to cool, but not to the point where the fragrance was lost.

Iqara dropped back onto her seat, balancing the coffee cup on the arm of the couch. "Me too. My father's house is always perfectly arranged. I hate it." She glanced around the room again, between sips of coffee. "It's not Danion's style either. The estate agent came in and aligned everything the first day she was here."

"Were you looking for him?" Sasha wondered why this possibility hadn't occurred to her earlier. Iqara's unheralded entrance must have flustered her more than she'd thought. "He went out, but he expects to be back this afternoon."

Iqara drained the coffee in a single gulp and placed the cup on the floor. "Interesting." Sasha assumed she was referring to the taste, not her brother's whereabouts. "I suppose I could get used to it, although I don't know why I'd want to."

She glanced at her hostess, consternation on her face. "Was that rude?"

Sasha shook her head. "Lots of people don't like coffee. It doesn't bother me."

"You *are* different," Iqara said. "I'd like to see Danion, but I came to meet you. Father said Danion had married a human, and I wanted to find out what you were like." Her face turned to mischief again. "I wish I'd been there when they met, don't you?"

"It didn't sound as bad as everyone expected," Sasha said. "After the first ten minutes or so."

Iqara had already gone on to something else. "Father told me not to come, of course. That's just like him." The vivid face had changed again, years shrinking away until she sounded like a child having a tantrum.

"Maybe I should send you away, then, if your father ordered you not to come." Sasha watched with well-concealed (she hoped) amusement as her volatile guest digested this.

"You wouldn't." Iqara could have been any teenager in the galaxy. "That would be worse than Reilu."

She looked so disgusted that Sasha—despite a momentary flash of sympathy for Reilu, who seemed to provoke everyone's dislike—lost her battle to keep from laughing. "So you admit that there is something worse?"

Iqara glared at her, then a smile crept out, and finally a tiny Tarkei giggle.

"That's better." Sasha decided to take a chance and ask the question that had pestered her since she first heard of Danion's first wife. "Tell me, Iqara-*chan,* if no one likes Reilu, why did your family make Danion marry her? It seems so odd to me."

Iqara leaned forward, her face solemn. "To me, too, but not to my father. I don't know if he likes Reilu or not; he may. I doubt he ever considered the question. He's the ruler of Tarkei, and his son is the future ruler. Royalty don't marry to please themselves, you know."

Royalty? Was this something else Danion had forgotten to mention? But Sasha felt more confident of her memory today, and it told her Tarkei was a republic. She said as much.

"Now," Iqara said, "and for the last two centuries, at least. But Tarkei live a long time, about half again as long as humans. My father's father ruled Tarkakhan and the surrounding area. Danion doesn't think of himself as royalty, and neither do I, but my father was raised as a prince in exile. He wants us to follow the rules."

"What rule is operating here?"

"Ah," Iqara said. "Reilu's family is as old as ours, and as prestigious. In the bad old days, they ruled the lands beyond Tarkakhan. Next to ours. Tradition says"—she made tradition sound like a dirty word—"that the oldest son of our clan marries the oldest daughter of theirs. They shift it about among the different branches, so we don't end up cross-eyed or simple-minded, but this time it was our turn, and that meant Danion." She pulled a face that made her look five again. "I don't know what Father thought would happen if he said no. That Orbfire would fall to earth, probably."

"And you?" Sasha, fascinated by these insights into a world she hadn't imagined, abandoned her usual restraint and asked. "Have you been married off, too?"

Five-year-old scorn became a pixieish smile. "He'd like to, but I have an advantage over Danion."

Sasha raised an encouraging eyebrow.

"Alienating prospective grooms' mothers with my outspokenness." Iqara giggled again. "Not to mention my hemlines."

Not laughing was impossible: Iqara looked so proud of herself. "And that works?" Sasha said when she could speak. "Your father hasn't guessed?"

"They don't dare tell him." Iqara was still giggling.

Sasha wondered how many Tarkei were like Iqara and her brother. It was reassuring, in a way, to believe that underneath they were not so different from humans.

But then, plenty of humans cared more about security and order than happiness. She should keep that in mind.

"Father's not a bad sort," Iqara went on, "when you get used to him. Sometimes I almost feel sorry for him, having two such rebellious children. I think he's resigned himself to my having no marital prospects." Another lightning change, and she became thoughtful again. "He misses Mother, I think, but he won't admit it. Not worthy of a Tarkei, you know."

The most important point she'd raised yet. Sasha's head spun with so much information. Perhaps she should let it go, but when would she have another opportunity? Danion might tell her if she asked, but he had steadfastly avoided the topic of his mother's death until now; she hated to push for answers that might cause him pain. "Your mother, would it hurt you to talk about her?"

"I don't know much about her." Iqara curled elegant feet in delicate high-heeled sandals under her on the couch, careful to keep her shoes off the fabric. "She died when I was six, so no, it wouldn't hurt, but I don't remember her well."

Six. That fit. The child she had seen looked about that age. On the flight here, Danion had said he was sixteen when his mother died. Later she had heard him remind his father that he was thirty-two. Which made Iqara twenty-two, even if she did act as though she were twelve, or two, on occasion. "I wondered what happened to her. She must have been quite young when she died, and as you say, Tarkei usually live longer than we do."

"Oh," Iqara said. "Well, I can tell you that. Kazrati killed her. It was an assassination attempt against my father. He's been prime minister my whole life. The perks of former royalty, I suppose. My parents were an arranged marriage, too, but they were happy together. She was a first-class pilot—she taught Danion—and my father had enemies, so she flew his shuttle. The Kazrati substitute their pilots for ours, you see, and since they look like us, sometimes they get away with it. But they didn't try to capture my mother. Instead, they blasted her out of the sky." The high-heeled sandals returned to the floor, missing the coffee cup by inches. "They got their facts wrong. Father wasn't there. She was on her way to meet him; otherwise we'd have lost them both."

"I'm so sorry," Sasha said. "What a horrible thing to happen, especially when you were only six." The grief she had sensed came back to her, revealing the source of Danion's ready sympathy—even when she first met him, when he sought to distance himself from her as much as possible.

"I don't think it was easier for Danion," Iqara said, "but yes, I still dream about it sometimes." She shivered. "Father said you were attacked by Kazrati as well. If everyone seems obsessive about it, I suppose you'll understand why."

That might explain some of Danion's anger, although he controlled it too well to make obsessive a fair characterization. "They haven't so far," Sasha said, "unless your father was reacting to it during his meeting with Danion. I didn't hear the details."

Iqara touched the empty coffee cup with her foot, then picked it up and played with it. "May I ask you a question?"

"If you like."

"How can you have married Danion? He is married to Reilu." Iqara's eyes fixed on her coffee cup. Her earlier insouciance had vanished; she looked like someone performing a grim mission she could not refuse.

So this explained Iqara's visit. No wonder her father's strictures had not deterred her. What was she imagining?

"Your father didn't tell you?" Sasha asked. "We didn't choose it, exactly. We married by joining."

The cup shattered against the floor. Iqara jumped and bent to pick up the pieces. "I'm so sorry." From her position on one knee, she stared at Sasha, the volatile face alight again. "You married by joining? That's so romantic. And no one told me!"

Sasha knelt beside her. Pieces of handle lay under the couch; shards scattered the rug. "Please, don't bother. Danion must have a cleaning robot somewhere."

Iqara stood, her hands full of broken china. Sasha, eye to hem with the peach dress, abruptly realized that here stood the solution to one problem.

"Iqa-*chan*," she said, "where would I go to buy clothes?"

9. Plans

THEY RETURNED TO THE house several hours later. The merchants had taken Iqara's orders to heart, and boxes littered the front hall. In their midst stood Danion, perplexed. At the sound of the door, he raised his head. "Iqa-*chan*," he said. "Now I understand."

He held out his arms, and Iqara ran toward him. As she reached him, he caught her around the waist and hugged her. Like that moment in the café, it made him look years younger. When he put her down, Iqara flicked his ear, and he did the same to her. "I am pleased to see you, Iqa," he said.

"And I'm amazed to see you, Dani-*chan*," Iqara said. "I thought you were stuck on that mountain and would never come home."

"Things change." Danion pointed toward the living room. "Go and say hello to Geoffrey. He's in there."

"In there?" Iqara's face glowed. She dodged boxes with consummate skill and headed for the living room, leaving Sasha alone with her husband.

Something else you didn't tell me, she said.

The boxes, although numerous, stacked easily. She began sorting them, piling them against the wall.

Nor she, it seems, Danion said. When did she arrive? Sasha, box in hand, thought. About three hours ago, she said at last. Not long after you left. We talked for a while, then we went shopping. You were in the middle of your meeting.

"I see you went shopping," Danion said aloud. His bantering tone was unmistakable.

"Some of it is for you. The shopkeepers had your size, Iqara said. I hope it hasn't changed in the last six years." Sasha dropped another box on top of the pile. "Plus a ton of dance wear. The company will reimburse you for that one day. This whole pile is pointe shoes. I go through them like that." She snapped her fingers in illustration.

Iqara returned to the doorway, Geoff and Thuja in tow. Danion said, "You didn't let Iqa pick my clothes, I hope. Last time she bought me a purple shirt with yellow flowers."

Geoff laughed until Sasha thought he would choke. "I remember that."

Thuja gave her lipless grin. "I, too. He gave it to me. I treasure it still."

"You didn't!" Iqara scowled at her brother, whose amusement visibly grew. "After all the effort I put into finding it! It was the latest style."

"But not mine, Iqa-*chan*." Danion touched his sister's cheek, but she continued to glare at him.

"I bought the clothes," Sasha said. Where was her own brother? Had the Kazrati killed him? "And if you don't like them, or they don't fit, we'll send them back."

Danion must have picked up what she was feeling, for he stopped teasing his sister and suggested they go somewhere else and compare notes.

I'm sorry, Sasha said. I think it's wonderful that you get along so well; don't change on my account.

We won't, Danion told her. No need to worry. Except about your brother. I hope we find him well.

"Somewhere with food," Thuja said. "Good food. I have been interviewing trainees since suns' rise, and I am starving."

"May I come?" Iqara bounced on the balls of her feet, as if in anticipation.

"Does Father know you're here?" Danion asked, expressing an omniscience doubtless born of long experience.

Iqara glared at him again. "No."

"Did he tell you not to come?"

"Yes." Like a schoolgirl, Iqara scuffed the toe of her elegant sandal against the rug, eyes fixed on the moving shoe.

"Then no, you can't," Danion said.

Geoff protested, and Danion relented. "Go home and get his permission, and if you do, you can join us. I just climbed out of one hole with him. I've no desire to fall into another right when I need his cooperation."

"I'll walk you there," Geoffrey said. "Where will the rest of you be?"

Danion thought. "Alcazar?"

The others nodded. Geoff said, "Fine," but Thuja's antennae waved wildly from side to side. "Their prey is frozen, Danion; how can you consider it?"

"The vegetables are fresh," he said, "but if not there, then where would you suggest?"

The antennae perked toward each other. "Antilles is better."

Danion shrugged. No one else objected. "Antilles, then," Geoff said. "I'll see you in half-an-hour." He grinned at Iqara. "With or without Iqa."

Iqara smacked him lightly on the shoulder. He grinned and followed her out the door.

Subconsciously, Sasha had expected Antilles to resemble the café where they had eaten breakfast the day before, which left her quite unprepared for the reality. The terminal at the door flashed the number seventeen when Danion punched in a description of their party, and Thuja almost hit the ceiling in her joy. Or would have, if the restaurant had had a ceiling to hit. "My favorite!" she shrieked, before a murmur from Danion hushed her. Even then, she led the way in huge bounds through the room. Danion shook his head and gestured for Sasha to precede him. They followed the Pannthu as discreetly as possible.

The room reminded Sasha of nothing so much as the fake New Orleans restaurant her father had selected to celebrate her tenth birthday: a grotto with a canopy of stars, a river running by, and pretend pirate boats. Here the stars were real, the center of the Milky Way splashed against the clear desert night. The grotto might be real, too: great blocks of granite reminded her of the area outside the sanctuary where she and Danion had met, and while sentient beings must have organized their placement, the rocks themselves looked as though no chisel had touched them.

Thuja's purple antennae bounced up and down from what appeared to be a cushioned pit ahead of them. In her efforts to attract their attention, the Pannthu was using the padded benches as a trampoline.

Danion descended into pit number seventeen. Sasha prepared to follow, but he reached up, caught her around the waist, and swung her down.

I can jump it, she said through the bond.

I know, Danion told her. He did not sound repentant.

Thuja stopped bouncing and settled at the far side of the table. She tapped the small terminal next to her chosen place, squealed in delight, and punched in an order. Sasha, brought to an abrupt realization of the advantages of darkness, sat cross-legged next to Danion and thanked the stars that she would not have to see what her most eccentric table mate had chosen.

The walls of the pit cut them off from the other diners, so that sky, breeze, and rocks seemed to belong to them alone. Late-blooming flowers perfumed the air, and only the hum of other voices broke the silence. In the dim light, Danion's white, open-necked shirt contrasted with the brown of his throat, the gray rocks, and the patterned cushions, which, although probably quite bright by day, blended into the overall setting at night. For a moment, Sasha wished Thuja gone, herself and her husband alone in the moonlight.

"Good, I found you," Geoff said. The spell binding Sasha and Danion broke as Geoffrey dropped into the pit and took the seat closest to the entrance and farthest from Thuja.

"You did not bring Iqa?" The Pannthu's purple antennae stood straight up—scenting gossip, Sasha assumed.

"Your father wasn't pleased," Geoff told Danion. "Disobedience cannot be rewarded, he said. She's to stay home and ponder her sins tonight, but after that, he's relented. He was trying to save you from another distraction; he had no real objection to Iqa's coming over, unless you count wanting to be the first member of the family to welcome your wife. Not that he'd admit the last."

"Not him." Danion punched his order into the console, queried Sasha by the link, and punched hers in as well. "I can't blame him for keeping her home, either, although you'd think he'd let her make her own decisions; she's twenty-two, after all."

"But if he wants to retain his authority, he must insist that she respect it, yes." Thuja lowered her antennae just as a plate rose from the center of the table. Sasha averted her eyes—not fast enough to avoid the sight of something that looked like a large snail inching across the greenery that surrounded it.

Thuja's antennae flashed out and sideways, forming a vee above her hair. "Yes! It is fresh. Come to me, my darling." The skinny arms reached for the plate. Sasha leaned her head against the rock behind her and closed her eyes. Hideous crunching sounds assailed her ears.

"This is the last time I eat with you, Thuj," Geoff said. Sasha, entirely in sympathy, opened her eyes and looked at him. He grinned the Cheshire-cat grin, his teeth white against the crimson glow of Orbfire rising.

"You say that every time, Geoffrey." Thuja, clearly unimpressed, continued cracking the snail. Sasha risked a glance. In the darkness, now that the Pannthu had dispatched her prey, the reality was no worse than a meal of oysters or clams. Nonetheless, much more exposure to Thuja's cuisine, and she would join the Tarkei in vegetarianism.

Her own plate and Danion's appeared at the same time, as he had ordered them. The aroma of garlic and spices blended into the perfume of the late-blooming flowers. Eight weeks on Tarkei had not proved long enough to educate Sasha on the complex and overlapping flavors of its food, but she had yet to encounter a dish she did not like.

This was no exception. Subtle differences of texture and taste reminded her of Indian cuisine on Earth: a sudden, vivid memory of smoky, chewy nan dipped in creamy spinach brought Danion's eyes back to hers. In response to her pleasure, both present and remembered, he gave her his half-smile.

I am glad you like it, he said through the link, although I must confess, I think Geoffrey is right. Perhaps we should not schedule dinner meetings with Thuja. She grows more outrageous by the day.

Sasha leaned toward him. Her shoulder brushed his, and she moved back a little. Like many dancers, her primary approach to the world was physical. Sometimes she had to work to remember that most people were less comfortable with casual touch than she—although Danion handled it pretty well, especially for a Tarkei. Another side-effect of the bond, perhaps?

She pushed the thought aside for later consideration and answered the point he'd made. She's coming with us, isn't she? Thuja, I mean? We can't avoid her every meal, so I think we'll have to get used to it. Across the table, the bits of broken shell caught her eye. She shuddered. If possible.

Space rations, Danion said. I will insist on it. Whatever mode of transport Geoffrey has secured, it cannot hold live prey for a battalion of Pannthu.

Absolutely not, Sasha agreed. Even if I have to fill the ship with shoes.

And tutus. The sparkle in Danion's eyes hinted at mischief.

Tutus, Sasha said. An excellent idea. They take huge amounts of room.

So I thought, Danion said. So I thought.

Geoffrey, having ordered his own meal and eaten half of it, was ready for business. "Who wants to go first?"

"I, I will go first." Thuja pushed the remains of the snail into the recycler, punched in another request (Dessert, Danion said, do not fear), and sat back. Her antennae curved forward again; she looked quite professional.

"Very well," Danion said. "Did your students prove satisfactory?"

"Twenty are fully trained and competent—I tested them. Ten more proved adequate, if lacking in experience. Sufficient for a reconnaissance force, but not enough to reclaim the planet. Will your father send reinforcements, Danion, if necessary?" Thuja's console made a burping noise, and the table disgorged her dessert, which did indeed appear innocuous—a Pannthu milkshake, perhaps. Sasha decided not to inquire into its composition.

"I will explain my father's position in a minute," Danion said, "after I hear from Sasha and Geoffrey." He gripped

Sasha's hand, her only warning of the emotional onslaught to come. "How many invaders were there, would you say?"

Screaming faces distorted with fury, raised guns, blue fire spun in Sasha's head. She clutched Danion's hand with both of hers, using his ability to segment his emotions, to shut them away, so that she could separate the shrieking demons and count them. The bond, silver as a pond in moonlight, flowed over her, and at last she mastered herself enough to answer.

"Tendak," she said, relaxing her grip, although she couldn't bring herself to let go, "the leader. And forty or fifty more—in the school, that is. More around the planet, I would guess. Four to six times that many? We didn't have a large population, and weapons were outlawed, even for hunting."

Geoff sent his plate to the recycler and leaned forward, elbows on the table in defiance of etiquette. Like Thuja, he could turn instantly from humorist to intent professional. "How many people in the school? And the company?"

Sasha thought again. Here the images she had to banish were broken bodies, not berserkers. "Fifty in the company, more or less. Thirty-two regular corps members, male and female combined, six apprentices, ten principals at various levels, Tonio, Elasi, Slava, and me."

"Tonio? Elasi? Slava?" Thuja slurped milkshake after each name, earning her a pained glance from Danion and a sharp comment from Geoff. She ignored them both.

"Tonio is my brother, Anthony Sinclair. He's company director as well as the alternate male lead. Elasi is his partner and his girlfriend; she and I handle most of the prima roles. Slava has partnered me since we were children." Emotion—jealousy?—flickered along the bond, silver shading to green around the edges.

Don't worry, she told Danion. *Slava and I are not lovers. We talked about it once, but we dance together so well we were afraid romance would ruin our partnership if it went sour.*

The bond narrowed, as though Danion were monitoring his thoughts—why, she could not tell—then opened again. Sasha heard his reluctance before he expressed it. "I regret the necessity," he said, "but we must know if we are to plan. How many of the company survived? And how many others, students and staff?"

The broken bodies piled high in her thoughts. Sasha forced them down, peered over them, and said, "Most of the active company was alive when I left. One or two corps members and one soloist were killed in the initial invasion."

Geoff flinched. "Not Sara," she hastened to add. She had told him several times already, but in circumstances like these, one could not repeat a reassurance too often. "In addition to my parents, perhaps half the teaching staff, and a quarter of the students." Pain like a burning sword pierced her heart. Danion's hand tightened around hers again, and she pushed the pain away; that, too, she would have to deal with later.

Her feet were growing numb. She moved them out of the cross-legged stance and hugged her knees to her chest. Behind her, the solidity of the wall anchored her in the present, but the warmth of the desert night seemed an eternity away from the ordeal that peaceful Xantera had become.

She shivered. "More students died in the uprising, and a few more company members as well, although most of them didn't react as fast as the youngsters. Tonio saw one of the invaders attack Elasi, you see, and he called the code they had chosen before the rest of them were ready."

Her voice broke. The silvery bond acquired cocoa edges that somehow communicated sympathy.

She waited, forcing herself into calm. "Perhaps sixty students were alive when I left," she finished, "and fifteen faculty members. Two or three secretaries, the cook, four gardeners. Altogether, with the company, less than 130 people. On the planet, I don't know."

"We could transport the company," Geoff said, "if we can free them. Not the rest, I'd say, unless they're fewer than Sasha thinks."

"How so?" Thuja's antennae straightened again. "Geoffrey, what have you done?"

"Went to see a man about a horse," Geoff said.

Pure devilry, Sasha decided, seeing the twinkle in those eyes. If so, it had the desired effect: Thuja squealed again and bounced on the cushions, sending her tormentor into peals of laughter.

"You're so predictable, Thuj." Geoff righted himself, the Cheshire-cat grin plastered on his face.

What a pair, Danion said to Sasha.

They deserve each other, she sent back.

Geoff, in another of his lightning shifts of mood, dropped the banter and leaned on the table. "Danion sent me to talk to one of his dad's friends. Someone who'd lend us a ship and not ask questions, as long as the project had

Jenat's approval. He can have a vessel for us within the week. Can you be ready by then?"

Thuja produced a surprisingly elegant shrug for such a skinny being. "Tomorrow, if necessary. Pannthu are always in training."

"Friday," Danion said. "Or Saturday. I have to follow up with my father and organize supplies. Where does that leave you, Geoffrey? Do you wish to bail out at this point?"

"Bail out?" Geoff's hands rose in the air until he looked as though he were praying to the night sky. "When my baby sister's in the hands of a bunch of thugs?"

"No, I see," Danion said. "What of your project, then? The journey will last eight weeks minimum, there and back."

"Sullivan can run it without my help. I'll call her tomorrow, in case she needs instructions, but she's more likely to hand me my hat and say good riddance."

"You will not tell her where we are going." Danion straightened, and the bond collapsed into a pale gold thread. Sasha jerked upright, but as Danion relaxed again, she leaned back against the rock once more.

"No way." Geoff's voice bespoke scorn. "Give me credit for a little sense, brother."

Danion apologized, and his friend went on. "How about you tell us what you did today? You're the only one who hasn't revealed a thing."

Danion shifted his position. "I went to talk to the diplomat in charge of negotiating with the Kazrati over Xantera," he said. "You knew that." Heads nodded around the table.

"At first, he treated me like an interloper, but after we talked for a while, he became more forthcoming. He confirmed most of what we discovered and provided additional information. The Kazrati disclaim responsibility for the invasion. They insist Tendak is a renegade, sent into exile for an attempted coup against the ruling military dynasty. They suggest he attacked Xantera to gain favor and win reinstatement."

"They would, wouldn't they?" Thuja swigged the last of her milkshake and dropped the cup into the recycler. "If Tendak is a renegade, no one has to answer for his behavior."

"Right," Danion said. "The allies are skeptical, and our own diplomat more so, but at the moment they have no proof of the Kazrati government's involvement. That is one of our tasks, to provide proof if we can find it."

Sasha watched the stars wheeling above her head. At the edge of her thoughts, a half-forgotten incident tugged, or was it an incident? A phrase heard and not understood? A reference without context?

Danion touched her mind, questioning, but the whatever-it-was ducked back into its hole and disappeared.

"Do Kazrati have private armies?" she asked aloud.

"If they belong to the upper classes." Danion sounded disappointed, and she felt guilty for her failure to force the whatever-it-was out into the open. "Tendak does, according to the diplomat."

Sasha frowned. "And ships?" she said, poking at the hole where the half-formed thought had vanished.

"He was a captain in their fleet before his disgrace." Danion's disappointment gave way to thoughtfulness but produced no answers.

Thuja smacked the table with both palms, drawing everyone's attention. "One ship would be enough, for the numbers you gave us. What are you thinking? Do not ignore Thuja! I must plan for my troops."

"Sorry, Thuj," Geoffrey said, although no one could have blamed him for the Pannthu's irritation.

"I don't want to leave you out, Thuja," Sasha said. "I don't know what to tell you. I almost remembered something. Only I can't force it out where I can see it. I'm taking stabs in the dark, asking questions in the hope of prying it loose."

"Ah." Thuja's antennae resumed their normal gentle wave, and she appeared mollified.

Sasha, turning back to the sky, pursued the elusive thought. "Not the troops. Not the ships, or ship. The memory-manipulation device? It was pretty advanced."

"Not for Kazrati," Danion said, killing that hope.

"I'm not going to get it," Sasha concluded, after several more attempts yielded nothing, "but it's there. Something I heard or saw. I'll have to wait for it to come back."

She sat up. "How frustrating!" From their expressions, the others agreed—yes, even Danion.

"It is becoming late," her husband said. "Let us talk tomorrow, and with luck, by Friday we can leave. Agreed?"

"But your father's plan?" Thuja said. "You promised to tell us. Does he send reinforcements?"

Danion relaxed. Facts always seemed to reassure him. "One ship, with a complement of Tarkei fighters trained against the Kazrati."

"So it's up to us to tell them where to strike?" Geoff asked.

"If necessary," Danion said. "We have yet to discover whether we face a small renegade force or an official army." Geoff nodded.

"Tomorrow, then." Thuja leaped out of the pit. Her navy-blue head peered down on them from the pathway. "Good night," she caroled. "May the stars smile on our venture!"

"Stars smile?" Danion shook his head, but Thuja had bounded from their sight.

Geoff followed more slowly. "What happened to that superstition of hers? The one about not walking in the streets at night?"

Danion stopped at the edge of the pit. Sasha vaulted out, in case he had forgotten she was as capable as he, and wrinkled her nose at him. Thuja was nowhere to be seen.

"She told me," Danion said deadpan, "that it operates only on Tuesdays."

Geoff smacked his shoulder. "I think you've been had, brother."

Danion's extended hand pointed him toward the entrance. "I too, my friend. Her love of gossip is indeed insatiable."

10. Journey

ON FRIDAY AT NOON, their journey began. Geoffrey, Danion, and Sasha reached the space port to find Thuja waiting for them. Thirty hand-picked Pannthu warriors stowed gear and swarmed over their assigned craft, a wedge-shaped beauty not unlike the original NASA space shuttle but matte black, made of steel-bonded aluminum, and at least five times the shuttle's size. Sasha saw no evidence of crew, except for the swarming Pannthu, who checked consoles, airlocks, and anti-gravity devices with admirable if chilling efficiency.

A sense of foreboding overtook her. "Who's going to fly this thing?"

Thuja turned, antennae in a vee of astonishment. Geoff's raised eyebrows made him, oddly, Thuja's twin. "Danion, of course," Geoff said. "Who else?"

She should have guessed. Iqara's voice echoed in her ears: "She was a first-class pilot," describing her mother, "she taught Danion." Danion, who had flown her to Tarkakhan from the mountain and now regarded her with a raised eyebrow of his own. He looked vastly entertained.

"He's the best they have," Thuja said. "He wanted to join the fleet, but his father insisted he become a scientist."

"Except at moments like this," Geoff added. "When they need to get a ship in and out without attracting the other guy's attention."

More patterns, Sasha asked, or was your father afraid he would lose you as well?

Both, I think, Danion told her. The men of my family either run the government or study at the Academy; the latter was more to my taste, although it is true, I like flying more than either. To Thuja he said, "I am a scientist. Do not let your love of scandal lead you astray." He held out a hand to his wife. "I am also, however, an excellent pilot."

"I know." Sasha thought of that flight across the desert, the unbroken sands and Danion's steady hands on the controls. A few days ago, but it felt like another lifetime. "Better you than me," she said lightly.

"But naturally. I would not dance your roles." A response exemplary for its Tarkei chill. Perhaps Danion had misunderstood. Without waiting for an answer, he disappeared into the ship.

Damn right, an annoyed Sasha told his retreating back. And you'd better get us there in one piece, too.

Don't worry, *kaleita,* he said. I have done this before.

Sasha muttered prayers for their safety under her breath. The others, intent on their pre-departure tasks, noticed nothing.

An hour later, they left Tarkei. Sasha, unable to contribute anything to the action on the bridge, wandered around the vessel in a distraught frame of mind. Worry over her friends and the remaining members of her family jostled relief that help was on its way and fear of what awaited them at the end of their journey. A small but persistent voice compounded her troubles by prodding her with the many things she had yet to learn about Danion: so much crucial information garnered in the last few days, but so much more that remained hidden to the point where she could not guess what to ask. Against that incontestable reality were those other moments when she and the man it was still difficult to think of as her husband had touched at a level she would not have imagined possible, in warmth and sympathy and, yes, passion.

Not that there had been much of the last since he kissed her on Tuesday night, but Sasha did not know if she wanted more. Her thoughts tumbled like cylinders in a lock, without opening anything.

She found the cabin that contained her and Danion's luggage, unpacked whatever she could, and did her best to make the place comfortable. When she was done, it still looked more like a hotel room than real living quarters, but for a few weeks it would do.

Bereft of distractions, she moved on. Since they would not let her near the controls—a wise decision—she needed space to practice what she did do, classical ballet being the most unforgiving of disciplines. An hour from Tarkei, and she already felt restless; several weeks without something to occupy her mind, and a nice padded cell would appear inviting.

A small lounge looked promising, although the floor was too hard and the crew would need it for relaxation. She walked on.

After a while, she heard a soft tapping from one of the bulkheads. She stopped. So did the tapping. Sasha stood still and listened. The tapping resumed. She took two steps toward it; it stopped again.

Two more minutes of listening brought nothing but silence. Frowning, Sasha looked around, but all the bulkheads looked the same. In the end, she passed the information to Danion through the link. He seemed unconcerned, so she went on.

On the fifth deck, at the very bottom of the ship, she found a large open space easily convertible to her needs. A cargo storage area, from the looks of it, but they were not a large enough party to need it. What made it usable were the wooden platforms that covered 80 percent of the floor; designed to keep goods away from the chill of the outer hull, they were varnished but not polished. They compensated for the metal floors that made jumping impossible and dancing on pointe risky.

The room lacked mirrors, but one could not have everything. It did have a railing that ran around three sides, which, if a little narrow and close to the wall, would serve as a barre. Sasha nodded happily and went back to the cabin for her pointe shoes.

The days passed in relative comfort. Tarkei's constellations gave way to a constant progression of stars—every one of them smiling, according to Thuja. Sasha, convinced that the Pannthu repeated it solely for the purpose of needling Danion, found it a comforting image anyway. Thuja's glee was infectious, and Danion did not really mind; in fact, she thought his pose of tolerant distance amused him. The ongoing banter between him and the Pannthu kept everyone's mind off problems they could not resolve, like what they would find on Xantera.

Despite Thuja's insistence on the smiling stars, a series of curious incidents plagued them. Items went missing from the cabins, and no one could explain their absence. The air rang with fierce denials in Pannthu, and tempers frayed. Food and water also had a tendency to disappear. Although it was impossible to account for every morsel, it did seem that the rations intended for human and Tarkei were more susceptible to loss—or was it just that there were fewer of them to start with, since nine-tenths of the crew were Pannthu? Either way, the asymmetry of the thefts brought more accusations and more huffy rebuttals, not least because Geoff, Sasha, and Danion were reluctant to switch to Pannthu food. That the three could not bring themselves to suspect one another, or Thuja either, added to the tension.

Amid so much stress, the relationship between Danion and Sasha, brimming with potential in Tarkakhan, languished. Preoccupied with his tasks, Danion spent long hours at the controls, which left Sasha as much at the mercy of solitude as she had been in the sun priests' mountain sanctuary. Again she took refuge in dance, honing her skills in the cargo area for what might have seemed like endless hours, had she not loved practicing so much. It was there, one day about halfway through their voyage, that Danion found her.

✳

He stopped in the doorway of the empty cargo hold, staring at the sight of his wife in arabesque, one leg extended behind her, her head turned toward him, over the arm that stretched forward. On pointe, it emphasized her ethereal air, transforming her into a creature in flight.

Except for the day he surprised her in the desert, he had not watched her dance. Danion heard echoes of the mountain, remembered the suns' rise, Sasha's feet pounding the sand. What might he learn about his wife, if he paid more attention to this pursuit that meant so much to her?

"Perfect timing," Sasha said as he walked through the door. "I need a partner, and you're elected. I'm sick to death of dancing solos."

Danion looked around the huge open space. Except for platforms and railings and a few empty cargo containers about the size of a large person, the room contained only Sasha and a small portable terminal emitting music he did not recognize.

His wife wore a dark-brown leotard and pink tights, a loose black overall made of cotton, and the pointe shoes that seemed as much a part of her as her hair. From the far right corner of the platform, she beckoned to him.

"I don't know how to partner." Danion stopped at the edge of the platform, which stood six inches above the floor, bringing his eyes to the same level as Sasha's.

"You will soon." In response to her imperious tone, Danion stepped onto the platform.

"I'm not asking you to perform by yourself," she explained. "Just to support me so I can dance some of the more interesting parts. You're strong enough to hold me,

especially since I do most of the balancing on my own. The most difficult part is figuring out where I need you to be, and that you should have no trouble with, because of the link."

Her vivid gray eyes sparkled, and a dimple formed in one cheek. "Please, Danion? You've been so busy lately that I hate to intrude, but if I spend much more time alone, I'll go round the bend."

That dimple was irresistible, and besides, she had a point. He *had* neglected her since they boarded the shuttle. For a good reason—a craft cannot fly without a pilot. But he could not blame her for desiring more companionship. And if she had missed him... He left the thought unfinished.

"Round the bend?" he asked, his lips curving, "and where precisely is that?"

She had won; he saw her elation reflected in the glowing pink of the bond. Sasha took his hand and walked him to the left-hand side of the stage, about halfway back. "Where crazy people go, my lamb," she said. "Did the inestimable Geoffrey leave that one out of your education in English idioms?"

"He must have," Danion said. Her hand, warm in his, reminded him of the morning they had kissed. His attraction to her drew him even as it fed a quiet apprehensive voice. He wanted her, he feared to lose her—so he had taken refuge on the shuttle's bridge?

An uncomfortable thought, that. "What do I do?"

"Stand there." She pointed her toe at the plank she had in mind. "And when I reach you, put both hands on my waist. I'll show you what comes next."

Sasha walked back to the spot she'd occupied when he arrived. "You'll have to imagine the costume." In her thoughts he saw a black velvet bodice with a full tulle skirt, both glittering with sequins, and black feathers in a semicircle about her head.

"Who are you?" Danion stayed where she had left him, hands at the ready, stalling for time, hoping to delay the moment when he would have to catch her. Suppose he misunderstood her instructions and she fell? Injured herself, even?

"Odile, the Black Swan." Sasha settled into fifth position, right heel pressed against left toes, then pointed her right foot, rounded her right arm, and extended her left arm to the side. She examined Danion impersonally, as though judging the distance. "Begin."

"Excuse me?"

"I'm talking to the computer." The music did not sound; the terminal was as confused as Danion.

"Wait," he said, "who is Odile?"

Sasha returned her foot to fifth position and her arms to her sides. "Odile is the daughter of the magician Rothbart, who has imprisoned a princess named Odette and turned her into a swan. She returns to human form only at night. One evening, while she is human, she encounters Prince Siegfried, who falls in love with her. Odette tells him that if he betrays her, Rothbart's power over her will be complete, and she will remain a swan forever. Siegfried vows to remain true, but Rothbart sends his daughter to trick the prince into thinking that she is Odette, so that Siegfried will declare his love to her and Rothbart will win. There's a famous pas de deux, which I, with your help, am

about to dance, where Odile imitates Odette so well that Siegfried—who hasn't the brains of a frog, but please don't take it personally—is fooled."

She extended her foot again. "I'm going to turn seven times—you can count them—and with luck, I'll end up right where you are. Ready?"

Danion held out his hands, resigned to his fate if not happy with it. "Ready."

"Don't worry, *kaleita*," his wife said with quite unnecessary delight. "I've done this before." While he searched for a reply, she looked at the terminal, then back at him. "Computer, begin."

She bent her left leg, stabbed her right foot into the floor, and spun seven times, her head whipping around. The last turn brought her right into his hands, and she stopped—poised on the toe of her right foot, her left leg extended behind her, bent at an angle of perhaps five degrees, so that it looked impossibly long. Sasha turned her face to the metal beams of the ceiling and stretched her arms back from the shoulders, curved like a swan's wings. While Danion stood, amazed that he had caught her, she tipped her head forward until she was gazing straight into his eyes.

A shiver, like a mild electric shock, ran through him. Sasha, as he knew her, was gone. Gone from the stage, and gone from the bond. Instead, he sensed Odile: ruthless, manipulative, seductive. The music changed, but Danion, mesmerized, did not hear it. In obedience to the pictures that ran through his head, he walked in a circle, his hands on Sasha's waist. The curved arms rippled, sweeping into an open circle above her head. She looked regal. Her eyes never left his face.

With his support, she bent forward, head level with her knee, left leg in its extended arc. The illusion in her mind communicated so clearly that for a moment he could see the nonexistent tulle skirt in a circle around her, feel it brush against his hands. The sequins that ringed the black velvet feathers sparkled against the frothy tulle.

Her head swept up, and she stepped away, raised arm forbidding him to follow her. He waited, and she soon returned, bending forward until her legs formed a straight line. Her tilted head assessed her effect on him as Siegfried. Danion promenaded her around again, then held her as she leaned back against him, off balance, left leg high and straight in front of her.

Just as he realized how pleasant it was to hold her like this, she moved away, but in a moment she was back, in arabesque, head inches from his shoulder. When she felt his hands close around her, she whipped the extended foot into her knee and turned, waist spinning between his hands.

Standing on pointe, she drew her left leg up to the side, one hand on his shoulder and the other above her head. Once she was balanced, she let go, running halfway across the platform before dropping to one knee. The other foot stretched out before her, and she held her arms high and wide, as though in welcome.

Danion walked toward her. The dancing itself began to draw him in; the music and the movement, the complex characterization; even in the role of prop, he could feel the magic of it, the joy in creation that she had called transcendence. As Odile, Sasha flirted outrageously, alluring and rejecting, innocent and self-assured, until

Danion felt as muddled as poor Siegfried, so callously dismissed as having the intellect of a frog.

The music changed again, and Sasha stopped dancing. Danion quirked an eyebrow at her. "It's Siegfried's part," she said. "This is where Slava gets to show off those wonderful muscles he works so hard for."

A flash of jealousy shot through Danion, startling him. He dismissed it as unworthy of a Tarkei, but of course, Sasha had sensed it. She stroked his ear, her expression not at all like Odile's. *I told you I'm not in love with Slava.*

Danion caught her hand. *You did. I did not mean it.*

Sasha pressed the hand, then let it go. *Maybe you should. Caring doesn't hurt.*

"My turn," she said before he could answer. She ran to the middle of the makeshift stage. "You can stand aside, if you like. You're done." Half-regretful, half-relieved to be free of his unasked-for responsibilities, he moved to the side of the makeshift stage.

The music changed again. Sasha brought her arms, one at a time, in those winglike curves over her head, crossing the wrists in front of her, then swept her pointed right foot from front to back, launching into a series of turns that made Danion's jaw drop. By comparison, Tarkei's most revered dancers looked like stumbling children. Her balance, her precision, and her discipline astonished him, but her ability to subordinate these to the demands of Odile's personality lay quite outside his experience.

After another brief pause "for Slava," Sasha returned to the center of the floor. "This," she said aloud, "you have to see. My *pièce de résistance,* as they say." She began to spin, not as she had the first time, in a line across the floor, but in one position, her right leg whipping out from the front to the side and back into her knee, over and over until it seemed impossible that she could complete one more rotation without collapsing.

Then, just when he thought she must go on forever, she brought the right foot down behind her and stopped dead, one arm straight out in front. For a split second, she stayed there, fighting a dizziness he could sense but not see, then she bent the front leg, pointed the back foot, curved the arms behind her like wings, and curtsied to him, her face alight with joy.

"Incredible," he said. "What was that?"

"The legacy of Pierina Legnani." Her breath came in short gasps, which didn't surprise him. "That, my lamb, is a fouetté. Thirty-two *fouettés rond de jambe en tournant,* to be precise, and if you hadn't had carpet on that living-room floor of yours, you would have seen them the day Geoff demanded I show him what I could do. They're not unique to me; any halfway decently trained ballerina can do them."

The music continued, but Sasha was no longer dancing. "It's nothing but barrel turns and spins from here," she said by way of explanation—at least, it might have been an explanation if he'd known what a barrel turn was. "Except for the final lift—which, believe me, you don't want to tackle."

She linked an arm in his, then stood on tiptoe to kiss his cheek. "The fouettés are spectacular, though, aren't they?"

Danion caught her around the waist and kissed her on the mouth. "Most spectacular." He kissed her again. "Odile, on the whole, appears to be quite a charming character, if somewhat unprincipled."

Sasha giggled. "Wholly lacking in principle, I'd say, although I suppose you could argue that she's defending Daddy's interests." The glittering edges of the bond indicated that she had correctly deduced what part of the Black Swan's behavior appealed to him. "Now if you want charming..." She let the sentence hang in the air.

Danion stepped back. "Are you about to insist that I partner you again?"

"No." Sasha said. "Although you did a good job, and I do hope you'll come back. I wasn't joking when I complained about being alone. For the moment, though, you can sit there." She pointed to the front of the platform. "And I'll dance Coffee. Continuing the theme, you know—well, no, you don't, but you will soon."

Bewildered but curious, Danion followed her suggestion.

"There's no plot here," she said. "It's a piece they put in to keep the fathers from chafing about having to take their little princesses to see *Nutcracker* every year." She went to the far right corner of the stage, sending him a wicked glance over her shoulder as if determined to keep him in the dark. And wasn't coffee something she drank?

"It's a solo." She wrinkled her nose at him. "So I've had lots of time to practice it."

Danion raised a hand in acknowledgment. In her thoughts, he saw the costume, which helped him clarify the idea behind the dance.

Coffee, Sasha said, is from Arabia, and this is an Arabian dance. More than that, you don't need to know.

She pulled her hair loose from its pins and braided it in one long strand down her back; in her mind, the strand was wound with gold thread studded with pearls. Except for jewelry, of which he saw a good deal, the image wore little—a long sheer veil, a bikini-like bodice, and a gauzy skirt that descended in waves from a narrow velvet band around her slender waist, fringed in gold. And pointe shoes, of course. The costume included gold finger cymbals on each hand, and their chimes became part of the music. You'll have to imagine them, Sasha said.

She talked to the computer once more, then shimmered across his line of sight, her body a whirl of motion too sensuous for even a Tarkei to ignore. The music crooned, an oboe or clarinet; he wasn't familiar enough with human instruments to know. The movements were simple—little running steps, often, although there was one memorable split—not sultry in themselves, but together?

And directed at him—the bond left no doubt about that. Danion would have had to have been made of the same material as the walls not to have reacted. When she at last sank to the floor, head on her chin, feet arched behind her, one touching her head, he sat, at a loss for words.

She stood and bowed. "Remember, Danion, when you're sitting at the controls, that life does have other things to offer." She picked up the computer terminal and walked out. Danion stared at the empty planks in front of him, thinking.

When he heard the door close, he stood and walked, dazed, toward the side of the stage. At the edge, his foot slipped, and he clutched one of the cargo carriers for balance. It tipped, and he tumbled after it, but the wall behind it kept it from upending. It stopped at an angle, breaking his fall. He heard the clunk of the carrier hitting the wall, followed by several smaller clunks from inside. That was odd; no one had used the containers on this voyage, and the previous crew should have emptied them before leaving.

Danion opened the door on the side of the container and peered in. Inside, he found a bench, one of the missing blankets, and several cartons of rations suitable for humans or Tarkei. He also saw eating utensils and toiletry articles taken from the crew; these had given rise to the noise.

He sat on the platform, considering his discovery. It seemed incredible that any of the crew, who had their own quarters and access to whatever supplies they needed, would have set up camp in such a fashion. Remembering the tapping noise Sasha had reported the first day they were in transit, he nodded. They had an intruder aboard.

11. Capture

HOURS OF INTENSE SEARCHING failed to reveal anyone not included in the ship's roster. The crew members were put on alert and sent back to their regular duties. Sasha, who had enjoyed the chance to participate, for once, in a group project, considered returning to her dancing and decided that she had had enough for one day. Unable to come up with a more appealing activity, she settled on a walk around the ship. In her haste to join in, she had forgotten to change; she was wearing her pointe shoes, but it didn't matter. She had danced on the shoes for a full day, and the fouettés had destroyed whatever strength they had left.

On deck three, she heard the tapping, right where she had noticed it the first time. No one else was in sight. Sasha stood in the hallway and listened. On her satin-encased toes, she could walk silently, placing each step with perfect precision. One toehold at a time, she inched down the corridor until she identified the offending bulkhead.

Should she call for backup? Danion would have a fit if she didn't, but help's arrival would most likely drive the intruder into hiding again. Sasha stood in front of the tapping noise and waited. Nothing happened.

It seemed a shame to bother Danion when she didn't intend to accept his assistance—especially after what she'd done to him earlier (not that he hadn't deserved it, after ignoring her for the better part of two weeks). But she ought to tell someone, in case the whatever-it-was proved to be more than she could handle, and he was the only one she could reach without making a racket.

Danion, she said, certain he wouldn't like her plan one bit, I think I've found our intruder. I'm on deck three, and someone is tapping right in front of me. I'm going to open the paneling, so if something goes wrong, you'll know where to find me.

No! If a person could shout mentally, he was shouting. Wait for me!

Sasha paid no attention. Despite their first meeting, her husband tended to forget that her ballerina's air of fragility hid the training of a professional athlete and the muscles to match.

But he was on his way down and in no mood to worry about how much noise he made, so if she wanted to capture their intruder, she had better move fast. Two decks would not hold him for long.

The panel felt cool against her hands as she grasped it and pulled. It came off more easily than she expected, knocking her backward.

She threw it to one side and grabbed the body that fell out with it, then opened her eyes to examine her catch.

It was Iqara.

Honey-brown eyes stared at her from under those pale blond bangs. Sasha let go and sat down in the same moment. It's your sister, she told Danion.

Danar take her, he said, his anxiety turned to anger, and you too. Why didn't you wait for me? What is she doing here?

Both rhetorical questions, Sasha assumed, but the latter was sensible nonetheless. She asked it.

"You were going to leave me behind," Iqara said in tones of deep outrage. "How could you!"

Sasha, about to remonstrate with her, bit her tongue. Danion's annoyance pricked at her thoughts, but her own frustration at her limited role loomed larger. Iqara was twenty-two, although everyone treated her like a child. Why stop her, if she had something to contribute?

"Why shouldn't we?" she asked her irate sister-in-law.

A chunk of bulkhead lay next to Iqara's right hand. She picked it up and threw it at the opposing wall. It hit hard and ricocheted off the ceiling before falling to the floor.

"Let's see." Her voice dripped sarcasm. "You're here, and Danion, who flies the ship. And Thuja with her toy soldiers, and Geoffrey for comic relief. Did any of you think to bring a doctor?"

Sasha, about to argue, regarded her with narrowed eyes. "You're a doctor?"

Iqara's pale brown cheeks turned the color of café au lait. "Not yet. But I will be in two years, and I know a lot more about medicine than any of you!"

"Pannthu medicine, too?" Sasha asked.

Iqara spread her hands. "Well, naturally. My specialty is xenobiology."

Not just a clothes horse, then. She should have expected better of Danion's sister. So should he, Sasha thought, although perhaps their six years apart explained his protectiveness.

Sasha stood and pulled Iqara up beside her. "Welcome aboard, although I'm not sure your brother will agree. He's foaming at the mouth right now, but I think it may be a good thing you decided to stow away."

Arms linked, the two women strolled along the corridor. "Which way are the medical facilities?"

"On deck two," Sasha said. "This way. Quickly, if you don't want to run into Danion just yet." The bond, glowing scarlet, made clear how little her husband appreciated this remark.

"Why were you tapping?" Sasha asked as they headed for the elevator.

"Checking the bulkhead," Iqara said. "Some of them stick."

That made sense. The tunnels weren't designed for frequent use. "How did you find us?"

Iqara had the grace to flush, although she looked more defiant than repentant. "I listened to your conversation at Antilles."

Sasha stopped dead, one foot between elevator and corridor. "You overheard us?"

"Of course," Iqara said. "My father wouldn't let me join you, but he didn't object when I said I had promised to meet a female friend in Tarkakhan. If I'd come to your table, Danion would have sent me home. He never used to be so stuffy, but you heard how he wouldn't let me go with you earlier. I took the next booth and listened, to find out which ship to board and when. Father told me you reached the sanctuary by stowing away on a cargo vessel. That's where I got the idea."

The cargo vessel, another mangled piece of Sasha's convoluted past laden with unexamined and often unbearable emotions. Her throat closed up.

No time for that. Dealing with her flight from Xantera would distract her from the needs of the present—meaning, at this moment, Iqara.

"I'm glad you're not a Kazrati spy," she said. "Stupid of me, but I didn't worry about being overheard."

"Why would you?" Iqara said. "There is no crime on Tarkei."

Speechless, Sasha followed her into the elevator.

Danion, simmering with annoyance at his sister, braced himself to confront his father. Jenat was tough to handle when in the wrong; in the right, he became intolerable. He must have been frantic, with his only daughter missing for two weeks. Or had Iqara fed him another dish of lies?

Apparently not, for Jenat looked haggard. "She is here, sir," Danion said.

His father glared into the screen.

"I did not ask her to come, nor did I permit her to come, but she is here. I will ensure her safety." A promise he might not succeed in keeping, but since in that case, he would be dead, Jenat could damn his ghost with a will.

His father did not look mollified, let alone happy, at this statement. "I would like to believe you, Danion, but if you are telling the truth, how did she discover your plans?"

Sasha spoke to him through the bond. Danion closed his eyes, cursed his sister, and prepared to face his father again. "When she pretended to meet her friend," he said, "she came to the restaurant and eavesdropped on us. Then she stowed away."

Jenat shook his head, more in disbelief than negation, his son thought. "She will be useful, sir," Danion said. "Her medical training fills a gap in our crew."

Jenat's glare intensified.

"No, I did not suggest it to her," Danion assured him. At the side of the view screen, Geoffrey materialized. His sympathetic expression almost made up for Jenat's fury, but not quite. Danion had worked hard for his father's acceptance and, medical knowledge or not, he would much rather send his sister home than jeopardize Jenat's good will at the very moment when it seemed they might work together.

"I am sorry, father," he added. "If I could, I would return her, but I cannot afford the delay. Xantera has already waited too long."

Jenat smacked the screen that separated them and muttered something about how different life would have been if their mother had lived. Danion waited, recognizing, with a clarity he might have preferred not to feel and an insight that could well be Sasha's, the pain that lay behind his father's need for control. His own anger dissipated like a cloud of space dust.

Jenat raised his hands in a gesture of resignation. "I have tried to protect her, and you, Danion. Maybe too much. She is an adult, albeit a young one. But please, watch over her. The two of you are all I have."

Danion, touched beyond expectation or belief, nodded at the screen. "I will, sir. I promise you, we will both return."

"May you bask in Danar's rays," Jenat said. For the first time that Danion could recall, his father looked old.

❀

"Please take over, Geoffrey," Danion said when Jenat had left the screen. "It's on autopilot, and we're twelve days from Xantera. We're not likely to run into trouble, but if we do, page me."

Geoff slipped into the pilot's chair. Thuja, for once, minded her own business. "Yes, sure," he said, "but if you're going off to wring Iqa's neck, I get to wring it after you."

"An old Tarkei proverb," Danion said. "'You cannot wring a neck and have it too.'"

Geoff acknowledged this poor attempt to lighten the atmosphere with a rueful nod. "I suppose we're stuck with her. Not that I dislike her—I'm quite attached to her, in fact, and her medical skills will prove useful, as you say. Still, the last thing we need is another headstrong civilian to keep out of trouble."

"Indeed," Danion said, thinking of Sasha's assault on the bunkhead, although strictly speaking he and Geoff were civilians, too. "But I am not going to scold Iqa. Since she is here, remonstrating with her serves no purpose. I cannot send her home, much as I wish to. I'm looking for a place to meditate on what to do next."

He entered the elevator, grateful to hear the doors swish shut behind him. Whereas his wife suffered from loneliness, he could not draw a breath without someone remarking on it.

Ironic. Sasha, used to constant company, had more solitude than she could stand, while he, who had seldom spoken twice in the day during the last six years, had to fight to get a minute to himself.

True, his obligations to the group had kept him from thinking about what he might find on Xantera, what he felt for his wife, and whether he wanted to return to the mountain. In the pleasure of flying he became absorbed, as dance swept up Sasha and took her beyond herself.

Until today, when their encounter in the cargo bay had blown the cover off his defenses, breaking the barriers rebuilt after those days in Tarkakhan. Rebuilt without conscious intent, he saw in retrospect—to protect himself from the potential consequences of the joining, his fear that caring for Sasha, loving Sasha, would leave him vulnerable to loss, to Reilu, to the demands of tradition, and to his father's unyielding grip on his life.

"Caring doesn't hurt," Sasha had said. But it did. Danion had not learned to meditate in the mountain sanctuary, but he had found peace in solitude. The joining had stripped that serenity from him and thrust him into a maelstrom of emotion he felt ill equipped to handle.

Yet Sasha had grounds for her complaint. He *had* ignored her. That situation could not continue. Danion walked the corridors of the shuttle, relieved that outbursts of temper no longer broke the silence, and sought a place where he could think.

He found it at last on deck four, as yet uninhabited by rescued dancers or crew: a room about twice the size of a large closet, with an unmade bed and a carpeted floor. Through a porthole he saw pinpoints of light scattered against a velvet background as black as Odile's tutu. He stared at the stars, trying to imagine how they would look from his desert perch.

If he concentrated, he could envision the granite blocks, the rocky soil, and Orbfire hanging low in a crimson sky. But instead of the silver birds he saw Sasha as she had appeared in his mind, an enchantress in black velvet and tulle. And as Coffee, who had ripped his pretense of indifference from him in one three-minute solo. Sasha, who had felt so warm and soft and desirable in his arms when he kissed her that he had understood why Tarkei did not kiss—the threat of disorder implicit in that passion was something they could not abide.

Could he? He could not blame today's indulgence on curiosity. She had kissed his cheek; he could have left matters there. He had not. Like it or not, resist it or not, he wanted her.

By Selassa's rays, Sendar had spoken the truth. The joining was real. Between strangers in a desert, the bond had formed, because he and Sasha belonged together. They had not recognized their compatibility, but the spirits of earth and sky had. And Sasha and he had welcomed the link, even though neither of them acknowledged as much at the time.

Which meant that the bond would not break. How had he fooled himself into believing otherwise? He could never return to the mountain, unless he traveled the path Sendar had taken.

Which would be the very result he feared. The reason he had resisted the joining in the first place.

And what of Sasha? She had demanded his presence this morning, and in general she appeared to welcome his touch. What it meant to her, however, was more difficult to say. Her casual approach to physical affection made more sense to him now that he had partnered her: it was part of her job, so much taken for granted that he had heard her reminding herself that other people—she meant him, although he had seen her brush Iqara's arm or Thuja's shoulder; she kept her distance only from Geoffrey, probably because his flirting troubled her—would not understand.

His own comfort with her baffled him more, but he attributed that to the joining. He could not remember touching Reilu, or wanting to, except as required by the wedding ritual. Thuja and Geoffrey—and Iqara, always in rebellion—had done much to break down his resistance, but his reaction to Sasha was different.

He probed the link, searching for clues as to what had motivated her to dance for him in that way, whether she had intended to affect him as she had. Typically, the answers were less clear than he would have liked. Danion sensed an impish amusement, not malicious but akin to Thuja's delight in rattling his composure.

After a while, the cool metal paneling behind his head transmitted some of its own impermeability to his fevered thoughts. He would talk to her. If she did not want him, he would try to convince her to stop her teasing.

And if she did?

Alone in the silent room, Danion shivered, wondering if he was, after all, ready for the next stage.

❋

In the mirror, Sasha saw Danion lounging in the doorway. Sparks flashed from his garnet earring; burgundy silk glowed softly in the dim light. She raised her eyebrows at her own reflection: in the months she had known Danion, he had worn only the most serviceable of clothes. This evening's high-necked shirt had been her gift; the dark red suited him, as she had guessed it would.

Black hair fell over her hands. She ran a comb through it and left it loose, curious to find out what brought him here. Most of his time during the flight had been spent at the controls or deep in discussion with Geoff and Thuja; this morning's exhibition must have unsettled him more than she thought if he had come to spend the evening with her.

Her long green dress brushed against her ankles as she walked toward him. The mirror told her she had chosen well, although, not expecting company, she had used comfort as her guide. The simple round neck and high waist, the full skirt that would flatter anyone, and the soft jersey fabric gave her a sense of freedom usually confined to her practice clothes. Her bare feet pressed into the carpet; she had not yet donned stockings, let alone shoes.

Danion watched without speaking as she came toward him. The bond, taut and gray, was tense as a steel wire, although he looked casual enough, leaning against the doorway with his arms crossed.

"Good evening," she said. The stilted greeting felt awkward on her tongue, but she had noticed that formality often reassured Tarkei. "Will you have dinner with me?"

"If you wish." Danion straightened, letting his arms fall to his sides. "I wanted to talk to you."

The tension in the bond increased. Never one to duck trouble, Sasha sank onto the bunk closest to her and extended a hand. "I upset you this morning. I'm sorry."

Danion sat at the other end of the bunk, one foot on the floor, the other leg bent in front of him. He did not take her hand. "Not upset. Confused? I don't always read human signals well."

"Nor do other humans." Sasha curled her feet under her, leaned back against the wall, and studied him, trying to decide how to proceed. Which signals did he want deciphered? And how would he feel if she deciphered them?

The way he'd kissed her this morning didn't suggest a man committed to the priesthood. But last she'd heard, he was determined to keep his oath of celibacy, in which case he might run like a frightened rabbit if she told him the truth.

Assuming she could figure out the truth, which itself was far from certain.

Danion was waiting. She sent her spiraling thoughts into oblivion and tackled the issue head on. "I don't know what you want—of me, of the marriage. I don't know what I want, either, except that this morning I wanted you to pay attention to me. If I hurt you, I'm sorry."

The tension in the link eased. Danion brought his other foot onto the bed, knee pointing at the ceiling. "I've neglected you. I apologize. I have, in fact, had a great deal to do, since I am the only trained pilot on board."

"I know that," Sasha said.

Danion held up a hand. "I hadn't finished. That's my excuse, but the reality is different. For six years, I have had to consider no one but myself. Even before that, I lived alone, except for the three months with Reilu. Most of which I spent trying to avoid her. My barriers have served me well, but they are not, perhaps, a good preparation for marriage."

That was generous of him, and it gave her a way to approach the underlying problem as well. "That's important only if you wish to stay in the marriage," she said. "If you intend to return to the mountain, the less contact we have, the better."

"Would you like me to stay?" Lord, he was quick. He had jumped on the one point she least knew how to answer and in the process turned the tables on her.

Sasha studied the opposite wall, which had nothing whatsoever to recommend it, not even a picture to break the monotony of beige plastic paneling. "I'm not sure," she said at last. "So much has happened to me, and in such a short time, that I can't focus on this, as I could in normal times, and ask whether I wish to go forward or not."

She turned her head toward him. Danion sat quietly, the way Sendar had when he visited her in the sanctuary, but beneath the burgundy silk, his muscles were rigid. "I don't want you to go," Sasha said. His shoulders relaxed. "I need time to learn more about you. About me, too. Before the Kazrati came, I knew who I was. But the memory manipulator changed me. I can't tell truth from lies half the time. It distorts my sense of myself. I don't trust my feelings to guide me. It's like living in a fairy tale—one of the gruesome pre-Victorian ones where people grind bones and chew them for bread."

Danion rose from the bed in one fluid movement, as though he could no longer sit still. "Not because of you," Sasha said.

He turned to look at her, his back against the far wall, his dark eyes open and vulnerable. His barriers had crumbled in ways she had not imagined possible. She held out her hand again. "Please, Danion, come here. I did not mean to be rude."

He took the hand and came to sit beside her, but she saw the tightness in his shoulders. With her free hand she stroked his ear, tracing the diamond outline and rubbing the garnet between her fingers.

"Try to understand," she said. Her voice trembled, despite her efforts to steady it. "The Kazrati tore my world apart. They stripped everything from me: my parents, my brother, my friends, my company, my memory, my integrity. Tonio is a year younger than I am, but I always protected him. Only I couldn't protect him from this. Maybe I caused his death. Most of the time, I can't handle it, can't think about it, even. I don't cry. I don't scream. I don't let the anxiety or the grief or the anger surface—especially the anger. I don't dare. Instead, I dance. Obsessively, constantly, so I won't feel anything except exhaustion. I know I'm doing it, but I can't stop. If I do, I'll collapse. Then I won't be strong enough to help when the time comes."

"Or so you believe." Danion caught the hand that was caressing his ear and joined it to the one he already held, then pulled her toward him. Sasha let him hold her, struggling to explain what she needed to say. What Danion, perhaps, needed to hear.

"You have barriers, too," she said. "You mentioned them just now."

"Of course." Danion rubbed the back of her neck. He hesitated, then added, "I expect you will not like this, but I did not know humans had them also. You are so open in your expression."

Sasha considered this. "I suppose. And some people do pour everything out. But others are not so different from Tarkei underneath. Even your friend Geoffrey keeps his heart well hidden, despite his apparent openness. Think of how he reacted to the news that his sister was in danger."

She rubbed her cheek against the burgundy silk, feeling Danion's arms tighten around her, but the images of Xantera would not stay outside the circle where they belonged.

She tried a different tack. "You know I'm attracted to you." Danion did not respond, although she could hear his acceptance through the link. "You must know I like you." More agreement. "I wouldn't have danced like that for anyone else." Of this, he seemed less certain.

Sasha raised her head and looked at him. "I would not," she said. "In performance, yes, but not in private."

"A narrow distinction."

A chilly response for someone who had his fingers tangled in her hair. Sasha frowned. "You're not helping me much."

The familiar glow of amusement returned, lightening his eyes but not Sasha's mood. In her experience, Danion used amusement to create distance, and that was not, in her mind, the purpose of this conversation.

"What assistance do you require?" Danion asked.

She had liked him better vulnerable. "So far, I've done the talking. What do you want?"

The direct attack startled him out of his remote stance. His fingers stilled in her hair, but he did not look away. "You," he said with a bluntness so uncharacteristic that it robbed her of any response she might have made.

Sasha bit her lip. She had asked. And there it was, out in the open, where she could no longer avoid it.

Danion released her hands and ran one finger down her cheek. "I cannot go back."

She stared at him, not understanding. "To the mountain," he said. "Already you mean too much to me. The bond will not break; my oath of celibacy has become a polite fiction. You are correct. Much has happened to you, and you have a right to your confusion, but the link complicates matters. If I'm not to impose my needs on you, I must withdraw. It would help if you did not play games with me."

Sasha placed both hands on his shoulders. The palms of his hands pressed against her waist. She wondered, with an odd sense of desolation, whether he would ever touch her again. "If by games you mean don't flirt with you as a way of getting your attention, yes. But withdraw—in what way? Am I not to see you? Are you going to barricade yourself behind your console and come out only at night? How will I decide what I'd like to do with our marriage if you hide yourself from me?"

The amused distance was gone, and Danion's half-smile seemed bittersweet. "I meant withdraw from the bond. If I can. To protect you from thoughts you aren't ready to hear. I did promise, once, not to impose the joining on you."

"Oh," Sasha said, for lack of a better response. It seemed reasonable—respectful, even—so why she feel so bleak?

Danion's arms dropped to his sides, and she sensed him preparing to leave. The demon of loneliness flexed its claws. "I only wanted to spend time with you," she said, searching for a connection that had already vanished.

Danion gave her another rueful smile and stood. "Let us have dinner, then."

"It will be my pleasure," Sasha told him, "as soon as I find my shoes."

Dinner was pleasant, and for a short time reminded Sasha of their meal at the priests' sanctuary, but by the end of the first course she realized that her relationship with Danion had changed irrevocably. Not because of anything he did; he listened to whatever she had to say and answered any question she asked, so long as it did not relate to him or his state of mind. Numerous details of piloting were made available to her, together with insights into Academy politics and the plans he and Geoffrey and Thuja were considering for the relief of Xantera. Huge quantities of trivia, but no personal information—no idle thought, no flicker of expression, no touch of humor, not even an inkling through the bond of what he might be feeling.

That must be what he meant by "withdraw." But how was he making it happen? Sendar had insisted the bond could not break, that it lay outside conscious control. Either he was wrong, or Danion wanted to break it now where he had not before, for the thread thinned until it was no thicker than a spider's.

Although it also proved to be as strong as a spider's: it only appeared fragile; it did not actually break.

Throughout the days that followed, Danion maintained his cool courtesy. He avoided Sasha when he could and made sure others were present if he could not. He moved essential supplies to another deck, leaving just enough in their shared cabin to keep Thuja from noticing and gossiping about their breakup. Or so Sasha assumed, after several days of bracing herself for the sight of avid antennae left her limp but free from interrogation. When she did see Danion, he looked tired, but he brushed aside expressions of concern—indeed, expressions, period. The spontaneous conversations that had enlivened the link were gone. He did not come to watch her dance again.

Thuja spent every spare minute putting her warriors through their paces, and Geoffrey seldom left Danion's side. After a few days of cataloguing medical supplies and organizing her department, Iqara had plenty of time to spare. Sasha stopped by often to visit her, and the two soon became friends.

But much as Sasha appreciated Iqa's company, she could not help missing Danion. The resulting onslaught of guilt and depression forced her into contemplation— about Xantera and her family, about the raid and its effect on her, but most of all about Danion and what he meant to her. At first, she felt manipulated by his withdrawal, but thinking about how he'd phrased it showed her that, at least in his own mind, he was respecting her wishes. By the third day of silence, she accepted that she, too, could not simply re-create the life she had once cherished. Danion had become part of her; she needed him.

Which left her worrying about how to broach the subject with him. The courteous stranger Danion had become might simply wait for her to finish and walk away.

In the end, Iqa—quite without meaning to—provided the solution. "I'm so bored," she complained. "The others stick to that bridge as if chained to it. I'll turn into a bulkhead if I don't get some stimulation soon. Even facing the Kazrati would please me better than sitting around waiting for something to happen. What do *you* do all day?"

"I dance," Sasha said. A truth of sorts.

"Oh." Iqa handed her a cup of Tarkei tea and slumped into a nearby chair. "Well, that won't help me. But that can't be the only thing you do."

"Pretty much." The cup of tea gave off the sharp tang of lemonade. In its golden depths, the reflected lights from overhead glittered like the three suns rising, as Sasha had seen them the day she met Danion. A thought flashed by, and she snatched at its butterfly wings.

In her mind, pictures coalesced, acquiring outlines and substance. Passages of music flowed around them like mists. She stared at the walls, forgetting her companion, letting the images unfold, nodding as they took the forms she wished. Enough time remained to make it work, and if she planned it right, it would shatter Danion's mental barriers as nothing else could do.

Iqara raised a delicate brown eyebrow. "Did I miss something?"

"Thank you, Iqa-*chan*." Sasha drained her cup and set it on the table.

"For what?" Iqara tossed the cup at the wall, which opened at the right moment and swallowed it.

"The answer I needed." She stood up, smiling at her bewildered sister-in-law.

"But what was the question?"

"You'll see. Oh, it's going to be glorious." And Sasha ran out the door.

12. Performance

THE DAY BEFORE THEY reached Xantera, Danion called a meeting of everyone except the Pannthu troops, who took their orders from Thuja. He included Sasha, the only person on board familiar with their destination. She agreed without protest, although he could no longer tell what went on in her mind.

Was the bond breaking? And why now, when he wanted more than anything to keep it? When he had been sure he did not want it, it had strengthened despite him. A surge of longing, tinged with desire, caused his hands to tremble; he hid them under the table and forced his wayward thoughts into submission.

The meeting took place in a small lounge that afforded a certain amount of privacy and, perhaps more important, an oval table big enough for five. Danion surveyed the assembled company. Iqara, stylish as ever, sat at his left, chin resting on one hand. Next to her, Thuja's antennae pointed toward the ceiling; her restless fingers tapped a tattoo on the table top. Geoffrey sat on his right, cheerful and competent; Danion, who needed his friend more than ever, gave silent thanks for Geoff's presence.

Sasha sat directly opposite, too far away to touch, so pulled into herself that he suspected even the link would not reach her. By now, he was afraid to open it and find out. She stared into her clasped hands; he could not read her expression.

"I asked you here," Danion said, "so that we can plan our approach to freeing Xantera. Since our forces are limited, I suggest we begin with the dance school and the company. It seems to be the only compact settlement on the planet, as well as the probable location of Tendak himself. Is that correct?"

Sasha moved her gaze from the palms of her hands to somewhere in the middle of the table. "That the school is the only concentrated settlement, yes. That Tendak is there, I don't know, but he was when I left. Nowhere else would make a headquarters." Her voice, cool and clipped like a Tarkei's, struck him as unnatural, like her pose. He tried not to shiver. Was she responding to him? Did he sound like that?

Thuja was staring at them, antennae perked— scenting gossip. Sasha and he had managed to keep their disagreement from the Pannthu so far, not least because of the many demands on her time, but it was too much to expect so avid a lover of scandal to miss the coldness between them when it was displayed right in front of her.

Thuja opened her mouth. Danion held his breath, but to his surprise, she remained focused on the task at hand. "I agree," the Pannthu said. "The school first. You said, I think, that there were perhaps fifty or sixty Kazrati there?" He exhaled.

"That was my estimate, yes." Sasha rested her wrists on the edge of the table. She had not looked at him since she came in.

Thuja was talking. "Sixty of them, thirty-four of us, and we have the advantage of surprise."

"Thirty-five," Sasha said.

"No!" Danion said sharply. Everyone stared at him, except Iqa, who so far had maintained an uncharacteristic silence.

Sasha glared at him. "Don't be ridiculous, Danion. If I don't go, how will you find your way?"

"She has a point, brother." Danion clenched his teeth. If Geoff took her side, he might as well stop arguing.

"There's a network of tunnels under the school," Sasha said. "No one knows about them except those of us who grew up on Xantera. My father..." She choked on the word, then forced her voice back to the level and went on. "My father blocked them off long ago. You can be sure the Kazrati have no idea they're there."

"Then tell us where they are," Danion said.

"No."

Danion considered and rejected half-a-dozen unforgivable responses, but before he could pick one, Sasha explained. "I can't. I haven't been in them since I was ten. I don't know what the entry point looks like these days, but I know where it is. I can show you."

"She should go," Iqa said. "It is her planet and her family."

Three against two already, and Thuja was far from a reliable ally. Danion tried to think of a counterargument. He couldn't find one.

"How far is the entry point from the school?" he asked. Sasha measured with her hands in the air. "Two, three hundred yards? I'm not good with distance."

This, from someone who could turn exactly seven times and land in his arms? But there was no point in challenging her. "I'm more concerned with whether we can approach the entry point unseen."

"With 98-percent probability," Sasha said primly. Iqa giggled.

She *was* imitating him. And in public, where even an apology from him would further alert those present to their disagreement. Danar take her. Did she not understand that he wanted to keep her safe?

"Be serious, please," he said, for lack of an acceptable alternative.

"I am being serious," Sasha said, her face stony. "The entry point is in the woods, and unless someone is standing in the clearing when we arrive, no one will see us or even think to look."

"Thank you." Danion prepared to raise the next issue, but Sasha stopped him. "And don't think you can dump me at the entryway and run off, because you'd wander around the tunnels for the rest of your life."

Danion gave in. His half-smile slipped out despite his annoyance with her. "Point taken. I bow to the force of logic. You may come with us."

"That's better." Sasha slipped her clasped hands into her lap, and the rigidity flowed out of her.

Danion controlled the urge to reach for her and, with a certain apprehension, signaled to Thuja to take the floor. "Next issue."

"Weaponry," Thuja said. "How are they armed?" He would bet that the Pannthu had not missed a single word, gesture, or expression, yet—Danar be praised—she had decided to maintain her atypical self-restraint.

And she had asked a reasonable question, one that Danion could answer. "Laser guns, from Sasha's memories. Standard Kazrati issue. Right?"

"Right," Sasha said. "That is, they had laser guns. If you say they were standard, I'll take your word for it."

"Laser guns." Thuja sounded thoughtful; her antennae waved from side to side. "Standard issue. And that means what? Last year's design?"

"Two or three years ago, I'd say." Danion frowned at the table top, trying to remember what he'd seen in Sasha's thoughts.

Thuja had moved on. "Good. We outgun them. That and the surprise favor us. And your father's troops?"

"Will come in when we give the word," Danion said. "When do you want them?"

"Why not bring them in right away?" Geoff asked. "Can't have too many reinforcements, can we?"

The antennae waved more rapidly. Thuja resented comments like this. Danion said, "We have to get in without being seen. One ship can do it, but I'm not sure two would succeed."

"He is right," Thuja burst in. "First we should secure the school. The other ship should remain outside the periphery. Either we can bring it in when we have completed our mission, or the crew will know, because they will not have heard from us, that we are lost. Then they can rescue us or report back, whichever seems more sensible."

"Why not bring some of them over now?" Iqa asked.

"I train Pannthu," Thuja said with great decisiveness. "Tarkei I do not deploy."

Danion glanced at Geoff, who was gazing at Iqa as if she held the answers to the secrets of the universe. The part of the pilot's position he disliked most was the way it made him impromptu captain; every dispute, every crisis came to him for solution. This time, too, it seemed he would have to coax Thuja to see reason.

"Iqa's suggestion is a good one," he said, ignoring Thuja's eruption of protest. "I vote to bring thirty of the Tarkei troops to this vessel, with an officer, if you so desire, Thuja. We need to match, as best we can, the size of our opponent's force."

"Oh, very well." The purple antennae drooped sideways until Thuja resembled a sulky caterpillar.

"We're agreed, then?" Geoff said. "We bring over the Tarkei for backup; we land as close as we can to Sasha's tunnels; we use the tunnels to get into the school; and we leave the rest of the force outside the perimeter in case of an emergency?"

Thuja muttered something that sounded like agreement.

"The dancers will help," Sasha said, "as soon as it's clear we're on their side. That's to our advantage as well."

Danion flinched. Placing his wife, his sister, and his friends at risk was bad enough; which of the suns had he offended that he should have fifty deaths on his head? Across the table, his eyes met Sasha's. Her annoyance had vanished, along with that unnatural quiet; her eyes sent sympathy.

The link thickened. Part of him yearned to accept the comfort she offered, but another part, sinking in an emotional sea, knew he could not afford to let her in. When he did not respond, Sasha looked away. The link thinned again.

"You haven't asked," Iqa said, "but I am ready. If Father's ship has additional medical personnel, however, I would like an assistant. Or more than one."

"Certainly." Danion's gaze traveled the room, touching each face in turn. With luck, they would all be here two days from now. For a moment he wondered what they thought they were doing—except that Sasha's friends and family were already at risk. Geoff's sister, too; he should not forget her. "Till tomorrow, then."

"Till tomorrow." The others rose to leave.

Sasha raised a hand. "After dinner—shall we say eight?—I invite you to come down to the cargo area on deck five. I have something to show you."

Danion watched her go. Thuja stared at him, antennae almost touching her nose. The strain must be showing, but he couldn't help that. Sasha intended to dance—what else would she do on deck five?—and watching her demanded more self-control than he could muster at this moment.

By inviting the others, though, she had made it difficult for him to refuse. If he did not attend, Thuja would have more than speculation to fuel her gossip. Danion clenched his teeth, eyes fixed on a blank steel door. A lifetime on Tarkei must have given him the resources to survive one performance by his wife. He hoped.

※

Nothing could make the cargo area inviting or the pretend stage less cavernous. Sasha had placed four chairs in front of the platform and turned Iqa's container residence into a dressing room, but the ambience wavered between a high-school gymnasium and a shuttle-craft hangar. As before, the portable computer terminal sat on the floor, ready to produce whatever music she required.

"I know," she said when they came in, "it makes about as realistic a theater as a silo would, but what can I do? Sets are beyond me; I had enough trouble producing costumes."

She wore a pale pink dance dress with a long, filmy skirt, as well as the ever-present pink tights and toe shoes. Her hair hung loose down her back, the front pinned away from her face. To Danion, she was beautiful.

"This is for you," she said. "The four of you, who have taken time out of your ordinary lives to help me. It's the only way I know to say thank you."

She swept a hand down the pink skirt. "First, I'm going to dance a solo from *Voices,* one of my brother's ballets. It's based on the life of Joan of Arc." For the sake of everyone except Geoffrey, she gave a brief summary of Joan's life. "This is from Act I, where she first hears the spirits."

The music, harpsichord with a Renaissance sound, spoke of quiet woods and gentle grasslands, an environment far from the desert where Danion had sought his own link to the divine. Before him, his wife, hands crossed over her chest, balanced on the toes of her left foot, her body parallel to the floor and her right leg high behind her. The dark hair fell forward, framing her face. She had said she was Joan, but she could as easily have been a spirit voice, so unearthly was her appearance.

Thuja nudged his ribs. "But how is it that she does not fall?"

"Balance," Geoffrey murmured from the Pannthu's other side.

Both Thuja's antennae pointed toward him, a sure sign of irritation. "Of course, she is balanced, Geoffrey. Don't be absurd. The question is, *how* does she balance?"

"Hush," Danion said. The antennae shifted in his direction. "You can ask her later."

Thuja, grumbling, hushed.

On the stage, Joan flitted in small running steps, trying to escape the voices that pursued her. An understandable reaction, Danion admitted. Briefly he wondered why, in the end, she had decided to trust them. What would he have done, if voices had begun speaking to him while he meditated?

Joan danced on, practicing warrior actions under the voices' direction. The barriers Danion had erected against his wife cracked. He saw her as she had appeared that day in the desert, stamping the sands in a flurry of fury.

Joan's trials ended, and Sasha disappeared for a few moments. When she returned, the pink dress had acquired an overskirt, draped scarves in many colors.

"*Tzigane,*" Sasha said. "It's Russian for gypsy. A piece by George Balanchine, the first great American choreographer, although he was Russian by birth. I'm only dancing the first half, because the rest involves more than one person."

The story concerned a young gypsy girl who, unable to sleep, walked out into the moonlight and envisioned the man she could love. A simple plot presented to a haunting violin concerto.

Ravel's, Sasha said. It was the first time he had heard her mental voice in days.

The girl's wistful air revealed the extent of Sasha's solitude since her arrival on Tarkei. That she could put together such a performance in not much more than a week underscored the many hours she had spent practicing, but here, in this solo, the depth of her loneliness was visible. Danion closed his eyes, wanting—and not wanting—to let the guilt surface.

Somewhere at the edge of his thoughts, he felt the bond flicker, as though someone were striking a match.

Sasha disappeared again, returning without the overskirt. "Juliet." She explained the story. Another young woman alone, but this one was playful, with the innocent abandon of a child. Danion had no trouble recognizing Juliet, either. Too much time had passed since he heard Sasha laugh.

The Prokofiev score changed tone, transforming the happy child through terror and heartbreak as Juliet struggled with a choice no fourteen-year-old should have to make. Should she abandon her love and fulfill her father's command or take the priest's potion, which might bring death instead of the relief it promised?

Danion tried to imagine Iqa in such a situation (not so great a stretch as one might think, given their father's views on marriage). His sister had been two years older than Juliet when he left for the mountain and wholly unprepared for life with a husband then; now she sat, a woman grown, leaning forward, her gaze fixed on the stage. Geoffrey sat next to her, looking more at her than at Sasha.

Through the bond, Danion felt his attention drawn back to the stage. The dance pulled forth his own sense of loss and rejection, first by the priesthood, then by the wife to whom the priests had, against his will, released him. Juliet took the potion, choosing Romeo, even if it meant death. Danion attempted to tackle his resentment with logic—his wife had a right to her feelings.

He failed, but to his surprise, the bond changed from a flicker to a glow, a gentle blaze deep in his thoughts, easing a pain he had not acknowledged until now.

Sasha returned in a white leotard, hair confined at the back of her head. "You'll have to imagine the feathers," she told them. Her gray eyes fixed on Danion and stayed there. "I need to keep my stamina for the last piece, and anyway, the Swan Queen is virtually impossible without a partner, so this is just a hint of her. But she's my favorite character, so I didn't want to leave her out. This is from Act II, where she accepts the love of Prince Siegfried and hopes that the spell binding her will be broken. It's several separate entrances put together."

The link transmitted a coda to the comment about needing a partner: unless you'd like to volunteer? Instinctively, Danion withdrew. He felt a flash of disappointment. The gentle glow faded to a candle flame.

From the far right corner, Odette shimmered across the stage, her arms rippling like wings. The Black Swan sprang into his mind. The day he had partnered Sasha, Odile had performed the same sequence of steps, looking at him (as Siegfried) to judge her effect. No wonder the poor prince had been befuddled: two swans danced by the same person, differing only in the colors of their clothes, one imitating the other's mannerisms. Although they were not in fact the same, he saw. Odile was imperious and flirtatious, Odette anguished but sincere.

Fascinated, he leaned forward. How did she convey the difference? The bond strengthened again.

One more costume change, and the pink dance dress returned. "This one," Sasha said, "is for Danion. It's my own creation. I call it *Pavane*."

Three heads turned toward him. Danion sat straight in his chair, more startled than they. Did you think I had forgotten our conversation, Sasha said through the bond, or that I haven't thought about what you said? I have. This is my answer.

The terminal began to play again, the shivering silver tones of a flute in Ravel's *Pavane*. Again, Sasha told him what it was. If he tried, he could see the pictures in her head, but not what they meant to her. She must be concealing it, pushing him to figure it out for himself.

Sasha crossed her feet in fifth position, then pulled her right leg up to the knee, extending it to the front, then rising on pointe and swinging the foot sideways until it reached shoulder height. Her right arm matched the line of the leg, and she turned her head so that her eyes followed the fingers out toward the ceiling.

Geoffrey let out a sigh. "God, she's good. Sara would sell her soul to dance like that."

Danion did not answer; he had no need. The dance spoke for itself. He knew next to nothing of ballet, whereas Geoffrey knew a good deal, but no one with eyes could fail to be impressed.

This is my answer, she'd said. But could he interpret it?

Sasha rolled through her supporting left foot and turned into the arabesque he had seen when he walked in on her before, the one that made her look like a bird in flight. Her extended leg bent, and both arms came above her head as she made a complete circle by shifting the position of her heel, one quarter-inch at a time. Back where she started, she brought the foot in toward her knee and again out to the front before closing. Fauré's *Pavane* replaced Ravel's, and the steps quickened into turns and jumps, each one precise, each one perfect.

Exquisite, without a doubt, but a message? Danion did not hear it.

Listen with your heart, the bond said. Listen with your body. Not all knowledge is found in books.

A heretical thought, for a Tarkei. Where to begin? His training so far had focused on the intellect, on conquering the emotions—even in rebellion, even on the mountain. Listen with your heart, with your body. What did that mean?

Well, he could guess what the latter meant, but he could not follow it: it prompted him to sweep her up and carry her off—and from what she'd told him before, that was not what she wanted. His heart, then, would have to do.

The steps continued, flowing one into the next, each one difficult, all superbly performed. None looked like anything he had seen on the mountain, or anywhere else.

My answer, she had said. In the steps lay a pattern— not a pattern imposed from the outside, Tarkei-style, but one generated from within and visible with the heart.

Sasha soared across the stage, her pointed foot inches from his face, landed in a whisper of toe shoe, and took off again in the opposite direction. She had been dancing for some time, and it seemed unlikely that she would continue much longer. If he could not decipher the message soon, the opportunity it presented would be lost.

Another jump. As she had on the day he introduced her to Geoffrey, Sasha arched her back and flicked her foot into the air. Through the pink film of her skirt, Danion saw the lights of the cargo area, white sparks and red intermingled.

The light exploded around him. Her dress became the wings of the silver birds, and for a moment he was there, in the desert at dawn, watching the three suns rise. The cosmic light he had never reached in training swept him up. If he were human, he would have laughed for joy.

In that moment he saw the pattern of the mountain, the pattern he had not seen when he lived there, the pattern hidden beneath Sendar's teachings, waiting for him to find it within his own soul. In the beauty of his wife's steps, in the discipline that formed them, in the serenity and trust that came from mastery, he saw the power of love, the balance on which transcendence depends. All that is, in harmony. Somehow, she had understood what he needed to learn and had found a way to communicate it.

Thank you, he told her.

The dance was over. Amid more applause than such a small group of people should have been able to produce, Sasha took her bows. No, she said. Thank you. And now we'll talk?

If you wish.

I do, Sasha said. I definitely do.

✺

The others left, chattering and laughing. Sasha, taut as a plucked harpstring after her performance, waved goodbye without really registering their departure. Her attention was concentrated on Danion, who lounged in his chair, long legs stretched out in front of him, feet touching the makeshift stage.

She folded her costumes into a neat pile, then went to sit on the edge of the platform, pointe shoes inches from his boots. The filmy pink skirt brushed the floor. She clasped her hands in her lap. How to begin?

Danion watched her with a disconcerting stillness. The link, although more active than during most of the last week, provided sporadic information at best. Sasha subdued the temptation to stare forever at her own pink feet and gazed into her husband's eyes.

For the performance he had worn the burgundy silk shirt she had given him, black pants, and black leather boots. The combination highlighted his air of quiet elegance even as it reminded her forcefully of the last time she had seen him in these clothes. It was appropriate, given that they were coming full circle.

"I've missed you," she said. "I'm glad you came tonight. I was afraid you might not."

"I considered refusing." Danion seemed fascinated by the far wall, but then he turned his head and looked at her. "I couldn't stay away. Fortunately. You gave me an extraordinary gift tonight."

"No more than you have given me." Sasha risked a smile. His eyes lightened in response, and she let go of a breath she had not known she was holding. "Can we go back a week or so and begin our conversation again?"

The gleam in his eyes became more pronounced. "Didn't you tell me one cannot go back, only forward?"

"That was Sendar." Sasha held out a hand, and after a moment's hesitation Danion took it. At his touch, the bond widened further; she closed her eyes, tightening her fingers around his, letting his presence fill her mind.

"Do you know, then, what you want?" Danion asked.

Her eyes opened. "I think so." Under the burgundy silk, Danion's shoulders tensed, as they had eleven days ago.

"I've thought a lot since we talked," Sasha said. Danion's hand became a lifeline, anchoring her to the present. "I had so much guilt—about what happened on Xantera, about escaping when the others stayed there, about taking you away from the mountain, about betraying Tonio."

Danion raised his free hand, but she brushed the interruption away. "Don't tell me these things weren't my fault." He lowered the hand and tilted his head to one side, listening.

"Thank you. I know, some were and some were not. I had little control even over the ones that were. It doesn't matter. The guilt was there, and the things that go with guilt. Grief and anger and fear. Self-hatred, even. I couldn't see straight."

She stopped. Danion's hand enclosed hers, strong and warm. If the bond would open completely, she would not have to say the rest; he would know. Or did he know already?

One of Danion's feet moved. The pointe shoes, flat on the floor, lay between his boots. A hand closed around her waist, then grew more insistent. Sasha followed its urging, leaving the stage to perch on his lap. Danion brushed the loose tendrils of hair away from her face. "And now?" he said in that soft, husky voice she had heard only once before.

Sasha put both arms around his neck. "I want to go forward. With you." She kissed his cheek. "If you still want to."

His arms encircled her waist. He looked deep into her eyes. Between them, the bond flowed, a river of gold breaking the dam they themselves had built. Desire lapped its banks. She welcomed it.

I don't even know how Tarkei make love, she told him.

Danion's laughter touched her, warming a heart near freezing, as though tapped by the Snow Queen's icy finger. *Would you like to find out?*

Sasha stroked the tip of his ear, traced the line of his cheek. *Yes,* she said. *I would.*

Danion stood, Sasha in his arms, then let her feet drop. He handed her the pile of clothes and picked up the computer terminal. One hand on her waist turned her toward the door. "Then let us go, *kaleita*," he said. "It seems we have much to say to each other."

13. Xantera

SASHA OPENED HER EYES on darkness. Danion's arm encircled her; his head lay inches from hers. His breath touched her cheek. In his dreams she could see images of herself, of their bodies entwined. She closed her eyes again, snuggling into his warmth, luxuriating in his presence. The bond flowed between them, clear and strong. So different from yesterday.

The knot of tension that had been present since the invasion loosened. For the first time in a month, she no longer felt alone. Geoffrey and Thuja, Iqara, even Danion could not replace those she'd lost, but they were becoming dear in themselves. The breach between her and Danion had hurt, but it was over. She could relax—for a while. Xantera must be only hours away.

Danion turned over, pulling her closer. Her back pressed into his chest; his mouth brushed the nape of her neck. He was awake. The bond intensified every exchange as long as they were in physical contact, deepening each interaction, enriching their love.

She sensed resistance. What would you call it then, if not love?

Danion did not answer. About to retreat again, Sasha stopped, curious. Danion rolled her onto her back, and she looked up into wide, dark eyes. His hand caressed her ear, brushed tendrils of hair from her cheeks.

Don't be hurt, he said. Tarkei fear love, as they fear disorder. My whole life, people have told me that love does not exist, not for Tarkei. My father married me to Reilu and never worried about whether we would like each other.

You love Geoffrey and Thuja and Iqa. Why not me?

I do. He sounded surprised. It's true. I did not think of that as love, but it is.

His mouth covered hers. Sasha wrapped her arms around his neck, pulling him down. His body pressed her into the mattress, his bare skin lay warm and smooth against her breasts. The bond glowed in the darkness.

Someone was pounding on the door. Danion did his best to shut it out, but it continued.

You'll have to answer it, Sasha said. I can't get up, and if I could, I have no idea where my clothes are.

Is that so? Danion trailed a hand down her side, verifying her lack of clothes. She arched her back like a stretching cat, a most satisfactory response, but the noise continued. "One minute," he said, unable to keep the irritation from his voice.

It stopped, but the respite would not last; it had to be either Geoff or Thuja, and neither had much patience. Danion stood and groped for the black pants, which had ended up on the other side of the room.

In fact, clothes were everywhere. He hoped the person at the door was Geoff. Thuja would break an antenna if she saw this.

It was Geoff, but Danion felt anything but welcoming. "Yes?" he said through six inches of open door.

Geoff must have drawn the appropriate conclusion, for with uncharacteristic sensitivity he refrained from inviting himself in. "We're holding at the perimeter, but we can't stay here. The Tarkei troops came aboard an hour ago, and there's at least one Kazrati scout ship too close for comfort. You're needed at the controls, brother."

Danion nodded. "Ten minutes. Pull back till I get there."

"Will do." Geoff's broad grin was back. "Tell Sasha that was a great performance, and I'm glad things are going better between you two."

"Don't you *ever* mind your own business, Geoffrey?"

"Not when I can mind yours, brother."

"Ten minutes." Danion shook his head. Geoff was laughing when he shut the door.

While they talked, Sasha had stayed under the covers, but when Danion returned to the bed he found her sitting up against the headboard. The blanket fell somewhere around her waist. He liked the effect, but not the anxiety that poured across the link with extraordinary clarity. He sat beside her, and she threw herself into his arms. Xantera, she thought to him. I'm so scared. What will we find? Is anyone left?

I don't know, *kaleita*. He stroked her back, black hair tangling in his fingers, but he couldn't stay. He told her so. We endanger ourselves and your family by remaining here.

The perimeter is crawling with Kazrati ships. We must hope Thuja is right, and that the stars will smile on us.

She let go at once. Danion cupped her ear with his hand and kissed her, then swept his clothes into a pile, dropped them in the recycler for laundering, collected a clean set, and headed for the shower.

When Sasha emerged from her own shower, clad in black pants and a cream sweater in which she could have passed for her husband's twin, she found him already gone. She braided her hair and tied it, grabbed a cup of Tarkei tea, and headed for the bridge.

As she reached the door, she stopped. The room was an awful mess; Danion, needed for piloting, had not done more than pick up his clothes. The tea went to the dresser while she made the bed. She patted pillows with a wistful glance: last night had been wonderful, and if things went wrong today, her relationship with Danion might die stillborn.

The tea, cooling in its cup, reminded her of the passing time. She swallowed it down, then dropped the cup into the wall unit and her nostalgia with it. They could be orbiting Xantera while she stood here.

Her own used clothes joined Danion's in the recycler. Except for the pointe shoes. After last night, she couldn't bear to throw them out, but what should she do with them?

A pen caught her eye. She picked it up. On the pink satin, she wrote in Tarkei, drawing on Danion's memories to guide her hands, "For thee, *kaleita,* may the stars always smile." A fitting tribute. She added her signature in Latin script and propped the shoes in front of the mirror for Danion to find when he returned. Then she left the room.

The bridge had not changed since Sasha's last visit, except for the addition of two Pannthu gunners. Danion seemed as cool as usual on the surface, but his air of serene confidence didn't deceive her. He turned his head when she came in.

"Buckle the harness," he said as she took a seat. "It's going to be a rough ride."

Sasha nodded, draping the heavy belt over her shoulders. By the time she had it fastened, Danion again had his eyes fixed on his console.

Geoffrey watched the view screen. He was navigating, meaning that he had to compensate for every course change Danion plotted, and there were many. Thuja was monitoring the location of enemy scouts, feeding the coordinates to the gunners. As far as possible, Danion wanted to avoid drawing the Kazratis' attention by firing, so the gunners were forbidden to use the coordinates. From the droop in their antennae, Sasha concluded that they didn't much like this state of affairs.

"Port!" Thuja said. Danion sent the ship into a roll that made Sasha, who had made the mistake of looking at the view screen, seasick. "Gone," Thuja said.

Danion reeled off a string of numbers, which Geoffrey punched into his console. The droop in the gunners' antennae increased by a fraction of a degree.

"Don't they see us?" Sasha asked when things had calmed down.

"Not if we're quick," Geoff said. "The shuttle has a special coating that blocks detection."

"Starboard!" Thuja interjected.

Danion turned the nose straight down. Sasha closed her eyes at Thuja's shout, preventing another bout of dizziness. The harness dragged her back against the seat, and she was glad of it.

"Nice," Geoff said. "We slid under him. Right, Thuj?"

"Or her," that lady said huffily.

"No," Danion said. She glared at him. "It's not my prejudice, Thuja. The Kazrati do not permit women in the military."

Was it Sasha's imagination, or did the gunners' antennae drift upward at that statement? Thuja must be a difficult commander.

Fifteen minutes passed, interspersed with ejaculations from Thuja, rapid shifts by Danion, and replotting by Geoffrey. On the view screen, when Sasha dared to look, Xantera grew larger. Continents, oceans, and poles became visible.

"Where do we land?" Danion said over his shoulder.

The shuttle was large, too big to land in the woods where the tunnels lay no matter how skilled the pilot.

"Do we have any kind of ground transportation?" Sasha asked.

Thuja flicked her gaze away from her screen. "Service vehicles. Enough, if we crowd. The Tarkei brought their own."

"Outside the woods, then." Sasha struggled to remember the coordinates.

Danion stopped her. "I can see them."

Everyone looked at him, including Sasha. The bond was stronger than ever, then. A good thing, too, because it would have taken her days to describe that location in sufficient detail for piloting.

"It's an uninhabited area," she said, recovering her composure, "so the Kazrati should have no reason to post troops there. With the service vehicles, we'll need an hour or two to get where we're going."

Danion nodded and turned back to his console. "Thuja!" he said, more sharply than she had ever heard him speak, "what is that behind us?"

Thuja's antennae shot into the air. "By the seven goddesses, where did that come from?"

"What is it?" Geoff said. Sasha clasped her hands and prayed.

"A scout," Thuja said. "Not good. I did not see him arrive, so we must assume he knows we are here."

A Tarkei curse lit the bond, but Danion didn't say it aloud, just tapped his fingers on the console. Sasha could hear him running options through his head.

"Geoff?" he asked.

Geoff's brown skin glistened in the cabin lights. "Do you wish us to shoot him?" Thuja said before Geoff could reply.

The gunners' antennae perked in anticipation.

"No," Danion said. Three sets of antennae drooped again.

"Can you dodge him, brother?" Geoffrey had ignored the by-play, sending reams of numbers into his console until it protested. "You're not more than five minutes from orbit."

"Sasha, does Xantera have a moon?" Danion stared at the view screen, fingers poised over the controls.

"Two," Sasha said, "and a half, if you count the asteroid in bipolar orbit."

"Bingo." Geoff ran his fingers over the touch keyboard one more time. "Here's your course."

"But what are you doing?" Thuja asked. Danion, intent on the controls, didn't answer. Sasha could see the plan in his mind—dangerous, but if it worked, no one would know they had been there.

Unless the scout had already reported home.

He wouldn't, Danion said, unless he was sure of his kill. Otherwise, he'd be held responsible for losing us.

"Two minutes," Geoff said. Xantera's asteroid was visible, a ball of granite the size of a mountain pockmarked with ice chunks. Except for the ice, it could have belonged anywhere in the Tarkei desert.

Thuja was not easily diverted. "But what—"

Danion interrupted her. "Thuja, mind your console, please. If that pilot sneezes, I want to know." Thuja grumbled under her breath, but she did as he asked.

"One minute," Geoff said.

Sasha curled her hands into fists and hoped her teeth would survive two minutes longer. Not to mention the rest of her.

"He's getting closer," Thuja said. "Beware."

The asteroid filled the view screen. "Now!" Geoff punched a final number into his console and leaned back, hands over his ears.

Danion spun the craft into a somersault, ending with the nose pointing straight up. He cleared the asteroid by what seemed like inches and ducked behind its far side. Thuja snapped the view screen into reverse. Above the asteroid, a ball of flame rose like a mushroom cloud and dissipated as they watched.

"Whew," Geoff said. "That could have been us." He grinned at his friend. "Always knew you were a damn fine pilot, brother."

Thuja bounced up and down in her seat, antennae waving wildly from side to side. "But that was marvelous! Shall we do it again?" Even the gunners brightened.

"Again?" Danion said. "Are you telling me we have another scout on our tail?"

"No, no." Thuja laughed so hard she nearly fell out of her seat.

Sasha propped her up with one hand. Honestly, she told her husband, sometimes I don't know how you put up with her.

Nor I, Danion said. He shook his head at Thuja and turned back to Geoffrey. "Thank you, my friend. And now, have we clear sailing to our destination?"

"Far as I know, brother, it's dead ahead." Unlike Thuja, Geoff looked grim. Thinking of what awaited them, Sasha guessed.

"Good," Danion said. "I'm taking her down."

They landed in an arid region not unlike the lands around the sanctuary but colder: a windswept plain bare of vegetation. Devoid of anything that gave color or life: bland rocks in shades of brown and gray lay flat against dry soil that sent up puffs of dust wherever they moved.

Danion stood in front of the shuttle, hands clasped behind his back. They had landed in a hollow, but that provided their only cover. "I would prefer to camouflage it," he said, referring to the spacecraft, "but I can think of no suitable method."

Sasha linked a hand through his arm. "No one will look for it unless they know we're here, and in that case, we're in trouble already."

"Yes." Danion was worried; she felt it quite clearly.

Iqara came up to them. "I'm ready. Are the Tarkei coming with us?"

"At least as far as the tunnels," Danion said. "Out here, they're too far away to assist us." Sasha could tell that he wanted to tell his sister to stay here, but he refrained. It would make no sense; she could not help them if they were injured, and if anyone did find her, she would have no protection.

Danion looked down at her. You see what a sentimental creature you have married, he said. One long finger traced the line of her nose.

Sasha tapped his ear. It's what I love about you—that you care. Even when you're pretending not to.

That startled him, she saw, but pleased him, too.

No one ever said they loved you? she asked. Not even your mom?

It's not our way.

How sad. Sasha tried to imagine a world where no one dared say, "I love you," but soon gave up the effort. Too bleak for words.

It would be too much to expect Danion to respond in kind, and he did not. She decided to let him off the hook.

For the next unknown number of hours, the mission demanded his full attention. "Let's do what we can to save the colonists, shall we?"

"Yes," he said, "let us begin." But as they climbed the rocky sides of the hollow, she could hear him puzzling over what he might have said.

14. Attack

THEY REACHED THE WOODS without incident, although not without a certain amount of reconnoitering and backtracking. After about thirty miles, the dust gave way to grasslands, which became shrubbery-dotted hillsides, then the woods they were expecting. Most of the journey was peaceful, even beautiful. Wildlife of various sorts romped and swooped and in general went about its business. Danion saw no people, but two burned-out settlements they encountered as they approached the hills served as a warning.

At last, they reached a point where Sasha suggested they hide the vehicles and continue on foot. About two hours had passed since their arrival on Xantera, and everyone was hot and tired and thirsty. Sasha led them to a clearing where the bushes came right up to the edge of the circle; ingenious cutting sufficed to wedge the service vehicles into the gaps.

No sooner had they finished than they heard footsteps. Danion grabbed his wife around the waist and ducked under a bush. Geoffrey, he saw, had done the same with Iqa. The Pannthu, trained and silent warriors, had vanished;

not one purple antenna remained in his line of sight. The Tarkei soldiers, too, had dropped from view.

Boots clomped by, half-a-dozen pairs. No concern about being overheard, he said to Sasha. A stick cracked not far away.

None that I can detect, she said. Not trained for forest work, either, from the sounds of it. The scouts of Earth fiction would drum this lot out of their corps.

It is to our advantage, so long as they do not stop to investigate the damage we did to the bushes. Danion heard her agreement, and something else—mingled anticipation and fear at being back on Xantera. Are you all right? he asked her.

Sasha leaned back into his arms. I'll be better when this is over.

The footsteps disappeared into silence. Danion, Sasha pressed against his shoulder, almost regretted their leaving.

They found a stream that Sasha said was safe to drink from and walked through the forest in the late afternoon sun. Above them, a canopy of green blended into the leaves of huge trees as wide around as Danion was tall.

It seemed incredible that the planet could have suffered an invasion; only the extraordinary paucity of people suggested the presence of anything untoward. Small blue-furred creatures hovered, leathery wings beating, before darting off into the overhanging branches. Copper fish leaped from the streams; unseen insects chirped; a reptilian with scales of gold scurried under a bush as Danion passed by. He held his wife's hand and tried to pretend they were out on an ordinary stroll, but he saw Sasha start at every noise and felt the tension in his own shoulders.

The sun hung lower in the sky. Sasha stood in another clearing, more open than the one where they had hid the service vehicles, her brow furrowed. Here Danion saw flowers: big puffy pink ones and small heart-shaped yellow ones. The clearing was both pretty and, like the rest of their trek, deserted.

"There," Sasha said, pointing at a large white bush with red cone-shaped flowers. Keeping her grip on Danion's hand, she crossed the clearing and pushed the branches aside.

The others crowded round. Sure enough, behind the bush lay a narrow tunnel, just large enough for an adult to crawl through.

"Oh, dear," she said. "It looked a lot bigger when I was ten." She released Danion's hand and dropped to her knees. The top of the tunnel came within inches of her head. "It will work, I think. They get higher farther in."

Danion had an unpleasant image of crawling the whole way to the dance school, but Sasha had already disappeared within the tunnel. So he treated Geoffrey, instead, to a raised eyebrow and received a shrugged shoulder in return. "Very well," he said, "follow me," and ducked into the opening.

The tunnel did widen and increase in height after a short distance. Danion stood gratefully and brushed fine clay off knees that hadn't had that much contact with the ground since he turned seven. Sasha touched his shoulder. No one had come level with them yet, so he stroked her ear. *You did well,* he said, not sure it was safe to speak aloud.

It's not, his wife said. *Clever of you to think of it. The tunnels echo like crazy. Let the others know: talk as quietly* as possible, and only when necessary. But no whispering. Whispers travel.

Danion passed the information to Geoff, who had joined them, and he murmured it in Iqa's ear. They were holding hands, Danion noticed. Interesting. His sister transmitted the message to the person behind her, and so it went along the line.

Outside, the sun must have set, for the tunnels had become too dark to navigate. With a portable lantern, Sasha led them far enough from the entrance to make camp. They ate packaged food and slept on the ground. Danion held his wife close under their single blanket, but the company of sixty-four others made greater intimacy impossible.

They rose as soon as the sun penetrated the tunnels enough for them to see one another. Not an entirely pleasant experience, Danion admitted. The clay floor of the tunnels must have defeated even the Pannthus' iron constitutions, for everyone looked tired. Thuja's antennae were wilted. Sasha, secure in his arms, had done better than most, but she too looked strained. Dark circles exaggerated her big gray eyes, and the grime on her face recalled the day he met her. Iqa's creamy skin had faded to a muddy beige, although somehow she managed to look like a fashion model even under these circumstances.

They sat in a circle, eating their packaged breakfast. Danion spoke quietly, mindful of the echoes. "How much farther, *kaleita*?"

"Not far," Sasha said between mouthfuls. The food tasted like straw and had about the same texture. She couldn't possibly enjoy it—and in fact, he could tell she did not—but no one knows better than a dancer that she who would exert herself must eat. "Lots of turns and twists, but even as children we could do it in fifteen minutes if we were late for class."

"You didn't have to refrain from making noise, however." Danion took a bite of his own ration. It tasted every bit as bad as he remembered from the night before.

Sasha's eyes widened. "You haven't met Camille yet, have you?"

A non sequiter, and cryptic at that. Danion grimaced, then quickly took another bite, lest he appear rude.

Useless, of course. He had forgotten the link. "We did have to be silent," Sasha said, "unless we wanted to spend our free time practicing. We weren't supposed to be in here. The difference is that we were a lot smaller then. Faster and quieter, and we knew where we were going."

Danion imagined them, a dozen mice scurrying through the tunnels. Sasha's image, naturally.

She swallowed the last of the miserable breakfast, washed it down with a swig of water, and held out her hand. "Come on. The sooner we start, the sooner it's over."

The maze wound under the woods, turns more constant and more complicated than the priests' sanctuary. How, after eighteen years, Sasha remembered them all (if indeed she did, and they were not going in circles, as sometimes seemed to be the case) baffled him. About fifteen minutes after they started, however, Danion found himself staring at a brick wall.

❋

Sasha put a finger to her lips and pushed Danion back to the entrance of the last tunnel. Sixty-five faces stared at her, including her husband's. She stood in the middle of the circle so that she could keep her voice as low as possible. "The entry to the school is that brick wall over there. The Tarkei should stay here, in case any of the Kazrati try to come through, unless they have reason to think the battle is going against us. Agreed?"

The Tarkei commander saluted, which startled Sasha. Salutes didn't often come her way.

"Pannthu go first," Thuja hissed. Her antennae had recovered from their morning wilt and stood straight up, battle ready.

"Well, naturally, Thuj," Geoffrey said. "That's why you're here." He pushed Iqara toward the Tarkei commander. "Stay with them, Iqa. Can't have them capturing the doctor."

Sasha intercepted a glance from Danion. Don't try it, she told him. Without me, how are the dancers going to tell you from the Kazrati?

He sighed. Must you be right about this? I only wish to keep you safe.

Sasha left the center, joining him on the far side of the circle. Out of the others' sight, she stood on tiptoe to kiss him. I want to keep you safe, too.

Danion beckoned to Thuja, but the Pannthu had already stationed her troops by the brick wall. Geoff on one side, Sasha on the other, Danion moved toward them.

❋

The brick shattered under the impact of high-quality lasers, and Pannthu poured through the gap. Sasha crouched in the entryway, Danion at her back, and considered where to go first. Until now, Xantera had shown so little impact from the invasion that her return had not been difficult, but the school, Tendak's initial target, gave evidence of intruders even in this side corridor. Broken windows and closet doors hanging from their hinges bespoke the Kazrati presence.

Her husband touched her mind, offering comfort.

Later, she said. I'll deal with it later. Let's find the dancers.

Do you know where they are?

It's past eight o'clock, Sasha said. If Camille is alive, anyone who can walk is in the studio. No one misses Camille's eight o'clock class. Which means most of the soldiers will be there watching for trouble. This way.

She stepped into the corridor. A blue streak of laser fire skimmed past her ear. Danion dragged her back into their manufactured entrance, tapped Thuja on the shoulder, and jerked his head in the direction she had planned to take.

Thuja waved her antennae and yelled something in Pannthu to her troops. They dropped to a crouch and half-walked, half-crawled their way down the hall, gaze focused, weapons steady in their hands. A small group stayed behind, guarding the backs of the invasion force.

Laser fire crisscrossed the air where the troops' heads would be if they were standing. The Pannthu crept, silent as cats, to opposite corners of the hallway. Screams marked the moment when they caught sight of the Kazrati.

One warrior, bolder than the rest, leaped around the corner, shooting. He fell, enveloped in blue, his antennae seared off. A comrade dragged him back. The smell of burning flesh assailed Sasha's nostrils.

Amid breaks in the firing, she heard other sounds: breaking glass, angry voices, soft thuds like stones hitting a sofa. More laser guns whining, but away from them, not toward them. She tugged at Danion's encircling arm, but it did not yield.

Even so, she sensed impatience. The bond, amber-yellow, said what Danion had not. If he could trust her to stay behind, he would join Thuja. She had no doubt that he knew how to fight, even if he belonged to a pacifist culture. Swift, strong, controlled—he would make a fearsome enemy. And he looked like the Kazrati guards.

Go, she said to him. I promise, I'll stay here till the shooting stops.

Danion tugged her long braid, bending her head back to search her face. Truly? he asked. You are not trying to get me to release you, so that you can help your friends?

She couldn't blame him for his skepticism. Cross my heart, she said. If you're going to waste your time worrying about me, neither of us can do much good.

Thank goodness for the bond. Her sincerity must have communicated itself, for he nodded and slipped down the hall. Sasha sat on the step, hands clenched into fists, and tried not to think about everything that could go wrong.

❀

Thuja had the situation under control, Danion saw. Six Kazrati lay on the ground—some writhing, others unlikely to move again. Only a few laser beams cut the air. Tendak must have grown lax during the months of success, or he would have posted more soldiers.

He went to the far end of the corridor, doing his best to ignore Sasha scrunched into a ball on the other side of the hole they had blasted in the wall. No comfort he could provide would work as well as seeing her brother alive— and if Tonio was not alive, no comfort would work at all.

The Pannthu at the other end had split into two groups and were moving down the corridor, their opponents already dispatched. Danion picked a direction at random and followed them.

The sound of lasers firing died away. Breaking glass gave way to the sobs and exclamations of people in distress. Sasha inched along the wall and peeked around the corner. Bodies littered the floor between her and the studio. Iqara would have quite a few patients, she saw. She hoped none of them were seriously hurt; the shuttle did not have the facilities to care for them.

Either way, they no longer posed a threat. Thuja and her troops had immobilized them.

At the studio door she stopped. The scene before her would have sent a tremor through the strongest heart. Dancers crouched in corners; more bodies lay on the floor. Camille knelt behind the piano, head in her hands. The once-beautiful room lay open to the elements, plate glass cracked, walls pitted with bullet-sized holes.

Sasha shivered as the reality of the invasion hit home again. Four months had passed since she was here, but the damage made the school look as if it had been abandoned decades ago.

Most of the bodies wore Kazrati uniforms, or what passed for uniforms; the invaders had not scrupled to steal whatever took their fancy from their hostages. Thuja watched, face bright with glee, as her soldiers slapped stasis cuffs on the fallen and laid them against the wall.

"Come in," she said to Sasha. She added a phrase in Pannthu, and four of her troops peeled off. "These will stand guard. We go to find the others. Geoffrey, if you please, ask the Tarkei commander to join us. He need leave only a small contingent to guard the tunnels."

Geoff did not respond. He had rushed forward and was bending over the body of a young woman.

Sasha felt her breath catch. Then she saw the woman extend a trembling hand. Geoff gathered it in his own.

"I'll go," she told Thuja. "I think Geoff found his sister."

Danion followed the Pannthu, waiting for them to clear each side corridor before proceeding. He had just passed a doorway when he heard a small, almost negligible sound, like the leg of a chair scraping against a tile floor. He ducked into the next alcove and waited. The Pannthu pushed on, leaving him behind.

When silence fell, he slipped back into the hallway. Pressed against the wall, he listened. Nothing.

Well, at worst he would make an utter fool of himself. Danion kicked the door open and dove through. A laser singed his shoulder as he rolled across the floor, grabbed the feet of his attacker, and pulled.

A heavy body slammed into him, but Danion, already in motion, had the advantage. He continued the roll, grabbing the wrist that held the laser and slamming it into the floor. The wrist twisted as its owner tried to pull it free, but the strength of desperation kept Danion from letting go. One good shot, and he was dead.

His knees held down the man's shoulders. He had seconds before the other, bucking like a wild animal, tore free. Danion raised his right hand and chopped the wrist that would not release the gun. At the same time, he yelled for assistance.

The man cursed, and the weapon flew from his grasp, skittering across the floor. Feet pounded the corridor as the Pannthu responded to Danion's call.

Danion settled back on his heels as the leader of the group he had been following burst into the room. A purple hand scooped up the laser gun and held it at his adversary's head. The man froze into stillness.

Danion looked down. Except for the blue eyes, it could have been his own face.

❈

He left Tendak in the Pannthu's far-from-gentle care and made his way back to the studio. The fight, fierce but short, had taken only a few minutes; even so, Danion was breathing hard. Perhaps that was why he didn't hear his next assailant until the knife touched his throat.

❈

By the time Sasha returned with Iqara and the medical kit, Thuja and her troops had disappeared, except for the four detailed to remain in the studio. Iqa ran to Geoffrey's side. Sasha watched them until she was sure that Iqa had the situation under control, then looked around. Slava, by the far wall, blew her a kiss; the big blond Russian looked gaunt and exhausted but appeared to have the full use of his limbs. More friends were gathering, but the face Sasha most wanted to see was not there.

Gathering, but not closing in. Her friends formed a circle about six feet in front of her and would not cross it. Camille dropped her hands and stood. "*Petite!*" She held out her arms, but even she did not approach.

From behind, Sasha heard a sharp intake of breath. She turned her head. A silver knife blade nicked the skin of her husband's throat. Danion stood perfectly still.

The young man who held the blade had light brown curls and eyes to match. He was slender and strong and a few inches taller than Sasha herself. He should have been smiling a welcome, but it looked as though he had forgotten how.

15. Reunion

"STEP BACK," THE YOUNG man said, speaking not to Danion but to the assembled dancers.

Do as he says, Danion urged Sasha. I do not want him to hurt you as well.

Instead, Sasha shrieked, "Tonio, no! He's Tarkei!"

While Danion was trying to figure out what was happening, she grabbed the young man's hand, snatched the blade from him, and threw it to the floor.

Dancers flooded in, until they were an island in a sea of bodies.

Danion rubbed his throat. There was a trickle of blood where the knife had nicked him, although it had come disturbingly close to a major artery.

"*Sasha*?" Tonio said. "Bloody hell! Where did you come from?" He caught her up, and she burst into tears.

"You're all right," she said between sobs. "You're not dead."

"Hey," he said, hugging her, "I'm fine. Really."

These reassurances did nothing to stem the flood. The tension of the last seven months released in a deluge of grief. Danion felt it as well as saw it, but this was his wife's moment of reunion; he didn't want to interfere, even though Tonio seemed at something of a loss.

As Danion watched, a big blond man walked forward and plucked Sasha out of her brother's arms. "There, there, my dove," he said, "don't cry. We thought you lost, and here you return to us. Amazing."

Danion recognized him from his wife's thoughts. Slava, her partner. Looking around, he realized he recognized most of them. The dark-haired Frenchwoman with the elegant bearing and the dramatic white streak in her hair was Camille Delagardie, the ballet mistress.

Tonio, of course, he would have identified at once if he'd seen him before the knife touched his throat.

Geoff and Iqa bent over a young woman. Geoff's sister, presumably. Geoff held her hand, but she did not move. Danion felt his stomach tighten.

Camille came over, pushing Slava away to hug Sasha. "Such foolishness. Come, *ma belle*, ignore them; they do not understand. Cry if you wish. What could be more natural?"

Against that motherly shoulder, Sasha's sobs gradually eased. "I'm so glad to see you, Camille," she said at last. "So glad to see everyone. I thought for sure that Tendak had killed Tonio, and maybe the rest of you as well."

Camille patted her head, as though she were a little girl. "*Bien sûr, petite,* but as you see, we live. Now you will tell us what happened, no?"

Throughout this interchange, Slava had been staring at Danion through narrowed eyes. "Are you sure he's Tarkei?" he asked. "He could be Tendak's brother."

Danion suppressed a shudder. "They do look alike," Sasha said. "I noticed it, too, the first time I saw him, but yes, I'm sure. Danion came with me. That's where I went, when I left here, to Tarkei. Although I didn't know it was Tarkei at first. I nearly lost my mind, thinking I'd gone all that way and landed on Kazratan."

"Maybe you did," Tonio said, "and they just told you it was Tarkei."

"I stayed there for two months," Sasha said. "It was not Kazratan. Danion is Tarkei. We're the rescue force. Or haven't you noticed the place is swarming with Pannthu? And Tarkei shock troops, so for goodness' sake don't sneak up on anyone else unless you know them."

This piece of sisterly advice provoked the sulky silence it deserved. While Tonio brooded, Slava, self-contained and dispassionate, asked, "How do you know he's Tarkei?"

Sasha exchanged a brief glance with Danion.

"Because he's my husband," she said.

That caused another explosion. Tonio's voice came through loudest. "Are you out of your mind? What does that prove? You weren't gone four months! How can you know anything about him?"

"You don't understand," Sasha said.

"Damn right," Tonio muttered.

"It's not what you think." Sasha looked around. Everyone was staring, waiting for her to explain.

Slava leaned against the portable barre and crossed his arms over his chest. "This should be good."

Sasha glared at him, although compared to Tonio's, his reaction was mild. Even Camille looked shocked.

"I'll tell you the whole story later," she said to her brother. "The important point is this. We are mentally linked. He couldn't lie to me if he wanted to. Danion is Tarkei, not Kazrati."

Tonio's skeptical expression did not change.

Sasha flung out her right arm, pointing at Danion. "Look at him, why don't you? Does he *act* like a Kazrati?"

Tonio examined him. Danion, forcibly reminded of his first meeting with Sasha, held out his hands, palms up. "I am not. We and the Kazrati come from the same stock, but we are not the same. Culture does make a difference."

Tonio focused on the floor, as though thinking.

"What your sister says is true," Danion told him. "We are mentally linked." He took a deep breath. However necessary, this was difficult for a Tarkei, but Sasha had reached out to him in the hollow. He had not then had the words to respond. "I love her. I would not hurt her."

The bond glowed rose, soft as the pink dance dress Sasha had worn for *Pavane*. She appreciated his openness even if her brother could not.

Tonio looked at Sasha, at Danion, at Sasha again. Then he walked over and held out his hand. "Sorry," he said. "I misunderstood."

Danion took the hand. "Apology accepted."

"And you're happy?" Tonio looked at Sasha, then back at Danion. It wasn't clear whom he expected to answer the question.

Danion released his brother-in-law's hand. "With your sister, yes. And Tendak is in custody." He did not say what role he had played. It felt good, though, to see the dancers' tension ease. "You are free."

The sea of dancers closed around them again, chattering. Danion touched his wife's shoulder and pushed his way through the crowd. The excited voices sounded odd in the ruined room.

Iqa looked over her shoulder as he knelt beside her and pointed to Geoff's sister. "She'll be fine once we get her back to the shuttle and give her a chance to recover."

Danion's stomach stopped turning cartwheels. "What happened?" Maintaining his usual calm tones took more effort than usual.

Geoff shook his head at his still-unconscious sister. "Couldn't stay out of a fight. That's what her friend over there says."

He pointed to a slender woman with short pale-green hair and silvery skin. The woman stood in the circle with her back to them, and Sasha's brother had an arm about her waist.

Elasi, Sasha's voice said in Danion's thoughts.

"Is she badly injured?" Danion asked Iqa. "Why does she not awake?"

Iqa raised a corner of the blanket that covered the woman from waist to ankles. A long, ugly slash ran from hip to knee.

"No," his sister said. "It's superficial, but she'll feel it for a while. And she's in shock right now. That's why I gave her a sedative."

"Clocked a Kazrati soldier with a rock. Can you believe it? My little sister!" Geoff sounded ebullient—with relief, no doubt.

Danion glanced at his own sister, bent like a seasoned professional over her patient. "They can surprise you."

Iqa gave him a half-smile to match his own. "Keep her warm," she told Geoffrey as she stood. "I have other patients to see."

With help from the two Tarkei medical assistants, Iqara had performed triage on almost everyone affected by the attack and had treated her brother's flesh wounds by the time Thuja returned, the entire battalion of Pannthu at her back.

"No one is here," Thuja said before she crossed the threshold. "We have captured everyone. Where is Tendak?"

Tonio turned his head. "In custody, your friend said. You don't have him?"

Danion intervened. "I left him with your subcommander."

"*You* captured him?" Sasha asked. How had he attacked Tendak without her knowing about it? She hadn't been *that* preoccupied, had she?

But apparently she had. Just as well, Danion told her, or you'd have been in the midst of it. And Geoff grumbles about Sara!

She was still crafting an appropriate response to this piece of absurdity when Thuja distracted her. The Pannthu's antennae pointed toward the ceiling, and her long, skinny arms waved in the air. "Oh, good for you, Danion!"

Tonio held out his hand again. "Now I am embarrassed. And here I thought you were the enemy." As Danion shook hands for the second time, Tonio said to Thuja, "I am

Anthony Sinclair, the company artistic director. And not coincidentally, Sasha's brother. And you are?"

"Thuja." The Pannthu clapped both hands on his shoulders. "Sasha's brother. How delightful! You are not, then, dead."

"Not yet." Tonio grimaced. "One busted Achilles tendon is all."

Sasha winced. A torn Achilles tendon. He might never dance again.

Tonio saw the wince. "If you're going to take the blame, don't. I planned the rebellion. It's my responsibility."

Sasha did not agree, but long acquaintance with her brother convinced her to save her arguments for another day.

Thuja ignored them, single-minded as ever in pursuit of her present concerns. "What did they want of you, the Kazrati?" she asked Tonio.

"I wish I knew. Hostages. Slaves. They killed most of the colonists and brought the rest here, to serve them." Tonio waved a hand at the room. "We were the hostages, the dancers and students. Any direct attack by the allied planets, and we would die. That's what Tendak told us."

Which explained why Jenat had backed the idea of a raid rather than a reconquest of the planet, but oh, how close she had come to losing the rest of her family! Had the Pannthu been less silent and less lethal... Sasha left the thought unfinished.

"Is that true?" Danion asked Thuja. "They killed those living in outlying districts?"

Thuja's antennae drooped at the tips, forming a pair of upside-down J's. "I cannot scan the entire planet, Danion, but it appears to be true. Those I sent into the woods found no one, and we ourselves encountered no living beings on our trip."

"It would make a horrible kind of sense," Sasha said. "They were a small force, and controlling the entire planet must have strained them. Easier to bring everyone here." The thought made her sick.

"We have prisoners," Thuja said. "Will they talk?"

"Kazrati?" Geoff left his sister long enough to join the discussion. "I'd expect them to die first."

"Geoff's right." Danion pointed at the studio clock, stuck displaying the hour as 9:28. "We must leave as soon as possible. Rather than rely on breaking the training of Kazrati warriors, let us fan out and search the school. They did not have time to destroy the evidence."

Those dancers capable of movement assisted in the search. Danion and Sasha walked together through the ruins of what had once been her home. The intense grief she had felt when she first saw the school had diffused into a dull ache that might weigh down her heart forever. Throughout the school, destruction and desolation reigned. The library that had been her father's joy lay broken, books tossed everywhere, carpet ripped. The room where she had slept provoked only disgust; when she convinced herself to cross the threshold at last, she found nothing worth saving. The kitchen was an ode to poor hygiene, the studio an exercise in gradual demolition. If Danion had not accompanied her, she would have given up and gone out to the garden to weep.

Tendak had taken her parents' room as his own. That was where Danion had captured him. Rage filled her as she stood in the doorway. The lace-trimmed coverlet that her mother had treasured looked like a large and noisome dishrag. The mirror that had reflected that beloved face boasted a crack that ran from one side to the other, and Tendak's discarded clothes lay in piles about the floor. How much of the damage had been done during his fight with Danion?

Not much, Danion said. I did not have the leisure to examine it at length, but I received a general impression of disorder.

A terminal of a type unfamiliar to citizens of Earth and its allies sat on the dresser. Lights flashed on the charcoal-gray screen, forming outlines of script that resembled Tarkei.

Danion, scowling, walked over to it. He punched a button, and the screen went dark.

"He alerted the fleet," he said. "We must leave at once."

He glanced around the room, his nose wrinkling in a revulsion that matched her own. Then his eyes narrowed. He crossed the filthy floor, kicked a pile of clothing to one side, and picked up a diamond-shaped gold medallion, no bigger than a fingernail. It lay in his palm, topaz center twinkling at her.

What is it? Sasha asked. The link glowed crimson with anger, but its golden edges suggested a certain satisfaction.

"It belongs to a Kazrati general," Danion said.

Sasha froze in place.

"In the secret police," he added. "Such men do not go renegade."

She felt her eyes widen. Had Danion discovered the proof they needed? He must have.

"The secret police kill anyone who tries to defect," he said.

❄

It was Thuja who found the powder. A vial half-an-inch across, filled with something that looked like red sand. Danion snatched it from her grasp as she prepared to test it by tipping a sample into her palm.

She tried to snatch it back, but he held it out of reach, aware that the dancers were watching the conflict open-mouthed.

Geoffrey ran toward them, his attention caught by her frenzied hops. "Good lord, Thuj," he said. "Don't you know what that is? Leave it alone!"

Thuja crouched, antennae at the ready. "No, what is it?"

"Tyrellian powder, from the looks of it." Geoff held out his hand for the vial.

Danion released it. "I am pleased that your sister will recover, my friend."

"Thanks, brother." Geoff put his thumb over the stopper, shook the vial, and stared at the sand as it fell back into place. "Were they making it here or trading it?"

Danion recalled the white bush with red flowers that had marked the tunnel entrance. It would produce red berries in the fall. "The first, I would guess."

Thuja's antennae perked. "Making it? In a factory? But what is it?"

"Feel-good powder," Geoff said. "A few whiffs, and you wouldn't care about anything else for the rest of your life."

"Except getting more," Danion added. "But not for long. You would live a few months, at best."

"And they made it here?" Sasha grabbed Danion's arm. "But where? We don't have factories."

"They did, though, sis." Tonio stood in the doorway. Everyone turned toward him, and he limped into the studio. "One. They put it up the week after you left. The Kazrati didn't tell us what they made there, but the colonists they didn't kill, that's where they worked them."

"That's horrible!" Sasha said. No one disagreed. "Is anyone left?"

Danion shook his head. "I predict few, *kaleita,* and the ones who survive will die soon. Those who prepare the drug cannot avoid addiction without special equipment, which the Kazrati would not bother to provide."

Sasha's face reflected his own outrage. "You should find the factory, though," he told Thuja, "and release those present. It is not their fault, and we should care for them."

Thuja dipped her antennae at him and departed, Pannthu troops at her back. Geoffrey, Tonio, Iqara, Danion, and Sasha remained in the studio, locked in an awkward silence.

"That's why they came, then," Sasha said at last. "Not because we were unarmed and reasonably close but in search of the raw materials for the drug."

Danion drew her long braid through his fingers, aware of her brother's eyes on them. "My guess, *kaleita.* I know no more than you."

"We must go," Sasha said. "Soon, before the reinforcements arrive."

"Agreed." Danion saw Tonio's instinctive protest and the way he bit it back rather than express it. "Your sister is right. Tendak alerted the Kazrati who monitor the perimeter; the longer we stay, the greater the danger. Your company is small enough for us to transport you, although if Thuja finds many colonists, they will have to wait until we can send reinforcements."

"She won't find many," Tonio said. "And yes, Sasha's right. It's difficult because we grew up here, but after the last few months I have no desire to stay. Can we bring the students, though? Not more than thirty of them survived, and most are children; they need their parents if they are to recover."

"We'll take them," Danion said. "The Tarkei soldiers will remain here for their ship. Their commander has already called for it. They can guard the prisoners."

"And Tendak?" Sasha asked.

"He must stay here. We have no security cell on the shuttle. My father's troops will guard him, too." He hated to let Tendak go, but allowing him to roam around the ship was unthinkable.

Camille clapped her hands. "Time to leave, boys and girls."

Danion led the way out of the studio, Sasha's hand clasped in his. Geoff installed his sister in a hover-chair and pushed it before him. A long line of dancers trailed behind.

✱

The Pannthu waited at the edge of the garden, Thuja at their head and the Tarkei troops at their back. As

Danion reached them, Thuja stepped forward. It took no acquaintance with her people to read this expression: she was angry enough to spit.

"They left no one," she said, biting off each syllable in turn. "No one. We found the factory and fifty bodies. Fifty, Danion! Dead no more than one standard unit of time." Her antennae spun in circles, she was so furious.

Danion could not blame her. He stopped, his arm around Sasha's waist, and allowed the others to pass him as he fought for control. "Tendak must have ordered their murders before he called home. They wanted no witnesses." His voice shook with rage.

Thuja held up another vial, much like the first one but larger. "I found this. What witnesses do we need?"

Danion took the vial from her and dropped it in the small pouch he had carried throughout the expedition. "None." He paused, wondering how to ask the next question, then pushed ahead. "And the bodies?"

"Vaporized. We did not have the luxury of arranging for their burial."

"You and your troops have done an excellent job," Danion told her. "Please accept my commendation."

With a jerk of her head, Thuja set her force in motion. She kept pace with Danion and Sasha as the group moved into the woods. "I accept it, Danion, and with thanks, but do not misunderstand if I say that I would have preferred a reprimand and living colonists."

The lavender antennae surveyed the silent planet, soon to be devoid of humanoid life.

"There is no cure for addiction to Tyrellian powder," Danion said.

Thuja stood in his path, hands on her skinny hips, the tips of her antennae pointing at him. "Are you saying they were better off dead?"

Danion turned her with one hand on her shoulder. "I am saying that the Kazrati are guilty not only of murder. They condemned these people, who had done them no harm, to an existence that may have made death seem welcome; they intended who knows how many others to suffer the same fate; and they did it either for profit or for revenge. We may have halted their campaign, this time, but no punishment can atone for what they did."

"Oh." Thuja dropped her aggressive stance, and her antennae returned to normal. "I am sorry, Danion. I did you a disservice."

"Think nothing of it, my friend," he said. "You were angry, and with good reason."

"But not with you."

Danion's hand still rested on her shoulder. "Fortunately, not with me."

The service vehicles sat in their woodland lair, and the shuttle in its hollow. Without the Tarkei soldiers, who agreed without protest to remain at the school, the group did not differ much from its original size. Once everyone was aboard and assigned to quarters, Iqara, who had treated the worst-injured dancers before they left the school, ordered those with wounds of any sort into the medical facilities, where she, with the assistance of two Tarkei medical technicians, bossed them mercilessly if to good effect.

Sasha stayed long enough to make sure her help was not needed before going to find Danion. She worried about him, although she suspected he would shrug off her concern. Except for Geoff and Thuja, needed on the bridge, and Iqara, doing the job she had come for, everyone else could relax—or collapse—whereas Danion had the responsibility of getting them safely past the Kazrati patrols and out into space. An hour's difficult flying, minimum, on top of two strenuous days.

She slipped into the seat she had occupied before, buckling the harness without being asked. Danion acknowledged her arrival in his thoughts, but he neither turned his head nor spoke. He was concentrating on his present task, although she sensed fatigue gathering—and his refusal to recognize it. Not sure what she could do to help, Sasha stayed. Perhaps some opportunity would present itself.

Danion and Geoff had returned to their seamless routine. Thuja, intent on her controls, monitored incoming scout ships; Danion flipped the shuttle this way and that until the flight resembled nothing so much as a roller-coaster ride; Geoff compensated for the numerous course changes, reeling off new lists of coordinates as a master of ceremonies reels off names.

This time they were luckier. Sasha counted eight near-misses and one last-minute correction that made her wonder if she would look in the mirror to find her hair turned to gray, but none of the enemy craft stayed long enough to detect them.

By the time Danion said, "We're through," though, her hands ached from the way she'd clutched them nonstop.

Even then, one lone scout slipped past them, necessitating a final dip and curve. The harness bit into Sasha's shoulders; she hadn't expected that sideways lunge.

Danion waited another forty minutes before leaving the pilot's chair. Sasha felt him unbuckling her harness and heard him ask Thuja which of her troops could relieve them.

He caught her as she tried to stand; only then did she realize how tense she had been. Her muscles were like rocks, and Danion's not much better. But when she looked into his eyes, she saw relief.

"We made it," she said.

"We did," Danion told her. Behind him, Thuja let out a cheer that could have been heard on Tarkei. Geoff punched a clenched fist into the air, then jumped up and ran out the door.

His sister, Sasha said to Danion. *I hope she's better.*

I too, Danion said. He pulled Sasha to her feet. *Time to rest, Sasha-chan.*

16. Giselle

DANION, ABOUT TO COLLAPSE onto the bunk behind him while he waited for Sasha to emerge from the shower, saw a pair of pointe shoes propped against the mirror, handwriting on one satin surface.

Curious. In the small cabin, it took minimal effort to stand and reach for the shoe. He held it up to the light to decipher the curves and dips of Tarkei script.

"For thee, *kaleita,* may the stars always smile," it said, and her signature, Alessandra Sinclair. Touched, he leaned back, caressing the silky fabric with his thumb.

Sasha appeared, wearing a fuschia nightgown that was more suggestion than covering. Danion, appreciating the effect of long legs honed by years of ballet practice, let his eyes linger. Her hair fell in a sheet down her back, ending just above her waist.

"Your sister picked it out," she told him.

Danion held out his hand. "Her taste is better where you are concerned."

"No yellow flowers." Sasha sat next to him. "You found the shoes, I see. So much has happened, I forgot I'd signed them."

"It is a custom, then?" Danion thrust his hand into the mass of dark hair. Her cheekbone lay solid beneath his hand, her ear soft against his fingers.

"Since the nineteenth century, at least. On Earth, companies sell shoes with their ballerinas' signatures."

"Truly?"

"People who love the ballet buy them as keepsakes or gifts." She smiled. "The inscription, though, is just for you."

"Thank you. I will cherish it. And you." He rubbed her cheek. "At this moment, however, I am going to take a shower before I fall asleep. Two days on Xantera have not made for optimal hygiene."

Sasha caught his hand and held it. "You were wonderful. Thank you so much."

"It was nothing," he said.

"It meant a great deal to me." Sasha kissed his cheek. "I'll be here, when you get clean."

And she was, although when Danion came out of the shower, wearing only a towel, he found his wife fast asleep.

The pounding started again. It must be a nightmare. Danion pulled the pillow over his head and did his best to ignore it. Only moments ago, he had been warm and comfortable, with Sasha curled against his shoulder and his hand tangled in her hair.

She scrambled over him, muttering about people who couldn't do anything for themselves. He forced his eyes open to see her rummaging in the bureau drawer.

"Grrr," she said. His largest sweater dropped over her head. It did nothing to diminish the effect of the long legs, but it did provide adequate cover. Sasha dragged her hair through the neck opening, shook her head to settle it, and opened the door.

Thuja bounced through, oblivious to any human or Tarkei preference for privacy. Her antennae swiveled in all directions.

"But this is good," she announced at top volume. "Very good indeed."

Danion groaned; he could not help it. His head ached with fatigue, and he felt as though he could sleep for the rest of the week. "Thuja," he said through gritted teeth, "tell me what you are doing here before I forget that Tarkei do not shout."

"But you must get up," she said. "Your father is calling."

Wonderful. The last thing he needed at the end of this hideous day. "Tell him I will call him back when I'm awake."

He did not have to see Thuja to imagine the state of her antennae. Her voice contained astonishment enough. "I cannot do that," she said. "He is already annoyed that I left to find you."

So his father intimidated even the Pannthu. Danion tried to bend an elbow as a preliminary to rising, but he could not make his arm move.

"Don't be ridiculous, Thuja," Sasha said. If he could move, he would hug her. "Can't you see he's exhausted? Give me five minutes, and I'll talk to his father."

Definitely he would hug her. Just as soon as he woke up.

Sasha dressed as fast as she could and followed Thuja to the bridge. The man on the screen did not remind her of her husband so much as of a snow tiger she had once seen in a zoo: coloring silver and black; too tall to be considered stocky but broad-shouldered and powerful. Although he lacked his son's lean elegance, he had the style found among men so accustomed to power that they take it for granted. At the moment, the resemblance to a caged tiger was particularly strong: Prime Minister Jenat was pacing from window to desk.

"Good morning, sir," she said to the screen. "I'm sorry to have kept you waiting."

Jenat spun on one booted heel, earning Sasha's unspoken admiration. She thought only people in books did that. "I'm not waiting for you, young lady, whoever you may be. Where's my son?"

"Sleeping," Sasha said. "I am your daughter-in-law, Alessandra Sinclair. And yes, I know you're not waiting for me, but Danion has had no proper rest for two days. He can't move, he's so tired. I volunteered to come and ask whether you would prefer him to call you later or to receive a report from me now."

Jenat dropped into his chair. "Well, you have courage, I'll grant you that. No one else bothers to tell me anything, and Danion needs someone to speak up for him on occasion. I'll listen to you. Where do matters stand?"

Sasha suppressed her sigh of relief and thanked the stars for the years of Camille's unrelenting demands that she present herself well. "The dance company and students are aboard, and we are heading back toward Tarkei." She checked the clock. No wonder Danion was so tired—he'd slept for less than one standard unit. "We crossed the perimeter some time ago. Danion evaded detection, with the exception of one scout ship on the way in, and that one he tricked into destroying itself."

"Excellent." Jenat tapped his fingers against the desk. "And the Kazrati?"

"Danion captured Tendak." That raised an eyebrow. "We left him with your troops, because they have a brig and we don't." A nod. "They're bringing the remaining guards as well: we didn't find many, and some were killed in the raid." Another nod, less curt this time.

"Any sense of who was backing him?" Jenat seemed unaware of her tension, or perhaps he was ignoring it out of courtesy.

"We had no opportunity to question the prisoners. Tendak had alerted the ships at the perimeter, so we left as soon as possible. But in the room he was using, Danion found a medallion belonging to a general in the secret police." Sasha straightened her shoulders and tried not to think about how tired she was.

"Secret police, eh? You did well, the pair of you. And my troops?"

"The transport landed without difficulty, but I don't know what happened after that."

Thuja circled a thumb and finger in the oddest approximation of the "okay" sign that Sasha had ever seen. "Thuja says they made it," she told Jenat.

"What happened to the colonists?" The unrelenting voice went on, but Sasha could not answer. She closed her eyes, sick at the memory.

"Tell me, girl." Jenat's voice sounded gruff. Perhaps not a snow tiger after all. More like one of those big noisy wolfhounds that wouldn't dream of actually hurting anyone.

Sasha forced herself to meet his eyes. "Not many of them were left. From what we could tell, the Kazrati invaded Xantera because certain plants there could provide the raw material for something Danion and Geoffrey called Tyrellian powder."

Jenat jerked in his seat. "Go on," he said, his face grim.

"Tendak used the colonists as slaves to manufacture the powder. They killed the few who were still able to work not long after we arrived." The horror of it hovered at the edge of her understanding, but she could not allow the reality to penetrate. Not yet, while she had to do this.

"People you knew, girl?" Jenat leaned forward, elbows on his desk, and his voice softened until he did sound like Danion after all.

"Most of them." Only her hands, digging into the back of the chair she had occupied earlier in the day, kept her from swaying. "I lived on Xantera my whole life. Even though it had a small population—maybe because it had a small population—sooner or later, I knew everybody."

"Your grief is mine," Jenat said. Perhaps the words triggered something. "And Geoffrey Anderson's sister? Is she with you?"

One piece of good news. "She is. Alive but injured. She threw rocks at a Kazrati soldier during the raid, and the guards shot her in the leg. She will make a full recovery, Iqara says."

Jenat's stern face relaxed. "A brave young lady. Tell Geoffrey I am pleased."

"I will," Sasha said.

"And now? What else need we do?" Jenat asked.

"Your troops are bringing the prisoners to Tarkei. They may need help. The rest of us are safe and mostly unhurt; we need nothing else for the moment." Our family and friends, our planet back, our lives—nothing Jenat had within his gift, so why ask?

He understood, she thought. His eyes looked sad. "Thank you, my daughter, for taking the time to come and talk with me. Tell Danion and that sister of his to call me later."

"Yes, sir," Sasha said. "I will." His image disappeared from the screen, and she headed for the door. "If he calls again," she told the inexhaustible Thuja, "don't wake me. In fact, don't wake me for anything less than a Kazrati assault. Agreed?"

Thuja wiggled her antennae. "Understood. But I must say, Sasha-*chan*, I am most impressed."

Sasha grinned at her from the doorway. "He wasn't so bad. You should have met *my* father."

Back in the cabin, Danion lay on his stomach. He did not so much as flick an eyelid when Sasha came in. She stripped off the hastily donned clothes and replaced them with the scanty nightgown, then rearranged the covers so that they provided some covering (much as she enjoyed the sight of Danion's smoothly muscled back).

How to slip in without waking him? After a while, she went to the foot of the bed and wriggled up against the wall, feeling like the heroine in a harem romance. She had reached the level of his waist when he rolled over and pulled her into his arms.

"I thought you were asleep," she said. His eyes, wide open and with a distinctly mischievous gleam, did not look in the least sleepy.

"I was," he said, "for a while. How did you get along with my father?"

"Fine." Danion stared at her, so obviously astonished that she couldn't help laughing.

"At first, I could have sworn he wanted to swallow me whole, but after about two minutes I figured out he was all bark and no bite, as they say, and after that I had no trouble with him." She traced the line of her husband's cheek. "By the end, he was positively sympathetic. Told Geoffrey how pleased he was and everything. He reminded me of you."

Danion's eyes widened, if possible. "Incredible," he said. "I shall have you conduct my conversations with him from now on."

"No, you won't. He said to tell you and Iqa to call him back."

"It was too much to hope for, I suppose." Danion flipped the covers over her, pulling her in until her palms lay flat against his skin.

"This gown of yours," he said. "It's very beautiful."

"Thank you."

"I am removing it," and he did.

Sasha pushed her palms harder against his chest, rubbing the hair between her fingers. "If you feel it's necessary."

"Oh, I do." Danion's hand stroked the curve of her spine.

"Pretty impressive, for an hour's rest," Sasha said. "And here I felt sorry for you. Maybe I should have let you talk to your father after all."

Danion's laughter sounded through the link. *Never think it,* kaleita. *Different stimuli produce different results.*

Is that so? Sasha said. *Perhaps you should show me how that works.*

An excellent idea, Danion said.

Slava and Tonio cornered Sasha as she walked through deck three the next morning. Camille, right behind them, wanted to talk about practice rooms. Sasha sent her down to look at the cargo area on deck five, but it wasn't likely to hold her for long.

Slava and Tonio were demanding the story of her marriage.

"I'll tell you," she said, hands in the air in surrender, "but for goodness' sake let's go to the crew lounge. No one's likely to be there at this time of day; we can talk in private."

"Well, if you insist," Tonio said, looking very much the younger brother. "Just don't think you can wiggle out of it."

"I don't want to wiggle out of it," Sasha told them. "I said it was private, not secret. But I'm not telling you a thing until Camille returns. She'll have a fit if I spill the beans before she gets here."

Slava threw a brotherly arm around her waist. "Come, Sashenka, pay no attention. You know how grouchy he is before he has his coffee."

"I am not," Tonio said, sounding grouchy as the proverbial bear.

"You are, too," Sasha said, "but don't worry. You can have coffee in the crew lounge."

Tonio acquired a spring to his step, if not enough to overcome the limp. "They have coffee? Isn't it a Tarkei ship?"

Sasha glanced at Slava, who winked at her. "I'm on it, Tonio. Isn't that enough?"

Tonio's brown curls danced as he swung his head. "Lead on, O sister. Story and java in one. I'm looking forward to a perfect day."

"Till Camille comes back from deck five, at any rate," Sasha said. "Or are you exempt from practicing?"

Tonio gave her the look reserved for the mentally disabled within one's own family. "Exempt? No one's exempt. You weren't gone long enough for dementia to set in!"

"Right." Sasha let her laughter bubble over. "So enjoy it while you can." She waved at the door, directly ahead, and it obliged them by opening. "There you go. If you're quick, you may manage two cups before duty starts calling, and in French."

Tonio headed for the console, Slava on his heels.

❋

"It will do," Camille said. Tonio handed her a cup of coffee, and she sank gracefully onto the seat they had left for her.

"So in two hours, I think, we will start. We have not more than eight weeks to prepare, although it is true, we have practiced a great deal already."

"Prepare what?" Sasha asked.

"*Giselle*. Have you forgotten, *petite*?" Sipping coffee, Camille looked every inch the grande dame, but surely even Sasha's favorite martinet did not believe she could erase the impact of the Kazrati invasion overnight.

"*Giselle*," Sasha said, buying time. "We're still planning to stage *Giselle*? At the San Francisco Opera House?"

Camille waved the coffee mug for emphasis. "*Bien sûr.* The sets are there, the costumes are there, the orchestra is there. Why should we not keep our engagement?"

Because we just went through seven months of hell? Camille would not understand that. One drowns one's troubles in work, *petite.*

And perhaps she was right. Xantera and everything it stood for were gone. Her parents were gone. And *Giselle* was a ballet about mourning. About pain and retribution and forgiveness. A ballet about remorse and the finality of death. If she could not mourn dancing *Giselle,* could she mourn anywhere?

In her mind, Sasha saw the Tarkei desert, the suns rising and the silver birds in flight. She sensed the stillness and the silence, the feeling she had tried to capture in *Pavane,* the comfort of meditation. Once Xantera had been like that, untouched and serene. If she asked him, Danion would take her to the mountain sanctuary; she could face her grief in the quiet assurance of her husband's company.

The others were watching her, waiting to hear what she would say. Sasha looked at the three beloved faces, one by one—her brother, her partner, and her second mother. She was their prima; they were counting on her. If she refused, they would mount the production anyway. Elasi would have to handle *Giselle* alone. And Sasha knew, not with pride but as a matter of fact, that Elasi did not dance as well as she and, perhaps more important for a company making a comeback after an experience that would break most people, could not draw the crowds that Sasha could draw just by putting her name on the playbill. That was, after all, how she became prima.

Danion waited in the back of her mind, listening for her decision. Do you mind? Sasha asked him. I can't let them down.

It never occurred to me that you would, Danion said. And why should I mind? That part of Earth is pleasant at this time of year.

Sasha held out her hands. "Fine," she said. "Let's do it."

17. Confrontation

"ALL RIGHT," TONIO SAID. "You've stalled long enough. I want to know what happened. One minute you're on Xantera with the rest of us, next you show up four months later complete with husband. Who is this guy, anyway?"

Sasha, startled, stopped to look at him, her coffee cup cradled in both hands. What had gone wrong? Yesterday he'd seemed to accept Danion, after his initial reservations, but now he sounded positively hostile. Hunched over in his seat, Tonio scowled as though she were deliberately keeping secrets from him, rather than restored to their company after four months away.

Rattled, she gave the first answer that came to mind. "He's a priest. Was a priest, anyway."

Slava smacked the arm of his chair. "You seduced a priest? Really, Sasha!" Tonio glowered at him.

"You know me better than that, Slava."

Her partner grinned at her. She explained the joining and how she had met Danion. Slava's ready acceptance comforted her. It testified to the depth of their friendship, or at least to his immunity from whatever specific concern had turned Tonio into a good imitation of a curmudgeon.

Camille did not comment, although she kept her eyes fixed on Sasha. Sasha did not worry. If the ballet mistress was disturbed by the story, she would say so in good time; if not, it underlined that the problem was Tonio's alone.

Her brother did not interrupt her, but when she finished, he still looked grumpy.

"A likely story," he said. "And how did you get off Xantera?"

Sasha left the gauntlet on the floor. "I stowed away on board one of the cargo ships," she said. "My memories were muddled, and I didn't remember what I was doing on Xantera. I felt an urgent need to get away. I saw an empty container in the kitchen. I didn't think, or I wouldn't have done it—it's a miracle I wasn't discovered."

Three heads nodded. Sasha stopped, a thought teasing the corners of her mind. Something she'd heard that day, something linked to the cushioned pit at Antilles where she'd sat with Danion. It had escaped her then, but it was so close, she could almost reach out and grasp it.

"Well?" Tonio said. "That's a beginning. You stowed away, and, thank the stars, you didn't get caught. What next?"

Sasha shook her head. "Wait. This is important. The cargo ship. What was it doing there?"

"Delivering supplies," Slava said. "For the soldiers, I suppose."

"What is it, *petite*? What are you remembering?" Camille, her hand warm from the coffee, touched Sasha's cheek.

"They were delivering that day, yes, but ... oh, this is so frustrating!" Sasha deposited her coffee cup on a small table that sat next to her chair. It hit harder than she intended, spilling coffee over the side. Without a word, Camille mopped it up with her napkin.

Sasha thought. Listen, Danion, she said. He was at the controls as usual, but given their distance from Xantera, his presence was more an insurance than a necessity.

As soon as she called him, she sensed his response. Should I come to the lounge?

No, just listen. Do you remember when we were at Antilles, and I couldn't think of what I'd heard?

Of course.

I almost have it, she told him. In her thoughts, she returned to the plastic crate. She'd worried that she would suffocate, but there was a tiny crack around the entrance hole, big enough to let in air without revealing her presence. Sasha crouched, terrified, waiting for the footsteps that would signal that her plan had failed. Much of her past was a blur; she felt like a trapped animal, desperate to escape.

Tendak's voice, not three feet from the container. Sasha curled into a ball, rationing every breath, but he gave no indication that he knew she was there or even that he cared about being overheard. The captain of the supply ship, a slimy alien of a species she didn't recognize, kept his comments to a minimum.

They were talking about the deliveries: arms and food, on this occasion. But then Tendak had said something else, about pick-up times and schedules. At the time, she hadn't known what he meant. He'd talked about powder, and it hadn't made sense. She'd thought he meant gunpowder, but that didn't make sense either, because they weren't using projectiles.

Tonio poked her foot. "Are you alive?"

"Stop it," Sasha said. "I almost have it."

The Tyrellian powder, Danion said.

Yes, I think so. The thought hung out of reach, like an apple too high in a tree.

Who was receiving it? Danion again.

That was it. The thought tumbled into her grasp, and Sasha relaxed. *Not who was receiving it,* she said. *Who was sending it. A faction within the Kazrati government. They planned to distribute it among the allies. Earth and the sister planets, Panntha, Tarkei.*

Thank you, kaleita. I will tell my father.

Sasha picked up her coffee cup. The three pairs of eyes watched her with greater intensity than before.

"You want to explain what that was about?" Tonio said.

She explained.

Tonio did not relent. "And you do this all the time? This talking to each other without words?"

So he was back to Danion. "Yes," Sasha said. "I told you, we're mentally linked. It's the Tarkei who define it as marriage. I accept their definition because I like Danion. In fact, I like him a lot."

"Are you lovers?"

Camille held up a restraining hand. Tonio ignored her. Sasha frowned, puzzled by her brother's belligerence. Slava, who had kept quiet since his comment about seducing a priest, leaned back in his chair, his thoughts and feelings well hidden.

"What difference does it make?" she asked.

"If my prima gets pregnant?" Tonio said in a tone so snide Sasha's palm itched to smack him. "No, why should I care?"

Her answer was not noticeably more polite. Sasha acknowledged this without letting it bother her too much. In her experience, her brother would walk over anyone who didn't bite back. "He's Tarkei, Tonio, and I'm not. What's the defining characteristic of different species?" It made her sad, in fact; she thought she would rather like having Danion's child, but it wasn't likely.

Slava snickered, but Tonio's glower intensified. Absurd as it seemed, he was jealous. He didn't answer, just sat there looking like a dam about to burst.

"Tut, tut," Camille said. "Such childishness. And where do you think Sasha will go?"

"Nowhere." Sasha picked up her coffee and found it cold, so she dropped it into the wall slot and asked for a fresh cup. "I'm not going anywhere. Except to deck five to rehearse."

"Absolutely," Camille said.

"Right, then, let's get started," Sasha told them. "As they used to say in films, we have a show to put on."

Alas, saying, "Fine, let's do it," did not prepare the company to do any such thing. At the best of times, *Giselle* would have been a difficult ballet to stage, for it was demanding in ways not often encountered in the twenty-third century. It dated from the era when pointe shoes were just dance slippers with stitching behind the toes and ballerinas were judged, first and foremost, on the speed of their footwork; even the repeated makeovers to which it had been subjected had not eliminated its Romantic obsession with jumps and spins. It demanded performers in tip-top condition, and Xantera Ballet had few at that moment. The Kazrati had protected their hostages to some extent, but only in comparison to the way in which they treated the rest of the colonists. Underfed, abused, and suffering from seven months of constant stress, the dancers were in worse physical condition than most of them had known in their lives. That they had hung on with grim determination while under assault merely made them more liable to collapse now that the danger was over.

Sasha, thanks to her early departure from the planet, had escaped the worst mistreatment. This, together with the endless hours of practicing that had been her defense against loneliness and anxiety, gave her a physical, although not necessarily an emotional, advantage over the others. Useful, since she was dancing the leading role, but she still had to struggle, and watching the strain on her fellow dancers was not pleasant. Slava, as her faithless lover, Albrecht, had a part as difficult as hers; and Elasi, as Myrthe, queen of the vengeful spirits who dominated Act II, also found her abilities stretched to their limits. Sasha listened to their endless complaints and made not a few of her own.

Tonio, barred from dancing, seemed to take it out in moodiness and fits of resentment over his sister's marriage. That hurt, too. What right had Tonio to grudge her the small amount of happiness she had managed to wrest from this dreadful situation, especially when she had no intention of leaving either him or the company?

Every day, from eight o'clock until past dinnertime, they spent in the makeshift studio. Regular class, pointe class, partnering practice, rehearsal, and more rehearsal until Sasha wished *Giselle* at the devil.

Yet in response to Camille's inexorable demands, the company restored its strength. The performances improved. By day fifteen, it seemed conceivable that they might open on schedule without disgracing themselves with an ill-timed fall or a missed jump. That *Giselle* had fallen so far from the postmodern dance repertoire that no critic alive had seen it, because no existing company had the technical expertise to stage it, helped. At the same time, it imposed a heavy responsibility, of which the dancers seemed acutely, even excessively, aware.

As technique became less of an issue, another problem surfaced, and this one affected Sasha more than the others. In its way, focusing on the steps had been a relief. Like a bandage applied to a wound, the opportunity to walk into a studio (even a pretend one) every morning and think of nothing but what her body had to do had protected her from touching the feelings that remained from her experience on Xantera.

Occasionally in the evenings, Danion prodded her to talk, or at least think, about what had happened there, but each time Sasha refused. I'm fine, she told him. Leave me alone. Because he was Tarkei and not human, he did leave her alone, moving on to other topics. Inside, she knew he was right and she was not, but it was too much to handle, so she pushed it aside, telling herself she would cope with it later.

Later arrived with a bang on day twenty. Tarkei lay four days ahead of them. Danion, with Geoff and Thuja, was as usual at the controls. Iqara, long since out of patients, had received permission to sit in on the rehearsals, but on this occasion she had chosen to visit her brother (more likely, Geoffrey—that romance seemed to be proceeding apace). Sasha and Slava were practicing the "mad" scene, in which Giselle, horrified to discover that Albrecht is not the peasant he has pretended to be but a nobleman engaged to marry another woman, relives her few moments of happiness before dying of a broken heart. An implausible scene for anyone not herself a Victorian heroine. Sasha kept wrestling with it, unable to establish a connection to this fragile flower.

This day proved no better than its predecessors. Sasha staggered artistically among the crowd of dancers who formed a semicircle around her. The woman dancing her mother sat, grief-stricken, at one end of the circle; Slava knelt at the other, filled with remorse. His fiancée stood behind him, distressed in a cool, condescending way. None of it helped. Sasha could have been parsecs from the scene, for all the impact it had on her.

Tonio exploded. The tension that had been brewing between them since she returned to Xantera and told him about Danion spewed out in a stream of fury. "God damn it, Sasha. Act like you know what you're doing! You're dancing like an automaton. You've lost the man you love. Could we see anguish? Caring? Heartbreak? Xantera's not that far behind us. You should be able to muster something."

Unforgivably, he added, "You can't be that happy with Tendak's brother."

Sasha whirled, the long Romantic practice tutu swinging like a bell. "You leave my marriage out of this! And don't lecture me on caring, Anthony Sinclair, because I won't put up with it. You try dancing this idiot who can't muster the gumption to punch Albrecht in the jaw and walk out. Make it believable, and I'll listen to whatever you have to say."

"That's your job," Tonio told her. "You're the damn prima."

"Not any more." Sasha tore the tulle skirt off and threw it on the stage. "Find someone else to bully."

"Sasha!" Slava said, but she paid no attention. If the door could slam, she would have slammed it on her way out.

The storm broke when she reached her cabin. Danion, listening to Geoff and Iqa banter, with occasional interjections from Thuja, gasped as pain crashed into his thoughts.

Geoff turned. "Are you all right?"

Danion stopped halfway to the door. "I, but not Sasha. Take over, please, Geoffrey."

"Wait, is she hurt?" That was Iqa, doctor to the core.

"No." Danion felt as though he were under assault, the others' concern on one side, Sasha's agony on the other. "I expected this. Since the beginning, she has avoided facing what happened during the invasion. Her brother, too, in a different way. Now they have chosen to express it by squabbling." A not uncommon human reaction, in his experience, but he doubted Geoff would appreciate his pointing that out.

"Oh," Geoff said. "Well, I can imagine that. So they've been yelling at each other and she's distraught. Better get down there, brother."

"Excuse me." Danion left.

In the cabin, Sasha lay on the bunk, drenching the pillow. Danion lay beside her, drawing her head onto his shoulder. He made no attempt to persuade her not to cry. Their marriage had given him a new appreciation for the value of tears.

In her mind, he could see jumbled pictures of people she had known, people the Kazrati had killed, her parents front and center. Scenes from her childhood formed a pastiche with later memories. A toddler watched her mother don a pink tutu and transform into a magic princess; he heard her determination to do that herself one day. A young girl played with a small boy with brown curls, watched by a sandy-haired man with warm gray eyes—Calum Sinclair. A birthday party, children cramming chocolate cake into their mouths and laughing at Calum dressed in a clown suit. Danion tried to imagine his own father in such a guise and failed utterly. People shouting, people hugging, people dancing, fear and comfort, hurt and reassurance—the full panoply of family life.

Sasha lay in his arms, no longer sobbing. You were right, she said. I needed to face it. In a way, I owe Tonio a debt of gratitude.

Tonio needs to face it, too, I think, Danion said. He has no reason to grudge you the little comfort I can provide.

Sasha kissed him. *You do yourself a disservice. This morning on its own would qualify you for sainthood.*

Danion pulled her on top of him. *I have no wish for sainthood. I have already experienced it. It has its advantages, true, but it is not really living.*

A concession indeed, my sun priest. Have I ever said that I love you?

Not that I can recall. Danion sensed her dismay, until she realized he was teasing her.

Well, I do. Sasha placed a hand on each ear and kissed him again. Her fingers caressed the diamond tips.

Will you be able to dance Giselle *now?* Danion waited, curious, while she considered how to answer his question. The whole process by which she created her characters was so foreign to him, he found it difficult to imagine.

Oh yes, she said at last. *She is like Xantera, you see.*

No, Danion said. *I don't see.*

She is betrayed by the man she loves, and she has done nothing to deserve it. She believes him when he lies to her, and when she finds out the truth, she's devastated. She wants to kill herself. She drags his sword around the stage, and in the original story, she probably did kill herself, but the Victorians couldn't accept that. So they made her die of a weak heart, which is absurd. But even after death, she loves him. She becomes a spirit, and she's supposed to be dedicated to destroying young men, but she isn't vengeful. Given the choice, she saves him from her sister spirits. Fights to save him.

And in that she is like Xantera?

No, Sasha said. He could hear the sadness, but it no longer overwhelmed her; she accepted it as a natural response to tragedy. She is like Xantera because neither one deserved mistreatment.

She dropped her head on Danion's shoulder again. With a sharp pang, he remembered his mother. No birthday parties, of course; no games, even; the stultifying hand of Tarkei tradition had weighed heavy on them all. But his mother had made her own rules, had taught him and Iqa to do the same. He remembered the pride in her face when he first flew a shuttle well enough to meet her expectations, the warmth in her eyes when he or Iqa did well, the agony of disappointing her, the safety of knowing she would always be there, ready to accept and respond. To love, although his family did not call it that.

Until the day she wasn't there any more. Then no one seemed to care, except Iqa, who cried in the night, and Danion, who tried to comfort her. The others acted as if dying was his mother's fault, the price she paid for not behaving like a good Tarkei wife. His father did not say so, but then, Jenat never spoke of his wife again. Only in adulthood could Danion recognize that his father's silence might have masked grief.

Yes, Sasha said. It's the same. You didn't deserve it either. Nor did she.

Danion hugged her, and they lay there, comforting each other.

Sasha entered the crew lounge next morning to find her brother alone. "I'm sorry," Tonio muttered. He looked sulky; this was as close as he came to an apology at first.

"I blew up, too," Sasha said. Tonio handed her a cup of coffee. He had put milk in it, but she drank it anyway. No need to throw his olive branch in his face.

Tonio dropped into an easy chair. "I'm being a pig about your marriage. Every time I look at your husband, or even think about him, I see Kazrati. I know he isn't. Lord, he captured Tendak! I want to like him, but I can't. Camille says I'm afraid of losing you, because I've lost everyone else. She and Elasi ripped into me last night." Over the top of the cup, brown eyes met gray. The sulkiness was gone. He was ready for a true apology. "I am sorry. God knows, the invasion wasn't your fault, let alone his."

"Just the opposite," Sasha said, twisting the knife to ensure that she got the point across. "Danion didn't only capture Tendak; he organized the rescue mission. His father's the prime minister of Tarkei, and he gave us a ton of assistance, but not until Danion pushed him. It wasn't easy, either. They hadn't spoken in six years."

His brown eyes became rueful. "Well, we have that in common, at least. Difficult fathers."

"I did notice a similarity." Sasha, about to sip coffee, felt her brother pluck the cup from her hands.

"I forgot you like it black," he said. "More accurately, I didn't think about the fact that I'd put milk in it when I handed it to you." He poured the coffee into the wall slot and gave her a fresh cup.

Truly on his best behavior, Sasha told her husband through the bond. "I am planning to dance *Giselle*," she said to Tonio. "Not that I wish to discourage any remorse you may feel like expressing, but I wouldn't let you down, you know. I am your sister."

Tonio grinned, a genuine smile this time. "Didn't think you could let it go." He held up a hand as she protested. "Yes, I know, that's not what you said. It's probably true, what you said, as well. But admit it, sis, it's a gem of a role. I can't see you turning down a challenge like that."

He was right, of course. The annoying creature knew her too well.

"Have you figured out how you're going to approach it?" He'd turned 180 degrees since she walked in. Typical. Her brother couldn't hold on to an emotion for more than two minutes.

"Don't fuss, Tonio," she said. "I have it."

He looked skeptical.

"I was angry with her for letting herself be victimized," Sasha said. "It cut too close to home."

"Oh." Tonio swung his injured leg over the arm of the chair. "Yes, I can understand that. But you can cope with it now?"

"Danion helped me," she said.

"A Tarkei?" His eyes were wide with astonishment, his laughter the epitome of disbelief.

"I told you, he's not what you think. Take the time to get to know him. You'll like him." Sasha sipped coffee, watching her brother ponder this. He was acting more like himself today; perhaps he, too, had made his peace with *Giselle*. He was always volatile, but not usually as unreasonable as he had been about her marriage—and his reaction to Danion did have a certain logic to it. "As for the ballet," she added, "it will be fine, you'll see."

The Tonio she loved looked back at her from behind haunted eyes. "Yes, I think it will."

❋

Tarkei filled the view screen, a copper globe hanging against the black of space, Orbfire glowing crimson behind it. From the pilot's seat, Danion watched it grow. His feelings on returning home were mixed. He knew, with a Tarkei's simple acceptance of reality, that their mission had succeeded, and that much of the credit for the success belonged to him. They had not only captured Tendak but unmasked him. They had discovered the Kazratis' plot against Tarkei and its allies and, at a minimum, delayed its execution. They had evidence his father and the diplomats could use to good advantage against their enemies. They had prisoners. Most of the dancers were safe, if not undamaged.

The mission had changed him. Six years on the mountain, and four at the Academy before that. He had almost forgotten how he loved to fly, how it satisfied him in ways his scientific experiments did not. In truth, in ways not even the mountain had.

Flying did not promise only excitement. Piloting often demanded no more effort than driving a ground car along long stretches of highway; the trick then was to stave off monotony. Still, space had enough dips and curves and nasty customers that it did not stay monotonous for long.

His father would oppose it, most likely. Sendar had already freed him to follow his own path. Sasha would be heart-broken if she lost him, but she would support him nonetheless. She was not Tarkei; she did not subscribe to the illusion that patterns tested by time guaranteed safety. The way was open, if he chose to take it. He just had to decide what he wanted to do.

18. Family

THE DRY HEAT OF Tarkakhan had a comforting familiarity. Sasha walked down the steps of the shuttle, jumped onto the flat rock of the runway, and stretched. The attar of a dozen different kinds of desert flowers mingled in the air. In the west, the three suns were rising, gemstones in a rust-colored sky. Against that incredible horizon, the land went on forever. How had some long-ago Tarkei ever guessed that his planet was not flat?

Tonio hopped down beside her. Literally hopped, for Iqara's best efforts had not cured his limp. It looked as though the Kazrati had indeed ended his dance career.

He had been surprisingly sanguine about it after his first wave of complaints ebbed. A born choreographer, he had so many projects he wanted to try, and so many responsibilities as artistic director of a soon-to-be-reborn company, that once the initial shock had passed, he might be relieved to give up the daily grind of practicing.

Sasha did not say so, however; her brother's temper remained uncertain, although in the last four days he had stopped treating Danion like a pariah. At times, he even succeeded in matching her husband's unfailing courtesy.

A hand touched her elbow, and Danion's lean form appeared in her peripheral vision. "This way," he said. On the far side of the runway a glass building stood ready to receive passengers. They headed toward it, dancers crowding behind them. Geoff and Iqa walked together, among the dancers but oblivious to them, focused on each other. Behind them, Thuja marshaled her troops. From the foot of the glass building, Tarkei with what Sasha assumed were baggage carts drove toward the shuttle.

As soon as they entered the terminal, someone handed Danion a message chip. He pulled Sasha aside, pressed his thumb to the "play" indentation, and listened. The chip verified his identity from his thumb print and transmitted its data.

A summons, Danion told her. They—together with Geoff, Iqa, Thuja, Camille, and the company principals—were invited (not to say ordered) to have dinner with the prime minister that evening. In return, Danion said, his father had arranged for the company to use Tarkei's only theater for as long as necessary to complete its rehearsals.

Camille clapped her hands on hearing this news. The others controlled their joy so well that Sasha decided they could all dance Melancholy in Hindemith's *The Four Temperaments*. Thuja's antennae drooped below her hairline, a feat that looked both impossible and painful.

Sasha herself did not worry. Since their previous conversation, Jenat had lost his power to intimidate her.

Geoff took Iqa's hand. "Well, he can only kill me once."

Sasha looked from one to the other. "Does that mean what I think it means?"

They have grown very close, Danion said. It seems sudden, but I think Iqa has been attracted to him for years.

She's quite young, Sasha said. They have plenty of time to decide what they want.

"It does," Geoff said, "but I don't plan to approach him tonight. I expect he has other issues to deal with. We wanted tell you two, though."

"You have my blessing, brother," Danion said.

Sasha kissed Iqa's cheek. "I wish you every happiness."

To her surprise, Iqa reacted with more astonishment than pleasure. "Happiness," she said with a bewildered expression.

Danion smiled at his sister, a gentle smile but a true one, not his usual curve of the lips. She looked more startled than ever.

"It can happen," he said.

Iqa stared at him, then at Sasha. "Oh! You are in love!"

Sasha slipped a hand through her husband's arm. "Yes," she said. "We are."

Danion entered his father's house for the first time in six years, Sasha on his arm, and almost walked into his first wife. He closed his eyes and opened them again, but Reilu still stood in the library doorway, chill and self-controlled as ever.

Sasha reacted instantly. Reilu? What's *she* doing here? I thought you said your father released you from the contract!

He did. Danion felt numb. He had trusted his father, and this was the result. How long would it take to convince Jenat that the match with Reilu had been a mistake? Or if not that, to respect Danion as an adult?

Geoffrey sent him a sympathetic glance. Iqa looked outraged; Thuja's antennae were perked for gossip. The others, having no idea who Reilu was, stood in a confused clump, staring.

Sasha waited, her hand on his arm. She could have been Odile, so regal was her bearing. Except that Odile stood in the library doorway, watching him.

"Reilu." His voice would have chilled wine, but it remained steady. "What a surprise."

"Danion," she said. "You haven't changed."

That could mean anything, although it was true, she had not changed either, at least on the surface. She had the cold prettiness of a marble statue—her black hair glossy, her green eyes so unusual among the Tarkei void of any expression except hauteur, her face unlined. Of course, she had yet to turn thirty, but her face seldom moved; he doubted she would have character lines at ninety.

Sasha's lips brushed his cheek. Go and talk to her, beloved, she said. Lord knows why she's here, but she must have known you were coming. You may as well get it over with.

Danion stroked her ear, not caring if Reilu saw. And leave you alone with my father?

I'm hardly alone. And if I find out he set you up for this, or even connived at it, he's going to wish you'd joined with Giselle. Besides, I think Camille is more than a match for him, don't you?

You are more than a match for him, *kaleita*. Very well. I will see you soon.

He crossed the hall and followed Reilu into the library.

❀

His father's library had changed no more than Reilu. Rolled scrolls tied with leather were propped along one wall, human-style books shelved against another; terminals and storage cubes sat on tables and desks.

"What are you doing here?" Danion said without preamble as soon as the door closed.

Reilu stalked across the room and settled into the chair behind his father's desk. A move obviously intended to place him at a disadvantage. Danion quelled a flash of anger that seemed quite out of proportion to the offense.

"I live here," she said. "Have you forgotten? Or did you think that when you ran off to join the priesthood, I would slink back to my parents' home?"

Danion frowned. Iqa had not mentioned this. In any event, it did not matter—except that he might have misjudged his father.

He took the chair opposite her, determined not to let her rattle him. "Forgive my surprise. My father said he would abrogate the contract. Did he not tell you I have a wife by joining?"

For an instant, her calm vanished. A spark of anger lit the green eyes. Then her expressionless face fixed on him again. "The woman who was with you? The human?" Her tone, frigid as the Xanteran poles, no longer deceived him. He had flicked her on the raw.

"Yes," he said, reluctant to expose Sasha to this fury's chilling wrath. "Don't misunderstand me, Reilu. I would not have left the mountain otherwise. Our marriage ended six years ago."

"It did not!" Reilu slapped the desk, then stared at her hand as though it belonged to someone else. Someone not obliterated by Tarkei training, someone with normal emotions.

For once, Danion could almost have liked her. Then she leaned back, as much the automaton as ever.

"You will not set me aside," she said, "for a legend. I will not be humiliated. Our marriage exists. It will continue to exist until one of us dies, whether you choose to acknowledge it or not."

Danion stood. "It does not," he said, his voice clipped. "And it will not. According to law, the joining supercedes it. I renounced you six years ago, but I could not break the contract. It did break, however, when I first touched Sasha. Accept that or reject it, it makes no difference."

Reilu raised her chin, glaring like a harpy out of human folklore. "My parents agreed to this marriage, and so did yours, Danion. No one can break it, not even you. Have your wife by joining. Ignore the truth if you like, but I warn you. One day she will be gone, and you will be mine."

"Are you threatening me?" Danion towered over her. "You will not touch Sasha. Do I make myself clear?"

She stood, the harpy submerged in sweet reasonableness. Danion clenched his hands into fists, shocked at how tempted he felt to commit violence.

"I don't need to threaten her, Danion. She is human. I will outlive her. It is the natural order of things." Her green eyes hardened again. "What I will not do is play the discarded wife."

Danion, too angry to speak, walked to the door before delivering his parting sally. "You are already discarded, my dear, and everyone knows it. You are the only one who refuses to recognize it."

Something smashed against the door as he shut it behind him. He did not go back to find out what it was.

Reilu did not crash the family dinner party, at least. Danion half-expected her to appear, if only to watch the other guests cringe. Instead, he had the dubious satisfaction of receiving an apology from his father: "Heard she popped out at you, boy. I'm sorry. I've been trying to send her back to her parents since we had our conversation, and the wretched woman won't leave. Just acts like she's deaf every time I bring it up."

Sasha came up to him then, sending waves of sympathy, and he put his arm around her waist and rubbed her earlobe. Even his father refrained from comment.

He was floating in remorse, she said. Tonio and I had to corral him and drag him off. He was all set to rescue you from the rabid ex-daughter-in-law, but we convinced him you could take care of yourself.

Thank you, I think. The—what do you call them?—the cavalry might not have been unwelcome, I admit.

I'm sure, Sasha said, but this way she heard it from you. Unless she's completely insane, that has to have an impact in the long run.

I hope. He had to agree: Reilu's insistence did hover on the edge of insanity, as though he were a toy she refused to relinquish. Perhaps he had been wrong, and she did want him.

He couldn't convince himself of that, though. In their short time together, he could not recall a single in-depth conversation. He'd had more fulfilling interactions with Sasha before she could confirm her own name.

Sasha was watching him, although the others had gone about their business. By now, they were accustomed to his and Sasha's unspoken conversations.

Is she hurt, do you think? Sasha asked. I thought you said she had no interest in you.

I don't think so, Danion told her. Her pride, perhaps. She kept saying she would not accept the role of displaced wife. It is the position she wants, not me.

Are you sure? Sasha stroked his cheek. You can be quite compelling at times.

He saw an image, Sasha's image, of them making love in the shuttle-craft bunk. Superimposed on it was his wedding night with Reilu six years ago. His ex-wife sat on the edge of the bed, hair unbound in accordance with the demands of the Tarkei marriage ceremony, stiff as cardboard under her white linen shift, feet squarely on the floor.

He heard his own voice, saying with a bitterness he could not conceal, "So, we are alone at last. For a moment, I thought my father would come in and manage this part of the ceremony as well."

And as clear as yesterday, Reilu's answer: "He has fulfilled his duty, as we must."

Unable to sit still, he had walked to the window and stood with his back to her, filled with a blazing sense of injustice that even then he knew had little to do with her.

Sasha touched his cheek. Danion caught her hand in his. I was unfair, he said. She asked for this no more than I did, but she accepted it, and I blamed her for it. I was furious, at my father and her parents and the whole situation. Reilu talked about duty, and it felt as though I'd married my father. I never touched her, not once in three months. Truly, I don't know what she felt. I did not ask.

Except that she spoke of duty, not attraction, Sasha said. That tells you something.

"Dinner, my children," Jenat said, "and my guests."

Danion placed a hand on Sasha's waist, guiding her toward the table. It changes nothing, he said. The joining exists, and she must accept it. He flicked her ear with his free hand. In the meantime, I intend to keep you safe.

Sasha laughed. I'm not Giselle, she said, and I'll be in San Francisco.

Danion corrected her. *We* will be in San Francisco.

So we will, Sasha agreed.

They had reached the dining room. Jenat beckoned. "Here, my daughter." He pointed to the seat on his right. "Danion, you may sit next to her, if you wish. And you, Iqara, over here." He gestured to his left. "Now I have my family. It is good."

The eternal manager. Danion shook his head—gently, so as not to offend his father.

He's a parent, Sasha said. They're like that. Who knows? Maybe you and I will be the same one day.

Parents? Himself and Sasha? A strange but appealing thought.

We can adopt, she said. He was mulling that one over when she turned to Jenat. "Will you come to see me dance *Giselle,* then, father-in-law?"

"There is no such expression in Tarkei," Jenat said with his customary severity. "One is family, or one is not. Father will suffice."

"Yes, father." Sasha's vivid face crinkled in amusement, and Danion watched in astonishment as his father's sternness evaporated into something perilously close to affection.

"I think I understand," Jenat said. There was a hint of sadness in his voice, more emotion (except for irritation) than Danion had heard in sixteen years. "She is very like your mother."

"It's true," Danion said, realizing it himself for the first time. "She is."

The company rehearsed at the theater in Tarkakhan for four weeks. Danion spent most of that time being debriefed by one official after another. He did not see Reilu again, in part because he insisted on meeting at his father's office. Jenat, who, judging by his occasional complaints, had made no impression on his former daughter-in-law, did not invite Danion and Sasha to his house, although he did make several unannounced visits to theirs. He even showed up at the theater one day, "to see this exercise his daughter made so much fuss about," as he put it. When he left two hours later, he seemed impressed. He agreed to attend the opening night in San Francisco, a concession Danion was not sure he appreciated.

Negotiations over Xantera proceeded at a slow but steady pace. The evidence of the Tyrellian powder and Tendak's connection with the secret police cracked open a few doors. Tendak himself was remanded for trial. The Kazrati, trapped by their insistence that he had nothing to do with them, could not press for his release, although their press vilified the allied planets, and Jenat in particular, every day. The diplomats held out for a court hearing but warned the survivors to expect Tendak's deportation.

That did not happen, however: justice proceeded swiftly on crime-free Tarkei; and within three weeks Tendak had been turned over to the allies for incarceration in their highest-security prison. Danion was satisfied. Sasha and the other dancers made occasional loving references to boiling in oil, but otherwise they accepted the punishment as just.

Earth and the sister planets, Panntha at their head, assumed responsibility for short-circuiting future Kazrati campaigns to induce drug addiction or worse, and Tarkei strengthened its border patrols. The allied worlds declared Xantera a military outpost.

Danion, thinking of that beautiful, untouched planet swarming with troops, shuddered at the news, but the company had no desire to return there, and no parent in his or her right mind would send a child to school there, so he did not protest. He doubted anyone would listen if he did.

He had yet to decide what he himself wanted to do. Sasha, deep in rehearsal for *Giselle,* came home just long enough to collapse before leaving again. Each night, he filled her in on the events of the day, but they had little time to spend in talk. Danion, convinced that Sasha would not want to hear about his problems, did not share his indecision with her. His questions could wait.

Iqa returned to medical school, and Geoff to his project. "You will come to the performance?" Danion asked as he said goodbye.

"Wouldn't miss it for the world, brother," his friend said. His sister Sara, well on the road to recovery, was scheduled to appear in Act I.

"I will hold you to it," Danion said. "Although that assistant of yours will become overconfident, spending so much time unsupervised."

The Cheshire-cat grin showed. "So much the better, brother. I can dump the whole show on her and move to Tarkakhan. I have to keep you out of trouble."

"And Iqa," Danion said dryly, under no illusion about why Geoff wanted to move back. "Myself, I expect to spend a considerable amount of time in San Francisco."

"Nice place," Geoff said, unabashed. "We'll come visit you."

Danion extended his right hand, human style. "Please. And thank you, Geoffrey. I could not have done this without you."

"Don't mention it. What's family for?" Geoff shook the hand.

Danion watched his friend cross the runway. At the door of the plane, Geoff turned and waved. "Hey, who's flying the boat to Earth?"

"I am," Danion said, startled. "Who else?"

Geoff grinned. "Just checking. Don't trust Iqa to any old pilot, you know."

Absurdity layered on absurdity. Danion waved. "Till San Francisco, my friend."

"Till San Francisco," Geoff said. "Call me when you guys get ready to go." He boarded the shuttle without waiting for an answer.

19. Prima

IT FELT GOOD TO be back in San Francisco, Sasha decided, standing in front of the pseudo-Baroque pillars of the Opera House. The air was cold after Tarkei; a chill blew off the San Francisco Bay, and fog rolled in from the Pacific, as it had done on each of the many mornings she had spent here during previous tours. In the distance, she saw golden hills, dotted with green shrubs and succulents, but the city remained damp and cool.

Danion felt the cold more than she. Sasha slipped a hand through his arm and led him into the beautiful old building. Once through the big double doors, she closed her eyes, drinking in the aroma of rosin and polished wood. It could be any theater in the galaxy. Then she opened her eyes again and knew she could only be here: white paint and gilt, murals on the ceiling and a great crystal chandelier, red velvet seats and that wonderful stage. It looked like a museum piece. She could not imagine a more perfect setting for *Giselle*.

Camille stood in the center aisle, bullying technicians. Practice barres dotted the stage. Dancers dressed in a motley collection of leotards, old shirts, leg warmers, and sweat suits stretched on the floor or did knee bends at the barres. In the pit, a real orchestra was warming up. Sasha hugged her husband, told him to pick a seat, and ran for the side entrance.

"Sashenka!" Slava tossed her in the air as she came out of the wings, as though he had not seen her yesterday and every day since the company left Xantera. Danion, no longer jealous, walked down the aisle and settled in the first row beside Tonio, who greeted him with a distracted wave.

"One more week," Tonio said, looking worried. "God knows if we're going to make it."

Camille spared a moment from bossing technicians to turn her head. "We will make it, *mon fils.*"

Tonio gnawed at his fingernails, earning himself a sharp reprimand. Danion repressed a chuckle, amazed at the ballet mistress's ability to monitor her surroundings. Tonio muttered something about it being easy for her to say, but not loud enough for her to hear him.

Jenat had the same effect on people. Danion leaned back in the plush seat, prepared to enjoy the rehearsal.

One hour before the performance, the house was packed. Since their arrival on Earth, Tonio had spent half his waking hours alerting every video journalist in San Francisco, as well as everyone he could contact throughout the solar system, to Xantera Ballet's upcoming premiere. His efforts had paid off. Ticket sales, always steady for a company considered one of the galaxy's ten best, had skyrocketed thanks to his publicity campaign. Entrance to the premiere had become an especially choice item.

Peeking through the curtain as she waited for the cast to gather in the wings, Sasha noted enough holo cameras to cover every news broadcast in the immediate area, ready to record the revival of the queen of Romantic ballets. Jenat had arrived not long ago, ushering in a large diplomatic contingent and an equally large staff before abandoning them to sit with Geoff, Iqa, and Thuja in a box to the right of the ancient stage. Only one empty seat remained— Danion's. She'd left him in the dressing room while she ran out here, and she had better get back before he came looking for her. He might take a wrong turn and end up in the lighting box.

Behind the scenes, chaos and confusion reigned. Danion, sitting in Sasha's dressing room and watching her make up, marveled at the contrast between the serenity she displayed and the clamor outside. Dancers milled about in the corridors, calling to one another. "Oh, no, my ribbon broke!" "Where's my eye shadow?" "Martine, do you have any lamb's wool? I must have left mine at the hotel." The list of accidents and inconveniences seemed interminable.

Sasha paid no attention to the noise. Dressed in her green peasant costume, her hair bound just tightly enough to prevent it from coming down before the time came for her to pull it loose, she stared into the mirror, concentrating on drawing an accurate line above her eyelashes. He decided that the sounds must be so familiar to her that she did not notice them. As the stage manager's voice sounded through the halls, shouting, "Curtain in five," producing a concerted howl from the dancers outside, she stood up, blotting her vivid pink lipstick against a paper tissue.

Danion stared at her. It was like viewing a stranger. The combination of gray and green shadow highlighted her eyes, and the dark eyeliner and mascara heightened the effect. She looked simultaneously exquisite and alien, like a clothing-store mannequin.

She must have heard what he was thinking, for she said, "On stage it looks quite different, you'll see. But only if you go and take your seat. That call meant the curtain goes up in five minutes, and if I'm not in the wings by then, Camille will be down here with a sledgehammer. So tell me to 'break a leg,' and go enjoy the show."

"Break a leg?" Danion said, bewildered. "Why should I wish you to do that? It would be not only painful but detrimental to the performance."

"Another idiom Geoffrey missed? Well, it's not surprising. I think only theater folk use it. It's considered bad luck to wish someone good luck, I don't know why. It's been around forever. So people say, 'break a leg,' instead. A sort of reverse psychology for the universe."

"Odd," Danion said. "May I say 'dance well'?"

She laughed at him. "If you wish." She stroked his ear, caressing the garnet earring. "I dance for you. Only for you. Now go, or you won't see it." She whirled out the door as she spoke, and he followed, touched and bemused. Her index finger pointed him to the correct stairway, and he left her standing on pointe in a square wooden box filled with some kind of off-white powder.

He took his seat as the curtain rose on a medieval European village. Geoff, in evening dress, sat on his right— next to Iqa, even more stunning than usual in tawny satin and high-heeled gold sandals. Thuja, whether out of devilry or a warped fashion sense, had worn the purple shirt with yellow flowers and indigo silk trousers. Iqa studiously ignored her. Jenat, imposing in dark brown velvet, sat on Danion's other side.

Jenat flicked his ear in greeting. Danion returned the gesture, more pleased to see his father than he would have believed possible three months ago. Geoff and the others had come to Earth with him and the ballet company, but the prime minister had flown in yesterday and then been so consumed with affairs of state that they had not seen him until now.

"I got that woman out of my house," Jenat said sotto voce.

"Reilu? I'm impressed." In fact, he was more impressed that Reilu had resisted for so long, but the news was welcome nonetheless. "She has accepted, then, that our marriage is over?"

"So I surmise," Jenat said. "It is her only real option, and your cousin is a fine young man. I am sure they will deal excellently together."

Danion, much better acquainted with Reilu than his father, made a mental note to avoid from now on whichever cousin had had the bad luck to win her. He also sent a silent prayer of thanks that the problem was solved.

The overture drew to a close. Hilarion, the hunter who loved Giselle, appeared. The ballet was beginning.

❅

Was it the combined effect of sets and music and costumes that made the two hours that followed so magical, or the atmosphere created in the beautiful dollhouse of a theater, where performers and audience interacted, for once, without the distancing influence of camera and screen? Danion, a virtual stranger to theatrical spectacle, did not know. Perhaps *Giselle* itself held the secret—relic of a more intimate era, it drew the audience in with its simple story and its extraordinarily light touch. The dancers spent most of their time in the air, in one complicated series of jumps after another; and Sasha, as the naïve, impressionable peasant girl, projected a luminous innocence not seen since the last Victorian maiden sank into a decline.

The audience adored it, and who could blame them? The music, although not complex, underscored the dancing; the performers, veterans of Camille's relentless quest for perfection and their own determination to succeed, outdid themselves in response to the enthusiastic applause that greeted every technical feat, and there were many.

Before the corps had finished its first entrance, Danion could see reporters jabbering into their headphones. He was glad, for the company had worked hard. Geoffrey could not contain his pride: Sara danced as skillfully as the rest of the corps in their bright blue skirts.

Danion touched Geoff's arm. "She did well, brother." Geoff nodded. Iqa, her attention caught by her brother's voice, ran a finger along the curve of Geoff's right ear.

Jenat raised an eyebrow at his son, who shrugged. The prime minister shrugged, too, and Danion let out a slow breath of relief. One more barrier crossed. The more time he spent with them, the more convinced he became that Geoff and Iqa belonged together. If Jenat could accept Anderson as a worthy addition to their clan, the future looked rosy indeed.

On the stage, Slava flirted with Sasha. Testing the truth of Albrecht's declarations, Giselle plucked a flower placed next to her bench and pulled the petals off it, counting them. "He loves me, he loves me not," an old village game.

Alas, he loved her not. Sasha pulled away, running to the wings. Behind her back, Albrecht picked another flower, counted hurriedly, tore one petal off, and presented the results as evidence of her mistake. Giselle, eager participant in her own deception, threw the flower away and linked arms with her partner, initiating another frothy airborne pas de deux. Not at all credible for a heart patient, Danion noted with amusement, but delightful to watch.

The story continued. Giselle's mother warned her daughter of the fate that awaited her if she stressed her laboring heart too much. Albrecht's real fiancée stalked onto the stage, complete with borrowed wolfhounds and a full retinue of idle nobility. Danion, unpleasantly reminded of Reilu, repressed a shudder. Giselle greeted her with sweet deference—quite a stretch for Sasha, a lady who seldom doubted her own mind.

The fiancée left, and Hilarion appeared again. The emotional tone of the production darkened. Hilarion carried a hunting horn and Albrecht's sword, a weapon that only noblemen could own. He ducked behind the cottage as Albrecht returned, but then, desperate at losing Giselle, popped out again to force the truth on her.

Giselle resisted; he insisted. The sword fell at Albrecht's feet. Hilarion sounded the horn, and the fiancée and her party reappeared. Albrecht, exposed, bowed his head.

The music became wistful, and the "mad" scene began. Danion leaned forward, curious to see what, in the end, she had done with it.

It was riveting. Even his father, that bastion of Tarkei tradition and master of the freezing phrase, could be seen surreptitiously wiping his cheeks. The anguish that had subsumed Xantera, the haunting sadness of those who had lived there, the murder of innocents, the sense of something irreplaceable, broken and tossed aside on a whim—all came through in Sasha's exquisite, understated portrayal. With tear-filled eyes and graceful hands, flying footsteps and slow, mournful passages marking the bittersweet memory of better times, she called them into another world, the world of archetypes, where love and death are inextricably linked.

Slava caught her as she fell. Albrecht, filled with remorse, realizing at last the enormity of what he had done, lowered her to the stage and bent over her, hand over his heart. But Giselle was gone.

The curtain dropped. Applause broke out around them, but the five in the box sat silent. Danion—thinking of that beautiful, untouched planet and his mother, shot down so long ago—could not have spoken if he had tried. To his right, Geoff looked as though someone had run him through a set of rollers. Iqa was weeping, Geoff's arm around her shoulders.

Only Thuja's enjoyment seemed unrestrained. "But she is astonishing," the Pannthu said. "To create a person like that, so unlike herself, and without words, even. How is it possible?"

"She is astonishing," Geoff said, his voice not quite steady. "The whole company's astonishing, if you ask me. Eight weeks ago they could barely walk."

"Indeed," Jenat said in his sonorous bass. "To be associated with such courage is a privilege." Across Danion's chest, he extended a hand to Geoff. "It is well that your sister survived, boy. She will go far, I think."

Geoff looked stunned. Danion, who suspected his friend had never encountered such an austere compliment before, sent Geoff his half-smile. The Cheshire-cat grin emerged, and Danion let his own smile broaden.

"Me too." Geoff shook the prime minister's hand.

Act II began with Elasi's glide across the stage. The veiled Myrthe, queen of the vengeful spirits known as Wili, called forth her minions, young girls dead before their wedding day. In defiance of custom, first Hilarion, then Albrecht, ventured into the woods where Giselle was buried, and each in turn fell into the Wilis' spectral hands. Hilarion, without a protector, suffered the fate of young men in this tradition and was forced to dance until he dropped dead from exhaustion. His pleas for mercy left Myrthe unmoved.

Albrecht, though less deserving, had better luck. Giselle, summoned from her tomb to join her sisters, threw her arms in front of him and won a concession. If he could live until dawn, he would be free.

The power of love over the power of death. More archetypes, Danion thought, but what an excuse for great dancing. The choreography of Act II, even more than Act I, floated and soared and skipped. Sasha drew one leg up to her knee and extended it, impossibly high, to the side. She looked like a flower opening. Danion could almost hear the audience holding its breath.

He thought of the desert, the three suns rising in the dawn glow. The silver birds had flown with that same effortless motion, so far beyond his reach that he could not have touched them. Except that he had. Sasha had shown him how. As he had on the evening she had danced *Pavane,* Danion relaxed into his feelings—his heart and his body, as Sasha would have said—letting the music sweep him up.

Slava lifted Sasha above his head. Her arms were extended in line with her ears, hands drooping from the bent wrists that characterized the Wilis' ghostly state. Her body formed a gentle curve, ending in arched feet crossed at the ankles. In her white tulle skirt, she could have been a silver bird. The light was there, on the stage and surrounding it, the life force of the universe glowing around them. Somewhere, Danion thought he heard his mentor laughing.

The silence lasted thirty seconds past the dropping of the curtain, then broke in waves of thunderous applause. Even the Tarkei stood, listening to the roar of "Bravo, brava, bravissima," without participating. The members of the corps stepped forward to make their bows, followed by the principals, and the applause, if anything, increased. Sinclair, his arms filled with roses, came out from the wings and presented them to his sister, who accepted them with the regality of a true prima.

Sasha stood with her partner on the stage, reveling in the audience's appreciation. So much work, so much heartache, but in the end it came down to this. This was what kept her going through the grueling practice times, the corrections and repetition and fatigue. And their triumph tonight was especially sweet. In defiance of everything the Kazrati had done to them, they had pulled it off. She saw relief in every face—shoulders free of tension, the smiles of survivors. The company was more ecstatic than its audience, because the dancers knew, as few out there did, just how great their achievement had been.

In time-honored tradition, she presented Slava with a single flower from her bouquet, and together they gave Tonio, as artistic director, flowers of his own. The conductor came up from the pit to kiss the prima's cheek, and Sasha had flowers for her, too. Any minute, the curtain would fall.

Out from the wings came a student, young enough to be awkward in her pointe shoes and dressed in the short classical tutu so much more familiar than Giselle's long Romantic skirts. She carried a glazed terracotta bowl, which she offered to the ballerina.

Sasha took it, and her lips parted. The pot contained a small desert plant in full bloom. Against the dark spiky leaves she saw a profusion of flowers, ranging in hues from palest pink through white to a glorious deep blue—an altanai.

Where had he found it? She looked up, toward the box where her husband sat, and in full view of the packed house blew him a kiss. I love you, she said.

Danion bowed his head in acknowledgment. And I you, my Altanai.

The curtain swung closed, but the applause continued, drowning out all other sound.

Danion landed the shuttle as the suns were rising. Framed by the stark beauty of the desert, the mountain sanctuary rose in jagged peaks against the rusty sky. He handed Sasha down from the spacecraft, expecting her usual protest that she could do it herself.

It did not come. Instead, she wrinkled her nose at him. I hate to be predictable, she said. Besides, I'm sure you've got the point by now.

He drew her hand through his arm. If Xantera had not convinced me, *Giselle* would have. Let us go and find Sendar.

His mentor knelt, fork in hand, before the altanai, where Danion had found him on the day he first acknowledged that more than chance linked him to the stranger he had met in the desert. The stranger who walked beside him, without whose warm presence life would lose its luster.

"Danion!" the older man said, joy in his face. He stood, brushing the dirt from his knees. "And Sasha-*chan*. How delightful to see you. Are you well?"

"Very well." Sasha held out both hands to Sendar and, when he took them, brushed her lips across his cheek. "I'm glad to see you again. I wish you could have come to San Francisco with us. You would have loved it."

Sendar seemed touched. "It is the price, my daughter, of not living in the world. But you will tell me the whole, will you not?"

"We will," Sasha said. "We have much news to share. I hope you have several days to spare."

Danion stepped forward, extending his hands in the gesture of respect.

Sendar touched his palms to Danion's. "And you, my son? I see you wear the earring still."

"And always will," Danion said. "In memory of a time that meant much to me." A hand around his wife's waist drew her toward him. "I cannot come back, Sendar, and that saddens me. But you were right about the joining, and that does not sadden me at all." He let his lips curve. "I have even learned to meditate."

Sendar's eyes twinkled. "Then indeed, my son, the age of wonders has not yet passed. And what will you do, since you cannot renew your oath?"

"I shall fly," Danion said. "Father, although not happy, has resigned himself to the assault I plan to commit on tradition by returning to piloting, and my wife tells me that I have her blessing so long as I neither crash nor fall foul of the Kazrati."

Sasha pressed against his side. He could hear her laughing through the link, and aloud as well; she had no reason to hide her emotions from Sendar.

"But that is wonderful, my son," his mentor said. "You have found your path, and I am glad. Come and tell me your story."

Suns' Set

CHOLI STARED AT HER teacher. An entire world had opened before her—one she had not imagined, of families and friends, of kindness and laughter and love. A world closed to a child of the streets until Danion took her in and made it real. Even now, she feared to believe in it, and she certainly could not bear to let it go. "But you're not married now. Did you leave her? Did she die? What happened?"

Danion lifted the shoe with the writing on it, balancing it on his hand and twirling it. The candle flame cast a peachy glow on the satin. The shadows obscured his face. "I did not leave her," he said at last. "How could I, given what I have told you?"

"I'm sorry." Choli felt very young. "I didn't mean to hurt you."

"It is nothing," Danion said, his voice so level she would have believed he didn't care, except that the pink toe shoe was shaking.

"It is." Above all, Choli did not want to alienate the one person who had been kind to her, who asked little in return. "I was thoughtless even to suggest it. But won't you tell me what happened? Did your friend and your sister marry?"

Danion looked not at her but at the wall, as though it might part and offer a window onto the past. "They did. A year later, and have lived long and happily together. Geoff is a professor; he and Iqa make their home in Tarkakhan. Her medical skills are much in demand. They have two adult sons, whom they adopted from among the survivors of Xantera."

In the light cast by the candle, the garnet earring flashed as Danion turned his head. For a moment, Choli was sure she saw a twinkle in his eyes.

"Thuja," he said, "is ageless. Her experiences with the rescue mission convinced her to abandon both science and life on a planet. She commands her own ship, terrorizing a new crop of recruits every year. We crossed paths often when I worked as a diplomat, but she will not visit Kazratan."

"What happened to Tendak? Is he still in jail?"

The twinkle vanished as Danion's eyebrows drew together. "Unfortunately not. He served his sentence and returned to Kazratan." His face lightened again. "Perhaps I should not complain. Your secret police is less forgiving than the allied governments."

Choli nodded, already focused on something else. "And your father?"

"Continues to serve as prime minister." Danion's voice grew warm with amused tolerance. "Terrifying everyone he encounters. Worse now, I think: he has a shock of white hair and the manner of a human Caesar. It's like talking to Danar. Sendar lives also, in his cell on the mountain. They have reached an advanced age, the pair of them, but they enjoy good health. At least, they did when I came here."

"He didn't frighten Sasha," Choli said, afraid to ask again yet hoping he would tell her what had happened to his wife. "Your father, that is."

"No." Danion bent over the candle flame. "Sasha loved him. She saw through the rough surface to the soft heart beneath. As you do."

Choli stilled, more startled by the unfamiliar compliment than by any amount of mistreatment. Not that Danion mistreated her, but many others had.

"You remind me of her, you know," Danion said. "No, I see you didn't know, but that was why I adopted you. When I saw you, with that tangled hair and dirty face but a spark in your eyes that said nothing could defeat you, it reminded me of her. Every day the resemblance strengthens. You have her courage and her resilience and her passion for life. These are rare gifts and should be nurtured."

The tears Choli had not shed in seven lonely years poured down her cheeks. Cursing her own weakness, she tried to brush them away, but more streamed behind them.

Danion put an arm around her shoulders and held her, as no one had held her since her mother died. "Weep, little bird," he said, "and do not fear. You are my daughter now."

One is family, or one is not. In that, Danion and his father thought alike. Choli cried into his shoulder for what seemed like ages. When the tears eased at last, she felt a soft cloth brush her cheeks. Danion shifted her to the not-damp shoulder, but he did not let go until she herself sat back on her heels.

"And Sasha?" she asked.

Danion placed the shoe on the floor beside him. "She is dead. As you guessed. But not to me. Nor to anyone who saw her dance. She lives forever in the Kingdom of the Shades, with the Wili and the fauns."

"But what happened? Did she just grow old?"

He drew back, until his face was hidden again, although in silhouette she saw him run his hand through his hair. He did not answer for a long time, and when he did, his voice, no longer steady, sounded as if someone had scraped his throat raw. "I can't, Choli. I'm sorry. She was my heart. I can't talk about it. Enjoy the happy ending. For it was happy."

Such hurt. When had it happened, that it still hurt so much? Or was it that he had loved his wife with such intensity that it would always hurt? And if so, did he love her, too? Choli wanted desperately to ask, but Danion sounded so sad, it would be unkind to probe further.

"Should I put them away?" She pointed at the shoes.

One long finger stroked the delicate pink satin, lingering over the Tarkei script. "No. Let's admire them for a while."

Moving On

Want to know what happened to Sasha?
Her story continues in *Kingdom of the Shades*.

Warning: Danion is in for a surprise.

If you enjoyed this book, please consider leaving a review at your favorite online bookseller and/or Internet book club. It will help other readers find it.

Ballet Terms Used in the Tarkei Chronicles

Adagio: A dance calling for slow, sustained movement.

Alignment: The positioning of the body—shoulders in line with hips, ankles, and feet—that exemplifies the upright stance characteristic of dancers. Correct alignment is essential to balance and prevents injury.

Arabesque: A position in which one leg is extended to the back while the dancer balances on the other. The arrangement of arms and legs determines the type of arabesque (first, second, etc.). Normally the head remains upright in arabesque; if the dancer tips the entire upper body forward, it is called penché (suspended).

Assemblé: A jump from one foot to two, in which the legs come together (assemble) in the air.

Attitude: Similar to arabesque, but with bent knee. Attitude can be performed to the front and, more rarely, to the side as well as to the back.

Ballonné: A step or jump in which the working foot shoots out, then returns to the standing ankle. Can be performed in any direction.

Bourrée: On pointe, a series of small traveling steps. Often the feet stay so close together that they seem to shimmer across the floor.

Cambré: A bend of the upper body, forward or backward or to either side.

Chassé: Similar to a two-step, where one foot leads and the other closes behind (chases) the first.

Échappé: A small jump from a closed position, usually fifth, in which the feet "escape" to land in second or fourth position.

En couronne: A port de bras in which the arms rise to create a circle framing the head, like a crown; also known as fifth position of the arms.

First (second, fourth, fifth) position: The basic starting and ending placements of the feet. First—heels together, toes to the side; second—same as first with a separation of 12–18 inches between the heels; fourth—one foot about 12 inches in front of the other, heels aligned to opposing arch (open) or toes (closed); fifth—feet together, heels aligned to opposing toes. Third position is a modified fifth used by beginning dancers, not professionals. Each foot position has an associated arm position, but the different national traditions vary.

Fondu: A step in which the working foot is placed at the ankle of the standing foot as both knees "melt" into plié, usually followed by developpé, in which both legs extend.

Fouetté: A turn in which the working leg remains stationary while the standing leg and body move. Often used as shorthand for fouetté rond de jambe en tournant, in which the working leg is whipped from front to side or side to back, depending on the national tradition; as the dancer turns, she brings the working foot into the knee, then extends it again to finish, as she started, in plié on one foot.

Frappé: A movement in which the foot shoots out from its base at the opposite ankle, striking the floor on the way to full point. It can be performed with foot flexed or straight. In a double frappé, the foot is stretched and beats both sides of the supporting ankle before striking the floor.

Grand allegro: A fast-moving dance calling for big movements, especially big jumps.

Grand jeté: A big jump in which the legs (ideally) form a straight line in the air.

Pas de chat: A big jump in which both legs are pulled up to the knee as quickly as possible, then returned to the ground. If one leg is bent while the other extends to the front or side, it is called an Italian pas de chat or grand pas de chat.

Pas de deux: Any dance involving two people, typically a man and a woman. A grand pas de deux is a formal version of this, in which both dance together, usually in adagio, then each dances separately, then they come together again for the finale—often the high point of a ballet. When it propels the action of the story, it may be called pas d'action.

Passé: A movement in which the working foot is pulled up the standing leg to the knee, then (usually) "passed" down the leg to close on the opposite side. Both legs are strongly turned out. A position often used in turns.

Penché: See arabesque.

Petit battement: A small, quick, beating movement of the foot at the opposite ankle, front to back or back to front.

Piqué: A stabbing movement of the foot into the floor, often the entry to an arabesque. It can also initiate a pirouette (piqué en tournant or piqué turn).

Pirouette: Any turn.

Plié: A knee bend. Used as a basic warm-up exercise, as well as to initiate and to end every jump and turn.

Pointe: The act of balancing on the tips of the toes. Although dancers use reinforced shoes (pointe shoes, more casually referred to as toe shoes) to sustain balance on pointe, the position is attained and held through a combination of strong feet and perfect alignment. The shoes are merely an aid. One can spring onto pointe in a single movement, but good technique requires the dancer to return to the floor by standing on the ball of the foot before lowering the heel (known as "rolling through" the foot), ending in plié.

Port de bras: Any movement sequence involving the arms, including cambré.

Promenade: A sequence of steps in which the dancer, by making small adjustments to the position of the supporting foot, circles while in pose (most often, arabesque or attitude). Often performed as part of an adagio, especially in pas de deux, when the man walks in a circle, turning the woman on pointe.

Relevé: Rising to stand on the balls of the feet or, if one is wearing the appropriate shoes, on pointe.

Renversé: A step in which the working leg makes a 180-degree turn, either front to back or back to front, while the body remains still.

Révérence: A curtsey, in which the placement of the arms often reflects the character portrayed, particularly in the Russian tradition. Also the last section of class, in which slow movements usher in the cool-down period.

Sissone: A jump from two feet landing on one.

Standing leg: The leg that remains stationary while a movement is performed. Also called the supporting leg.

Temps de flèche: The "arrow" step, a jump involving two kicks to the front, usually with straight legs.

Tombé: A step that ends lower than the step preceding it, into plié from a normal standing position or into either plié or heels flat on the floor from relevé.

Tour en l'air: A big jump, most often performed by men, in which the dancer turns 360 degrees—once, twice, or three times—in the air before landing in fifth position plié.

Turnout: The dancer's ability to rotate the legs from the hip socket. Ideally, the feet form a straight line. If the dancer can rotate 180 degrees in this way without training, (s)he is said to have "natural turnout."

Working limb: The leg or arm that performs a movement.

Acknowledgments

ONCE UPON A TIME, I decided to write down a story that had occupied my thoughts for years. One scene led to another, and soon I had a quarter of a novel. It grew and evolved, and as it did, thanks to comments from my friend Wendilee Heath O'Brien, it turned into a book. So large a book, in fact, that I ended up splitting it in two. *Desert Flower* is the first half, and *Kingdom of the Shades* the second.

Thanks go also to my friend Eve Levin, who during a long-ago performance of *Giselle* at the Mariinsky Theater in St. Petersburg (then the Kirov and Leningrad) first mentioned the echoes in the ballet of a suicide rather than death due to heart failure; to Jon Sherman and Sharon Friedler, who have made it possible for me to indulge my love of ballet by permitting me to take Jon's class for twenty-five years; and to Catherine Thomas Nobles and Colleen Kelley, who read and commented on both novels before publication. And to the great classical ballerinas Nina (Nino) Ananiashvili and Alessandra Ferri, whose exquisite artistry and phenomenal technique became my inspiration for Sasha. When I started work on this story, they were at the height of their careers; they have since retired from most active performances, although they continue to dance on special occasions.

Although I finished the first draft of these novels in the late 1990s, it took much longer for me to feel confident writing fiction. Helped by comments from my fellow-members of Five Directions Press—Ariadne Apostolou, Courtney J. Hall, and Diana Holquist—I published three other novels before deciding that this story had grown up enough to face the world. I thank them for their many contributions along the way—and, as always, my husband for his love and support.

And for those who may have read *The Not Exactly Scarlet Pimpernel,* the idea of two characters in mental communication had its origins here. I adapted it for the later novel after convincing myself that the Tarkei Chronicles might never see the light of day. But times have changed, and here they are.

May you enjoy Sasha and Danion's world as much as I enjoyed bringing it to life. They have been and remain dear to my heart.

The Author

As a child, C. P. Lesley thought everyone told themselves stories to help themselves fall asleep. It never occurred to her that anyone would pay her for them, and for a long time, she was right—no one would. But after years of producing horrible prose, reading books about novel writing, and pestering hapless fellow-writers and friends to read her drafts, some of the advice stuck, and she finished *The Not Exactly Scarlet Pimpernel.*

In addition to *Kingdom of the Shades,* the second part of Sasha and Danion's story, she has published *The Golden Lynx* and *The Winged Horse*—books 1 and 2 of Legends of the Five Directions, a series set during the childhood of Ivan the Terrible. She is currently working on Legends 3, *The Swan Princess.* Find out more about her and her books at www.cplesley.com.

When not thinking up new ways to torture her characters, she edits other people's manuscripts, reads voraciously, maintains her website and blog, and takes classes in classical ballet. She also hosts New Books in Historical Fiction, a channel in the New Books Network (http://newbooksinhistoricalfiction.com).

THE NOT EXACTLY SCARLET PIMPERNEL
(EXCERPT)
C. P. LESLEY

FIVE A, 5B, 5C, 5E, 5F: where was 5D? I had checked every seminar room on the fifth floor of Widener Library a zillion times. No 5D. I'd begun to think it lived in an alternate universe, restricted to the talented few like Avalon in the Arthurian legends and hidden from the uninitiated—meaning me.

I had no idea where I'd gone wrong. In eighteen months at Harvard, I'd never had this much trouble finding a seminar room. In fact, I rather prided myself on my ability to navigate the campus. Yet here I stood, on the brink of arriving late to my graduate seminar on the French Revolution. Which wouldn't matter, except that it threatened to sink me with David Houghton, the professor I wanted to supervise my doctoral dissertation. David had built a career on studying the psychology of committed revolutionaries—exactly the area where I planned to specialize. He'd also made no bones about having more students than he could handle. And since I had no less than four potential competitors for any remaining slots in his roster, I preferred not to grease the skids under myself by failing to show up on time.

To make matters worse, my feet hurt. I had bought my black fake-leather pumps two-for-one at Fantastic Footwear, since my usual thrift-shop forays didn't include shoes. Now I knew why the store put them on sale: they had an evil buttoned strap perfectly positioned to rub the bone above my big toe raw. A grad student income doesn't include funds for Manolo Blahniks, although I suspected that, if I could afford them, they might prove no more comfortable than my Hot Pincers.

My woes didn't stop there. The dust of century-old books made me sneeze, and my backpack had carved a permanent furrow into my left shoulder. I kept trying to shift it to the right, but it was one of the ergonomically correct one-strap sort that aligned to one shoulder or the other. Guaranteed to turn anyone into a hunchback. I imagined myself as Shakespeare's Richard III, doomed to limp around the fifth floor until I dried up and mingled with the dust on the shelves. In the distance I saw David's head clear the stairwell.

My heart accelerated, and with it my breath. A hollow cough alternated with the sneezes. I ordered myself to calm down. Obviously, I had located the general area where I was supposed to be. In a pinch, I could follow David there. So what if he held my tardiness against me? If he refused to accept me as his student, I could work with someone else. Not on the French Revolution, but on something. Turkish peasants, maybe. Sure, I wanted to know about the Jacobins, but I could adjust. No one would send me to the guillotine for arriving late to class.

Besides, I was exaggerating. David wouldn't turn me down for such petty reasons. Would he?

Clued in by the direction of David's footsteps, I spotted a tiny corridor that had escaped notice during my first sixty rounds and made a beeline for it. When I reached it, I discovered an index card, yellowed with age, bearing the notation 5D, with an arrow, in old-fashioned fountain pen. As I limped down the hallway, subdued voices guided me. I stumbled into the right room just as the campus clock chimed two. The usual library seminar room: one large oval-shaped table, a bunch of chairs, lights, and a white board topped with a tube that might hold maps. Not even a window opening onto Harvard Yard.

Four students looked up, startled by the clamor I created as I crashed through the door. Two thoughts darted through my head at the same time. One, they had found the place without trouble. Two, did I look as wild-eyed, shaggy-haired, and dirt-strewn as I felt? I headed toward the only other woman in the group: Suzanne Henderson, a cute brunette whom some people would describe as my opposite number. Whereas I spent my time trying to figure out what drove people to commit to a life based on violence, Suzanne focused on the victims. Specifically, she had an interest in the French noblewomen whose lives the revolution destroyed, who wound up penniless and often friendless in England, Austria, and elsewhere. After three semesters of shared classes, she was also the closest thing I had to a friend. She'd tell me if I resembled something the cat dragged in.

On either side of her sat Simon Gray and Tony Kent. Simon played football, although not well enough for him to attend some Midwestern school instead of quarterbacking our pathetic excuse for a team. Dark brown hair, gray eyes, solid, the kind of muscles you'd expect from a football player, big but not linebacker enormous. He and Suzanne had arrived at the same time, already a couple. I liked Simon, although I found it hard to imagine what he and Suzanne talked about. He had a gift for picking the kind of research topic that makes people think academics don't quite connect to the real world: crop failures that affected some itsy-bitsy village in the middle of nowhere from 1734 to 1736; age at marriage in Provence before and after the Fronde; the long-term impact of silk factories on shepherds—you get the picture. If Suzanne worried me to the extent that I doubted David would want to take us both on, Simon bothered me because if David succumbed to the lure of shepherds, I figured I didn't have a snowball's chance in the Inferno.

Tony—medium height and build, super-smart, African-American—tapped the conference table in front of him with long musician fingers. Marking rhythms for his next cello concert, I guessed. Or for the revolutionary songs that were his chosen area of specialization. "Ça Ira," "La Marseillaise"—Tony had a bottomless store of anecdotes about where they came from and how people used them to mobilize the poor. He was younger than the rest of us, but so knowledgeable and focused he seemed older than his true age. Under present circumstances, I had to consider him something of a triple threat.

That left Ian Campbell, my personal bête noire, although no one would think it to look at him. To reach Suzanne, I squeezed past him. Ian was very tall, with chestnut hair, hazel eyes, a mild expression, a charming smile that he didn't often show, and a hint of Scots accent even though he insisted he came from Chicago. Whereas Tony had squeaked past twenty-three last month, Ian had twenty-eight years under his belt, four more than I do.

That extra experience gave him a self-assurance I couldn't match. It had attracted me at first, before I tried and failed to get him to confide two words about his past. Since then, I'd gone out of my way to avoid him, only to discover that the structure of the Harvard history department made that impossible. He appeared in every class, excelled at every assignment, aced every exam. Naturally, I detested him. He even had the best-developed and most interesting dissertation topic: he wanted to learn more about the bystanders—conservatives, revolutionaries, ordinary citizens, whoever. If they played both sides, "spoke Jacobin" (to borrow a phrase) while retaining their previous loyalties, or just ducked under the radar, Ian yearned to find out what made them tick. An idea so appealing I wished I had thought of it first.

And unless David had developed a mad yen for crop failures, he would pick Ian for sure, leaving the rest of us, as usual, fighting not to end up in the cold. Another reason Ian and I did not get along.

"Hello, Ninel," he said as I pushed by. "Nice stockings."

Determined not to let him rattle me, I suppressed a groan. I hate my full name, imposed courtesy of my dyed-in-the-red-wool grandmother in memory of a certain famous Bolshevik (read it backwards). Other than Babushka herself, no one but Ian ignored my preference for Nina. And my leggings, until the library covered them in dust, had been a precious find at the campus rummage sale, held outside Memorial Church last month. Candy striped, like the ones you see on Christmas elves, hence in tune with my sweater (pine trees). A little off-season for February, but Boston, winter, dull snow-laden day—it worked. I had worn the leggings to give myself confidence. Now Ian Campbell made them seem garish.

"Thanks," I said, for lack of a brilliant comeback. Suzanne smiled in sympathy and patted the chair on her far side. "Do I look like a scarecrow?" I whispered as I slid onto the seat between her and Tony. She shook her head.

I'd skidded in just in time. The minute I stuffed my too-loud leggings under the table, David arrived. "Glad you could make it, Nina," he said by way of greeting. "Busy day?"

Drat. He'd seen me scurrying down the hallway—hobbled by the evil shoes. I hadn't gotten away with anything. But excuses wouldn't help me, so I bit my tongue and waited while he settled himself at the head of the table.

I should explain that David was in his early thirties. That's why we used his first name. A prodigy, he'd made his reputation even before he earned his doctorate. Brilliant, quirky, innovative. The bright young star in French revolutionary studies. Also outrageously handsome—dark, slender, blue-eyed, medium height—and blessed with one of those plummy English accents that make everyone sound like Lord Peter Wimsey. Harvard had lured him from across the Pond, offering tenure and freedom from the UK's routine assessments of faculty progress, and he'd been inundated with student requests since he arrived last fall. This was my first course with him. Of course, I knew not to get moony over a professor. But if I were to lose it, David Houghton would be worth the sacrifice. As he studied us, I had to work to keep my jaw in line.

He sat at the head of the table, pulled out a piece of paper, and called our names. "Pennington" didn't normally put me last, but this class was the exception. "Very well," David said. "Everyone's here. Before we start, I want you to understand something. All five of you have requested that I supervise your doctoral dissertations. I already have fifteen students, and with only so many hours in the day, I can't accept five more. So this course will, in a sense, determine your fate. The two students who come out on top—I'll explain what that means in a moment—will work with me. The rest need to find other advisers. The course centers on a computer simulation based on *The Scarlet Pimpernel*—"

A gasp went around the room. Only Ian made no sound. As if he already knew what David meant by a computer simulation. He would.

Childish, Nina. Stop grousing and listen. I listened.

"Yes," David said. "As a group, we are going to recreate *The Scarlet Pimpernel,* the Emmuska Orczy novel published in 1905. The original, let me add, not any of the film or television versions. The experience will be similar to a computer game, but live. At least, you will be performing live. The company running the simulation supplies sets, costumes, and players for the roles not covered by the six of us. The game lasts a fortnight—the last two weeks of the course—and will take place at a warehouse in Concord. Alert your families that they will not be able to reach you in that period, although they can contact the university in an emergency. If any of your other professors object, tell me, and I'll arrange a way for you to satisfy the requirements for their classes. If you drop out, though, you are also choosing not to work with me in the future."

Two weeks of running around in some warehouse in Concord in eighteenth-century dress—was the man nuts?

Nuts or not, David was still talking. "In week nine, based on the syllabus I'll hand out in a minute, you turn in a paper discussing how Orczy's novel shapes and distorts our historical perceptions of the French Revolution and contemporary England. To come out on top, you must write the best paper and win the game."

He'd lost his marbles, for sure. Syllabus, paper—those were old hat. But hanging my entire future on winning a game? And this was the guy I'd picked for my dissertation adviser!

At the same time, chills ran down my spine, and not just at the implicit challenge. Everyone has a book that defines a crucial stage in her life. Okay, not everyone—my sister Nessa probably has a ballet. But bookworms have books, and future historians tend to glom onto historical novels. Mine was *The Scarlet Pimpernel,* which I had loved ever since an aunt gave me a copy for my fourteenth birthday. The book marked my feeble attempt at teenage rebellion, in a sense. Since Babushka pretty much had a lock on the Radical Left, I moved right. Orczy made the perfect anti-Babushka—convinced that the French Revolution was a major international catastrophe, just as the collapse of the Soviet Union seemed to my grandmother. I devoured the book in secret (to avoid lectures about the downtrodden masses and the five social formations), relishing my wicked admiration for a long-gone and no doubt deservedly forgotten aristocratic past.

Of course, I had matured since then. These days, I understood that history looked different depending on where you stood. The downtrodden masses had as much right to life, liberty, and the pursuit of happiness as did the bluebloods and the merchants. Even so, I remembered *The Scarlet Pimpernel* with pleasure. I could ace this course in my sleep!

David moved on to asking each of us about ourselves. Again, as the "P" in the room, I came last. I half-listened to Ian summarizing where he stood with the bystanders. I paid even less attention to Suzanne, who shared her progress with me every other day. Tony, as always, had a few good anecdotes to share. Simon surprised me by abandoning the crop failures and the unwed teens, expressing an interest in the French royal family's intrigues with Austria. Then he threw in the silk industry and the shepherds, claiming he needed help deciding. The potential excitement of international espionage must have given him pause.

David gave a noncommittal nod and said, "Nina." Although I'd watched him on and off as the other students talked, his expression did not hint at how he felt. I had no clue whether one of us had impressed him more than another. Now that it was my turn to talk, how could I make my dissertation stand out, convince him I merited his attention?

"My grandmother was a revolutionary," I said, "in Russia. She still reveres Joseph Stalin today. Even though she lost classmates and an uncle in the Terror, she believes that the victory in World War II justifies their sacrifice. I want to find out how that kind of indoctrination happens, to study memoirs and letters—of people like Robespierre, yes, but also ordinary people who supported the revolutionary government even after the killing began. To understand how cognitive dissonance works. And how it doesn't: why some people draw back, as Marguerite does in *The Scarlet Pimpernel.*"

Was that a gleam of approval in David's eyes? I subsided, happy with my succinct presentation. Big idea, method, mastery of concepts, last-minute reference to the novel chosen for this seminar (no one else had managed that)—and I'd left out the sticky stuff, like the fact that my grandmother was the family outlier. Only I showed any interest in understanding Babushka's point of view, mostly to figure out what kept her mired in the past.

David held up a plastic sandwich bag containing slips of paper. "So. Each of you has an area of interest that you can pursue through the simulation. We have revolutionaries, exiles, bystanders, and music as a motivating force. The factories won't get much play in Orczy's novels, but she does hint at high-level international politics. I suggest you focus on that, Simon, and worry about the shepherds later."

"Yes," Simon said, lacking any alternative. The only shepherd in a *Scarlet Pimpernel* novel would be Sir Percy in disguise.

"First step is to dole out the parts," David said. "Then you can keep your assigned characters in mind as you tackle the syllabus and the paper. *The Scarlet Pimpernel* has three major characters and numerous minor characters. There are six of us. This bag contains three male names and two female ones. The company running the simulation will fill the other roles." He handed the bag to Ian, sitting on his right. "Pick a slip of paper and pass it on. If the name turns out to be the wrong gender, pick again. If your selection strikes you as a horrible fit, feel free to switch with another player."

Ian picked Sir Percy, aka the Scarlet Pimpernel, right away. Simon landed Sir Andrew Ffoulkes, Sir Percy's chief sidekick—another good part, although Simon pulled a face that suggested he had hoped to play the hero. I suppressed a giggle. Who would have guessed Mr. Crop Failure concealed a longing to become Errol Flynn? (Not that Ian made a likely swashbuckler.) I wondered if Simon would try to talk Ian into switching, but I couldn't imagine why Ian would agree. Percy had the best part in the story, by far.

Suzanne showed her paper to the crowd: Lord Antony Dewhurst, third in command of Sir Percy's League of the Scarlet Pimpernel.

Tony reached across me and plucked it from her fingers. "I'll take that one. Seems like a natural." He grinned.

Suzanne yielded the slip with a laugh and reached into the bag again. Only two slips remained, and both were female. Would she get Lady Marguerite Blakeney, Percy's wife and the main woman's role, or Marguerite's best friend, Suzanne de Tournay? I doubted David would have chosen any women's parts except those two, since the others were little more than walk-on roles.

Suzanne's fingers closed around a second scrap of paper and drew it forth.

My stomach tightened. I was torn. On one hand, I had no desire to spend two weeks as Ian Campbell's estranged wife. On the other, Marguerite, a bourgeois radical who switched sides, fit my dissertation topic better than Mademoiselle de Tournay—just as Mademoiselle, a noblewoman sent into exile, was the better match for Suzanne. Could I persuade her to switch, if push came to shove?

Suzanne unrolled the paper. Her face lit up, and she held it out to Simon. "Suzanne de Tournay!"

Great. That left Marguerite for me!

"That's settled, then." David handed me the last slip and dropped the plastic bag into his briefcase. "Ian, Percy. Nina, Marguerite. Simon, Sir Andrew. Suzanne, Suzanne de Tournay. Tony, Lord Antony. Let's talk about the syllabus."

"What about Chauvelin?" Ian asked. In *The Scarlet Pimpernel,* Chauvelin is the villain. Excuse me, Sir Percy's main antagonist. Chauvelin doesn't regard himself as evil. He genuinely believes that his opponents deserve to have their heads chopped off. Babushka's kind of guy.

David flashed his showstopper smile. "I'm taking Chauvelin. Your job is to thwart me. Change the plot, if you can. If I capture or kill you, you lose. If you capture or kill me, you win. Otherwise, the last two standing take the prize and—assuming you write decent papers—become my students. Got it?"

FIVE DIRECTIONS PRESS

THIS BOOK WAS TYPESET using Athelas, a body font inspired by British literary classics, with headings in Cochin Italic, a display font produced in 1913 by Georges Peignot based on the eighteenth-century engravings of Nicolas Cochin— here intended to evoke both the classical formality of ballet and Tarkei script. The desert flower type ornaments come from Poetica Supplemental Ornaments.

www.ingramcontent.com/pod-product-compliance
Lightning Source LLC
Chambersburg PA
CBHW020911200626
46814CB00001BA/288